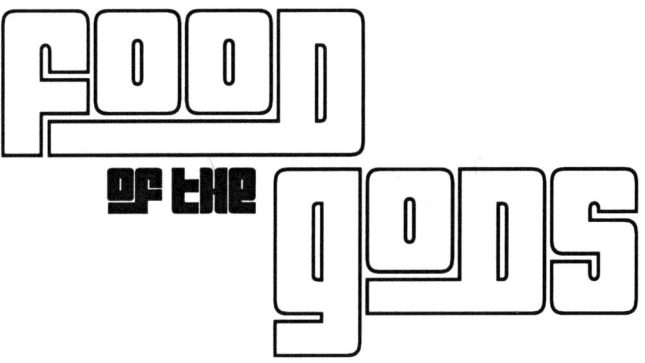

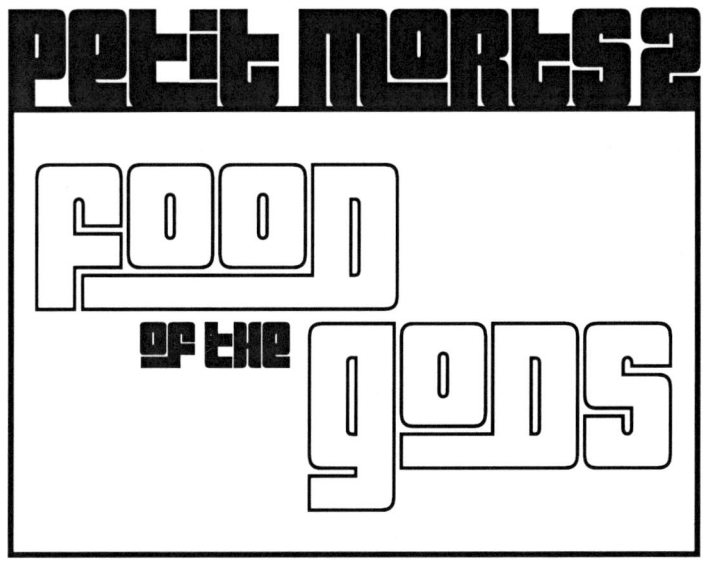

PETIT MORTS 2
FOOD OF THE GODS

Sean Kenndy • Josh Lanyon • Jordan Castillo Price

jcpbooks.com

First published in print in the United States in 2011
by JCP Books
www.jcpbooks.com

This book is a work of fiction. The characters, incidents, and dialogue are drawn from the authors' imagination and are not to be construed as real. Any resemblance to actual events or persons, living or dead, is entirely coincidental.

Petit Morts 1: Sweets to the Sweet. Copyright © 2011 by Sean Kennedy, Josh Lanyon and Jordan Castillo Price. All rights reserved. No part of this book may be used or reproduced in any manner whatsoever without written permission except in the case of brief quotations embodied in critical articles and reviews.

First Edition

ISBN: 978-1-935540-23-6

CONTENTS

Pretty Ugly by Jordan Castillo Price...1

Sort of Stranger than Fiction by Josh Lanyon..........................47

One Less Stiff at the Funeral by Sean Kennedy......................103

Critic's Choice by Josh Lanyon..141

Wishink Well by Jordan Castillo Price.......................................191

About the Authors..233

Pretty Ugly
Jordan Castillo Price

A SWELTERING SEPTEMBER Tennessee afternoon had settled into a cool, hazy night. When Mimi Van der Berg appeared at the top of the grand staircase, Dominic could have sworn she was glowing.

The light in Cypress Mansion was nothing at all like the light in Hoboken by which Dominic had learned to shoot. Here in Nashville, the days were tinted gently blue, unless it was raining, in which case the light took on a subtle, cool, diffuse quality. Twilight gave a delicious carnation cast to white skin, and a striking amber highlight to black. And evening—which should have been the same as anywhere else in the civilized world, lit as it was by ambient incandescent bulbs and his cherished Nikon SP900 speedlight—held a magical radiance he had never seen anywhere but Nashville.

He stood in the foyer shoulder to shoulder with everybody who was anybody in the Cypress Estate Preservation Society. On one side, he brushed elbows with a tall historian in a tuxedo, and on the other, a twenty-something kid in a string tie and a spray tan.

Dominic braced his elbow against his chest and captured a shot of Mimi just as she drew breath to welcome her exclusive guests. He might not be able to capture the exact quality of the light, but he'd damn well try.

Mimi was a vision in orange, crowned by a severe silver wig. Most women her age—mid-eighties if she was a day—would have chosen a traditional black dress, or maybe a muted earth tone, if black made them feel as if they were celebrating their husbands' funerals prematurely. Not Mimi. Orange was a difficult color to wear, but standing there, framed by the meticulously restored banisters, Mimi beamed down at the throng as slender and graceful as a daylily.

Dominic couldn't think of any other person who'd attempt a wig like that, aside from Lady Gaga. But Mimi Van der Berg worked it as if she'd been born with it.

"Welcome, one and all, to the grand re-opening of Cypress Mansion." Her accent was southern, and incredibly genteel. There was a hint of throatiness to her voice, not from cigarettes, but possibly bourbon. "We at Cypress Mansion are opening our doors for the first time since February, when the restoration of the dish pantry and the family dining room began."

If Dominic had retained an assistant, he would have positioned that lucky soul to Mimi's side with a gold reflector to smooth out some of the less flattering shadows. But since most people had a hard time acting natural with a crew of assistants and interns around them, Dominic usually worked alone. It just meant he needed to look more closely for the opportune shots.

"While last spring's unprecedented rains delayed some of the restoration, thankfully Cypress itself escaped the flooding with minimal damage."

Toward the foot of the stairs, a hand popped up out of the crowd as if someone was gauche enough to interrupt Mimi's speech with a question. Light from the overhead chandelier glinted off shiny black plastic: a cameraphone.

Mimi gestured toward the door without breaking stride. "It would have been such a shame if harm had come to this mansion. Cypress is a rare and wonderful example of the Italianate style, which was very popular in the North at a certain dark time in our history, but is quite uncommon in Tennessee." Just as Dominic, who was a Yankee through and through, was wondering if he should look dutifully ashamed of the Franklin-Nashville Campaign even though his predecessors had been scattered throughout Europe at the time, an extremely tall and disturbingly broad man in a tuxedo and an earpiece pushed past him, and escorted the woman who'd attempted the Hail Mary shot with the cameraphone toward the exit.

"I am truly delighted to present the fruits of the labors started by the Society in 1973 with a viewing of the latest renovation, made possible by all of you. Won't you please join me for a glass of wine in the family dining room?" Dominic took another shot of Mimi descending the staircase like American royalty. As she reached the bottom, and the crowd shifted to give her plenty of room, she added, "If you'd like a photographic memento of the evening, call the Society's secretary Monday morning and have him put you in contact with Dominic Mann who, of course, you all know. Mr. Mann is tonight's *official* photographer."

She beamed in Dominic's general direction, and he captured a shot of her with the chandelier in soft focus behind her. "Mr. Mann's latest photographs of the upstairs library appeared in Harper's Bazaar, so his work should certainly be adequate for all of your needs."

Mimi swept her imperious gaze over the crowd, daring someone else to attempt an unauthorized snapshot. No one dared. Satisfied, as always, with weight of her own authority, she turned and led the way to the new restoration.

Dominic passed through the main hall, the downstairs library, the map room and the women's parlor, all of which he'd photographed for the Cypress' website when he first moved to Nashville. He didn't remember the rooms themselves so much as his images of them. If a piece of bric-a-brac that appeared in one of his photos had been moved to a new position, he noticed. And yet, overall, the place felt unfamiliar, museum-like, and not particularly welcoming.

He'd never been beyond the women's parlor. Along the walls of the narrow hallway, prior inhabitants of the Cypress stared down at him, stiff and pale-eyed, from tintype prints. In the exterior shots, the building looked much like it did today—minus the group of townhomes and bungalows that had sprouted up around the building in the 1920's, when Lydia Van der Berg had sold much of the grounds to pay off her late husband's gambling debts. He passed beneath Lydia's silvery stare, and emerged into the newly renovated family dining room.

The addition of the word "family" to the dining room had conjured up images of relatives relaxing together, passing plates of scones and offering to top off that mint tea. That wasn't the case. This "family" dining room seated twenty, and was filled with enough faux-Italian scrolling metalwork to shock the Pope.

Dominic braced his elbow and poised his camera, but instead of shooting right away, he looked. At times like those, the camera was more of a prop for him, a way to let the people around him know not to disturb him, because he was looking.

The other members of the Cypress Society streamed around him, their numbers doubled as they reflected in the gilt-framed floor-to-ceiling mirror on the opposite wall. Dominic spotted himself in the center of the reflection as the only person who was still, and turned to scan the rest of the room before he picked his mirror image out of the crowd in any great detail. He'd lived with himself long enough to know exactly what he'd see. Immaculately tailored suit. Passably fit, for a guy in his forties. And plug ugly.

Dominic turned away from the mirror. There was a buffet against the west wall brimming with wine. Beside it, Carlton Jeffrey from Jeffrey Imports & Exports stood, scanning the crowd, most likely anticipating who would call him Monday for a case of the Pinot they sampled at tonight's event. His gaze lit briefly on Dominic, then hurried on without lingering. Such was the way of one-night stands that never had enough momentum to develop into anything more.

Dominic allowed his attention to slide past Carlton—no hard feelings, pal—and on to the second buffet on the north wall. The top groaned under a spread of flowers and fresh fruits, and among that precisely coordinated swath of color and shape, on gleaming silver pedestals, the star of the show: chocolates.

He snapped a few shots of the crowd filling the room, then turned away from Carlton, and away from the mirror (wondering how the family dining room had become an obstacle course of avoidances) and made his way against the tide of cocktail dresses and suits to the chocolate buffet.

The spread couldn't possibly have been laid out by an amateur. Dominic knew all the top food stylists in town. He tried to place the work. Ashford? No, not formal enough. The Robinson Sisters…if it was them, it was the most graceful arrangement he'd seen them do yet.

"Beautiful, isn't it?" Mimi drifted up beside Dominic and looked upon the buffet with such pride, he wondered briefly if she'd arranged it herself. That wasn't Mimi's style, though. Mimi didn't do things herself; she hired skilled artisans to do them for her. "That young man is a genius. When Blanche Montague sold her shop, I braced myself for some terrible chain store to open in its place. But Sweets to the Sweet blends in with those lovely old Victorian storefronts just like it's been there for three generations."

Dominic framed a shot of the candy, and clicked. Immediately he spotted another. And another. It seemed as if he simply couldn't find a way to aim his camera that didn't result in a dynamic, engaging composition.

"Pretty as it may be, we're celebrating the restoration tonight," Mimi reminded him, "not the catering." Dominic lowered his camera. He felt slightly dazed.

A young couple approached the buffet and helped themselves to a piece of candy. They did it furtively, as if they felt guilty for touching it, but simply couldn't help themselves. "It's *so* good," the girl whispered to her beau as they sank back into the crowd with their guilty pleasures.

"And where is your date for this evening?" Mimi inquired. "I specifically invited you to bring someone."

"Nah." Dominic's Jersey accent contrasted with Mimi's soft southern cadence as if it was another language entirely. "I just wanted to focus. It's too distracting to have someone tag along to a shoot."

"I see." It was perfectly clear that she did. "Forgive my candor, Dominic, but there's no reason at all that a man of your quality should need to remain single."

"Quality." Dominic laughed out the word before he could stop himself. "Is that the southern equivalent of a great personality?"

Mimi didn't deign to answer. "You never know. Maybe you'll find something in common with a member of the Society. We have our fair share of 'bachelors,' you know."

Dominic knew. He'd entertained one or two of them, though none had ever seemed interested in a repeat performance.

"Don't sell yourself short," Mimi said. "You have plenty of important connections. A younger man might be very appreciative if you help him launch his career."

The very thought of it made Dominic cringe inside. "How about you cut me a break, Miss Mimi? What can I say—I'm an incurable romantic."

Mimi was not deterred. With a subtle gesture of her chin, she indicated a young man nervously sipping his wine in the corner. "I could introduce you to him. Actor." She cut her eyes to another nubile gentleman admiring a painting. "Or him. Artist."

Dominic couldn't think of any way to tell Mimi, who was twice his age, and who undoubtedly counseled her female friends it was perfectly acceptable to marry for money rather than love, that her matchmaking left him embarrassed rather than intrigued. Some guys in his position wouldn't think twice about being served some fresh meat. They figured a little hookup was their due after a few decades of building their careers. Not Dominic. Looking into a set of sparkling young eyes and realizing the attraction was not about him, but the idea that he was a coveted rung on the ladder to fame and fortune, made him feel like a pathetic old troll. "C'mon. When you say Cyrus, those kids think you mean Miley, not Billy Ray."

Mimi swept the room with her regal gaze, and stopped cold. "That one. Trying to break into music. Johnny Palomino—he'd be perfect for you." A broad-shouldered brunet in a vintage western-cut suitcoat stood with two guys in tuxedos, smiling modestly. The coat was a real showstopper, black with a piebald yoke framed in red piping, and the aspiring musician wearing it carried off his flashy finery like it was his birthright.

One of the tuxes bookending him owned a radio station; the other, a dark, broad, goateed man whose waistline was putting a strain on his cummerbund, Dominic didn't recognize. "Palomino's handsome," Mimi said, "but look at the corners of his eyes. He's got to be at least thirty—a little long in the tooth for a breakout act. I'm sure he'd be appallingly grateful to have some head shots taken by the illustrious Dominic Mann."

Dominic opened his mouth to dismiss Mimi's suggestion out of hand—but he couldn't. Johnny Palomino had stolen his breath away. Dominic had grown up among plumbers and hockey and meatball hoagies. Cowboys were the stuff of fantasy; they might as well have been superheroes or Martians.

Sexy Martians.

"You see? There's someone out there for everybody."

Mimi began to raise her arm to summon the would-be singer over, but Dominic stopped her. "Wait. Not yet. Just lemme see if…."

"He already knows who you are, darling. Everyone here does."

"I know, I know. I was just hoping it'd feel a little more natural if I tried to strike up a conversation myself."

"Do have one of the waiters flag me down if you change your mind." Mimi primped her lustrous silver wig. "I've always thought 'natural' was highly overrated."

TWO

THE NEED TO maneuver around the dining room table resulted in some interesting traffic flow, but at least it made Dominic's meandering approach seem less obvious. He took a few shots on his way to the spot he'd last seen Johnny Palomino standing, photos that would not only be snatched up by the *Tennessean's* Style section, but would also give him a good excuse to work his way around the room.

The big guy in the tux was gone by the time Dominic approached, but Stanley Beloit of WOPR had practically backed the musician through the wainscoting. Stan held a fresh glass of wine, and a waiter was just leaving the scene with two empties. Johnny Palomino was hardly a victim, since he could have picked up Stan and tossed him into the butler's pantry if he was anywhere near as cornered as he looked—but he was probably well aware that burning bridges wouldn't be very healthy for his career.

Dominic butted in just as Stan began to punctuate his sentences with overly-familiar tweaks to the arm of the singer's cowboy jacket. "How's about a nice smile for the camera?" Dominic said, and reflexively, both men turned to face him and flashed their pristine dental work. Stan never let go of the musician's sleeve, but Dominic was undeterred. "How ya doin', Stan, nice to see ya."

He shook Stan Beloit's hand, which gave Johnny Palomino an opportunity to reclaim his arm. An opportunity he took, Dominic noticed. He turned from Stan to shake the singer's hand.

"Johnny Palomino."

"Dominic Mann." Dominic tested the handshake—and not just Palomino's handshake, but his eye contact, his stance, the set of his shoulders and whether he leaned in, or away. He didn't drop the handshake, even when Dominic held it long enough to turn it into a question. Better still, he leaned in.

"That's a nice-looking jacket you got on. Vintage, right? Come over here by the window and let me grab a couple of shots."

Johnny nodded a polite leave-taking to Stan Beloit as Dominic hustled him away. Stan narrowed his eyes at Dominic, but left it at that. The night was young, and there was plenty more time for the old hunter to snap up his prey later.

Dominic guided Johnny to the east wall, which was a bit less crowded than the rest of the room, seeing as how it was opposite the wine. "Stand over there by those red curtains. There you go." Palomino hitched a thumb into his pocket and dropped his closest shoulder as natural as a print model. Hell, maybe he'd actually been a print model, but figured singing would take him farther than modeling.

Mimi might have looked at Johnny's eyes and seen "over-29" etched in the corners. Dominic saw character.

"Whaddaya say we step outside and take a few pictures in the garden? They got that lit up real nice; shoots like a dream."

Johnny Palomino dropped his gaze and smiled to himself, that unassuming look again that even from across the room was positively magnetic, and Dominic felt his pulse start pounding. He slipped an arm through the crook of Johnny's elbow and began leading him toward the hallway. The crowd made way for Dominic, or maybe for the 3-pound Nikon around his neck with the whopping 20mm wide-angle lens.

The air outside was no warmer or cooler than the air inside the old mansion, but it smelled like real, vital things like grass and smog and hot asphalt rather than the stifling dryness of plaster and gilt. The outdoor can lights shone up the façade of the Cypress, throwing the trellises and the climbing flowers that clung to them in high relief. "Stand over there," Dominic said, "Between those two lights."

Johnny framed himself between the fixtures. It wasn't quite a pose—and Dominic was glad, because he hated it when models posed too much—but Johnny sure did know how to stand so that he looked good. He tilted his head so that his eyes weren't lost in shadow.

Bluish outdoor lighting, a trellis of flowers, and that wild spotted coat. A flash would kill the effect, but without a tripod, it was probable that even with his fast glass, Dominic wouldn't capture anything more than noisy grain. He cranked the aperture, took a few deep breaths, braced his elbow to his chest and then double-braced it by grabbing his forearm, exhaled, and shot.

Johnny pivoted and glanced over his shoulder, again, not like he was posing, but like something had happened to grab his attention. Dominic captured a shot, took a few steps closer, and snapped another.

"There even any film in that thing?" Johnny asked. His voice had a soft southern twang to it. He leaned back against the trellis and crossed his arms. Right there—that would be the perfect album cover.

Dominic captured it. "'Course not. It's digital." Johnny smiled at him and he caught the moment when those perfect, white teeth glinted in the darkness. He noticed Johnny was being just as careful as he was to be very, very still. And so he crept forward another few steps.

"So you make a tripod with your body. I've never seen anyone do that before."

"It's a wedding photographer trick. I shot a lot of weddings." When I was your age, Dominic nearly added. But the urges that had started gnawing at him, more hungrily every time Johnny struck a pose-that-wasn't-a-pose, suggested to Dominic it was better off to leave certain things unsaid.

He machine-gunned another dozen shots, then let camera drop to his chest. "Okay. We got it." He didn't step back—he just sized up his model and waited.

Johnny Palomino leaned toward him. Dominic leaned, too. When he sensed no resistance, he closed the deal.

Johnny's mouth tasted like Pinot. He hadn't shaved, part of the whole "cowboy" image, most likely. The stubble rasped against Dominic's chin. Johnny took hold of Dominic by the lapel—no, by the camera strap—and dragged him forward so their legs brushed. Johnny's thighs were stair-climber hard. Dominic ran his fingers up the front of Johnny's red-piped jacket. His chest was hard, too.

Something about his kissing didn't quite match up to his physique. With a build like that, Dominic would have expected Johnny to really nail him with some tongue—show him who was boss. And later, maybe bring out the lasso and the bullwhip.

It wasn't so much that Johnny was timid, more like he was…polite.

When it came down to it, Dominic supposed, Johnny was still the wannabe, and Dominic was the star.

But who knows? Maybe he'd bring a lasso along if I told him we could use it in a studio shot.

Dominic eased back and picked out the glitter of the can lights reflected off Johnny's eyes. "Look, normally I'd ask you to ditch this thing and come back to my studio, but I should probably stick around 'til at least midnight since Mimi's counting on me."

"And my manager's probably wondering where I went."

"But if you want to hitch a ride with me after that…."

"Oh." Johnny seemed genuinely surprised. "I…I'd like to, but…sorry. I can't. I've already got plans."

Dominic took a few steps back and adjusted the weight of the Nikon so it wasn't chafing its usual spot across the back of his neck. "Okay, no problem."

"But what about tomorrow?" Johnny said in a rush. "Are y'all comin' to the tea reception? We could get together then."

Dominic did have an invite to the tea—a smaller, more intimate gathering than the wine gala. He'd been on the fence about showing up, but if cowboy Johnny was going to be there, waiting on him….

"Sure. That sounds swell." And hopefully, Johnny wouldn't develop cold feet once he got a load of Dominic by the cruel light of day.

He fiddled with his equipment while Johnny rejoined the party, so as not to put the kibosh on whatever the kid's "plans" might have entailed, then followed him in discreetly a few minutes later.

The crowd inside was more wine-lubricated now, and Dominic picked out a few more dynamic shots. He'd always had a soft spot for women in red lipstick laughing. The third round of wine was usually where the most red-lipped smiles made their appearance.

Zoom in. A ruby pair of lips filled the frame. Motion, a hand. Dominic expected the rim of a wine glass to edge into the shot, but instead, it was a single, lustrous, perfect piece of chocolate. He took the shot just as the woman bit in, but he hadn't been prepared for it, and he'd probably moved and blurred it. He braced his elbow and tried to find her again, but she'd turned away, and the moment was gone.

Some people considered chocolate to be a magical food group, but Dominic had never been plagued by an insistent sweet tooth. He'd always considered his indifference to sweets to be a lucky thing. However poorly he'd fared in the looks lottery, at least he had no trouble keeping his weight down. Even so, although Dominic could take chocolate or leave it, he could tell the new caterer was some really big deal.

A majority of the crowd had now shifted from the wine buffet to the chocolates, and Dominic was struck by the body language of the partygoers. It wasn't as if they were actually enjoying the candy. They looked more like they were worshipping it, with equal parts of lust, awe, and even a bit of fear. It was the sort of posture he'd seen around a mirror full of coke lines, back when he was fresh out of Parson's, and people did that sort of thing in semi-polite company.

He framed a shot of the crowd that featured a swath of newly-restored Italianate metalwork, but he didn't take it. There was a decadent edge to the crowd that wouldn't translate well into Cypress promotional materials. Something even a bit sinister. Sexual, too.

Eh, why not?

Dominic fired off a dozen shots. That was the beauty of digital. It took a lot longer to blow through memory cards than good old Kodachrome.

A wisp-thin socialite bit a piece of candy in two, then tucked the other half into the mouth of the middle-aged woman at her side. A friend, or a stranger? Dominic took the shot, then lowered the camera and tried to figure out what was off-kilter. It was subtle, but if he looked, really looked, he saw it. The bubbles of personal space most people carried with them were non-existent around the buffet. Men brushed up against women, women against men, men against men and women against women, old and young and everything in between. All of them were so hypnotized by the chocolate that they hardly noticed they were touching—or maybe a good old-fashioned orgy was getting ready to break out, right there on the floor of the newly-restored family dining room.

That'd sure give the Style section something to write about.

Dominic's thigh butted up against something hard and unyielding, and he realized he'd drifted all the way up to the buffet as he shot without even realizing he'd done so. He lowered his camera, disoriented, and found the caterer, dressed in black and red chef wear, standing profoundly still amidst the chocolate bacchanal.

He said, "You must be the official photographer…Mr. Mann." His voice was low and smooth. It sounded like the silky, dark pieces of chocolate looked. "That's quite a lens."

Dominic glanced down at the camera as if to reassure himself it was still there. The caterer wasn't exactly Dominic's type, too androgynous, too pallid and thin—but his eyes were riveting. He smiled. That was fantastic, too, although something in his body language suggested he wasn't exactly flirting. The ambiguity of his attitude was intriguing. "I'm Chance. You've seen my shop?"

"No, I ah…I've heard of it."

"Well. Don't believe everything you hear. Most people are filthy little liars." He smiled again, as if he'd made a joke. Or maybe he'd been dead serious, but felt it was polite to pretend he wasn't.

"Only good things," Dominic said.

"All the more reason to take them with a grain of salt."

Chance pulled a platter out from a tiered cart at his side and began replacing the candies that had been decimated by the sudden greed of the crowd. His hands moved with unerring accuracy, grasping each piece by the fluted paper cup and placing it just so among the foliage and fruit. Every chocolate landed in just the right spot. He never repositioned a thing. He worked quickly, too, and before Dominic realized it, the platter was empty, and Chance tucked it into the vacant slot on the cart.

"You'd make a real good hand model."

"I'll bet you say that to all the boys. I can only imagine what the casting couch entails."

Dominic laughed, and Chance's smile deepened at the appreciation of his joke, if it even was a joke. Dominic thought it was funny, anyhow. "I'm serious.

You're not tall enough for runway, and you don't have the right look for doing print in Nashville. But you've got good bones, good skin and nails, too. And you hold your hands nice and still."

"That's very kind of you to say." Sarcastic? Dominic couldn't tell. Chance brought out a second platter and began to repopulate another plundered section of the buffet as they spoke. "I don't think I'm really the type to go for modeling. Successful entertainers thrive on attention; I can take it or leave it. Being on the other side of the camera seems far more interesting. What is it they always say—photographs are the mirrors of the soul?"

"I think the expression is *eyes*."

"Is it? Ah. You're right. Mirrors tend to get me all turned around."

Dominic hefted the camera in a "May I?" gesture, and Chance gave him a small shrug in return. Dominic took a few shots of his long-fingered hands moving through the fruit and flowers, and then he tilted the frame up to Chance's face. Chance looked up just as the shutter clicked, then looked back at what he was doing, clearly unimpressed.

Daunting. If Dominic's clout was meaningless, then what did he have to fall back on—his scintillating conversation? That'd be the day.

He turned away from the buffet and scanned the room, not for shots this time, but for another look at Johnny Palomino. It was really none of his business who Johnny had agreed to meet for a private after-party…but he couldn't stop himself from feeling curious.

In his peripheral vision, he saw Chance look up and follow his gaze. "I take it you couldn't lure the Boston Buccaroo into a more private photo session."

"Boston? If that kid's from Boston, I'm Elvis' love child."

"You're sure he's not from Boston? Judging by what? His accent?" Chance lifted the final piece of candy from the platter, held it up between them so they could both judge its chocolaty perfection, and said, *"Col cioccolato tutti i guai sono dolci."* Italian? Dominic couldn't say, with only his grandmother's pidgin-English to compare it with. Maybe it was Latin. He shifted his focus from the candy to Chance's eyes. "Not everyone defines themselves by the way they speak," Chance said in a subtly Tennessee-tinged cadence. "Just like some of us aren't defined by what we do, or how much money we've squandered, or what we look like."

"Easy for you to say." It came out louder and more agitated than Dominic had intended. The members of the Cypress Preservation Society on either side of him began to ease away and pad the distance between them. Chance, however, leaned in closer. The corner of his mouth curled up. Dominic gestured at his patrician features. "You look like…well, like that."

"And that's all that matters?"

"I didn't say—"

"Think about some of the most iconic photos in history. Are they of pretty people? Or the migrant dustbowl mother with her scrappy daughters hiding their faces in her neck? Or the Vietnamese children trying to outrun napalm?"

Dominic tried to think of a single important photo of a beautiful person, but the unbidden image of the children's screaming faces blotted out everything else.

Chance placed the final chocolate on the buffet, and then a hand with a cocktail ring set with an emerald the size of a lens cap snaked around Dominic and plucked the candy from its spot before the fluted paper cup had made full contact with the table. Mimi Van der Berg bit off a corner of the chocolate, took a sip of merlot, then repeated, all the while looking Dominic and Chance boldly up and down. Once she was finished savoring her chocolate, or maybe her wine, she asked Dominic, "Are you harassing my favorite chocolatier?"

"I don't think he's capable of being harassed."

Chance, in the midst of handing out red paper napkins to a pair of tittering young debutantes, smiled to himself.

"Well you certainly don't look like you're having any fun. It's as if a black cloud has settled over this end of the room."

"We were talking photography," Dominic explained. Mimi looked to Chance, who neither confirmed nor denied it. In fact, the way he simply went about his business, Dominic might have just ceased to exist.

"Less talking, more doing," Mimi said, but she was flush enough with merlot that the threat was plainly halfhearted. She even snagged another chocolate from the buffet before she strode carefully away on her wine buzz and high heels.

"Not everyone's got the calling to be a photojournalist," Dominic said defensively.

"It's obvious you care for what you do; I wasn't besmirching your career choice." Chance planted his hands on his hips and surveyed his buffet. It was full again, for the moment. Once he was satisfied with what he saw, he raised his eyes and nailed Dominic with a look. "I'm merely wondering about your core values."

Dominic laughed, for a moment. The laughter quickly died when he realized the caterer was serious. "You're saying I'm shallow?"

Chance's eyebrows rose. "Why else would you be so smitten with John Horowitz?" The smile crept back into his expression. "Or, should I say, Johnny Palomino?"

"Then sue me. I happen to like cowboys." Even as he said it, Dominic blanched at the notion that not only was his "cowboy" a Jewish kid from Boston, but that he'd damn well figured as much all along. He turned away from the buffet, hoping to end the conversation before it tanked even further.

"So, that's it?"

Dominic flinched as Chance's voice cut through the hubbub of the crowd. He turned back around. Chance's shadow of a smirk was firmly in place.

"You come here and take pictures of my exquisite hands, and then you leave without sampling even one tiny piece?"

Dominic released a breath he hadn't realized he'd been holding. He wasn't sure how much more of a beating his Johnny Palomino fantasy could take. Candy was a much safer subject. "Well, I…."

"You don't like chocolate? Yes, now and then I do meet someone who claims that's the case." He drew a smaller tray from the catering cart and presented it with a quiet flourish. "Try one of these, then—they're from my special stock, the ones that sell for five dollars each at my shop, if you can even find them before they sell out. The pieces with the tiny pink dots are topped with peppercorns. The oval pieces are infused with cedarwood. They're all so painfully artistic, you can hardly even call them food."

They didn't look like food, either. They looked like props, too perfect to be eaten. The thought of biting into something too precious to be consumed felt decadent in a way that very few things did anymore. Dominic's hand hovered over the tray. Neither peppercorns nor cedarwood sounded very appealing, so he opted for a third piece instead, a diamond-shaped chocolate, so dark it was nearly black, with a purplish texture on top that glinted subtly when the light hit it just so. It was too small to bite, so he placed it in his mouth whole.

And he wondered if it was even chocolate. He kept his expression as neutral as he could, but even so, he suspected his surprise was apparent. It tasted like he'd just put a pellet of soil into his mouth.

"The thing about chocolate," Chance said, "is that its melting point is just below the temperature of the human body."

That would explain the way it was spreading over Dominic's tongue.

"Now that it's started to melt, exhale through your nose, gradually, in stages, so you'll be able to pick up all the undertones."

What Dominic really wanted to do was either spit the thing out, or swallow it whole to get it over with as quickly as possible—but he could hardly do either of those things with Chance looking right at him. He exhaled. It smelled like dirt, too.

"And now, before it's melted completely, bite into it so you can experience the snap."

Dominic did so, promising himself that it would all be over soon, and then he could wash it all down with a nice glass of cabernet. The chocolate didn't snap—it crunched. Whatever was on top scoured against his teeth. Gritty. And then that, too, began to dissolve, adding a saline, mineral flavor to the dirt.

"Himalayan salt."

Dominic swallowed convulsively, unable to keep the chocolate on his tongue any longer. He glanced around to see if there was wine, water, anything at all to clear the taste from his palate.

"Wait for it…" Chance murmured.

"When you said it didn't taste like food, you weren't—" Dominic swallowed again. When he'd opened his mouth to speak, the air that played over his tongue had released a string of flavors: bitter, moist, dark, musky, rich, salt… and finally, delicately, sweet.

Chocolate.

He sat with it, very still, mouth slightly open, while the flavor mellowed on his tongue. All around him, he was vaguely aware that other guests who'd been listening in to Chance's instructions were now in varying stages of holding chocolates on their tongues, exhaling through their noses, biting into them, and then exclaiming to their friends. But the jolting experience he'd just had was so transcendent that he could tune the partygoers out as easily as he might close down his aperture.

Chance was watching Dominic with that eerie stillness of his. "Looks aren't everything. Don't you think it's about time to go deeper and find someone you can really connect with?"

Dominic wanted to object, but his mind had just been well and truly blown. Where he would have normally protested, he found all he could do was stare.

"If you looked for something more than a slick attitude and a pretty face, you might be surprised at what you'd find."

"That's not fair," Dominic blurted out. Chance raised an eyebrow. "I don't only date showbiz types." He searched the crowd, and picked out Carlton Jeffrey pouring Mimi another glass of merlot. Carlton looked passable in his jazzy notched-lapel tux jacket, but he wouldn't be appearing on the cover of any magazine except *Wine Spectator*. "Looks aren't everything."

Dominic steeled himself for the glib repartee, but it never landed. He turned back to take the insult like a man, and found Chance was looking, really looking, at Carlton. The silence extended far past the state of comfort, and finally, when Dominic began to edge away from the buffet, Chance narrowed his eyes and said, "Interesting."

When Chance drew a tiny red napkin from its stack and handed it over, Dominic sensed he was finally being dismissed, and took it without hesitation. Their fingers brushed. Chance's model-perfect hands were as cold as a February night in Hoboken. A chill so profound raced up Dominic's arm, he thought he might have been having a coronary. Dominic shuddered, but Chance didn't seem to notice. He turned away, drew another tray from the candy cart, and went back to work. "Do take care, Mr. Mann," he said casually. "I hope you find what you're looking for."

Three

THE CYPRESS WINE gala was a rapidly fading memory from the night before as Dominic stared into his bathroom mirror and considered his options.

One: he'd snapped. Mental illness didn't run in his family, unless you counted his cousin Louie who liked to collect empty beer bottles, who'd actually amassed so many he needed to rent a storage unit to house his collection. But there was always the chance that Dominic would turn out to be the first completely delusional member of the Mann clan.

Two: that piece of "chocolate" he'd eaten at the party had been spiked with something a hell of a lot more potent than Himalayan salt.

Three: well…there really was no third option. Either Dominic was crazy, or he was on drugs. Unless he really had been experiencing a coronary, a fatal one, and whoever was in charge of his afterlife possessed a totally fucked-up sense of humor. He supposed that was just as likely a scenario as the other two.

The same face had been staring back at Dominic from medicine cabinets, chrome toasters, hubcaps, and photographs ever since he could remember. Especially photographs. He recalled full well the way his mother's face fell when he brought home his kindergarten class photos, and she looked like she would have liked nothing better than to sneak them right back out with that week's trash collection.

The face in the mirror this morning was most definitely not that face. This face was…handsome.

Dominic leaned in so close, his forehead bumped the mirror. He pulled down his cheek and peered into the slick, pink pocket that cradled the lower curve of his eyeball. It sure looked real, all right. He ran his fingertips over his whiskers. Felt real, too. He tilted his head back and traced the edges of his stubble. Not only did it look and feel real, but it looked and felt the same way it always looked and felt when he shaved. The exact same way.

If anything, Dominic knew faces. He took a few steps back to get a good, unbiased look at himself, and convince himself that his place was *behind* the camera, definitely not in front of it. His eyes were the same hazel. His eyebrows were still thick and dark. Even his nose still had a little bend to it. But for some reason, his eyes were trying to convince his brain that together, it all looked good. Not just good—great.

The sound of bells floated in through the window—Church of the Nazarene calling its faithful to 10 o'clock mass—and the Cypress Mansion tea popped into Dominic's head. It started at 11:30, early enough for churchgoers to arrive straight from mass, but late enough to allow anyone who'd had too much wine the night before to sleep off at least some of their fuzzy-headedness.

He had time to figure out what was going on with him. Not a lot. But some.

Though he hadn't shot angsty self-portraits since he was a desperate and lonely sophomore at Parson's, Dominic was sure he could find a picture of his own face on his computer that would remind him what he really looked like. A lighting test. A group shot at a restaurant. Something.

He powered on his desktop and began poring through the collections. There wasn't a single shot of himself—not that he'd actually remembered taking any, just that it seemed that out of thousands and thousands of shots, there might be at least one he'd done with the autotimer. He scrolled, and scrolled, and scrolled. Nothing. He sat back in his chair, rubbed his eyes, then glanced at the tiny clock in the corner of the screen. If he was still interested in showing up at that tea, he needed to leave in half an hour, and he hadn't even shaved.

Although he was still hallucinating that he was now one of the pretty people, Dominic managed to shave without hurting himself. His face felt familiar, from the rise of his Adam's apple to the curve of his jaw, to the concavity under his lower lip he always took extra care to scrape, so as not to end up with an inadvertent soul patch. Guys like him just couldn't get away with it—ugly guys.

Or could he?

Ridiculous. He splashed away traces of shaving cream and blotted his face dry. Whatever it was he thought he saw in the mirror, he'd be a fool to let it get to him. He was a double-bagger, always had been. And he wasn't about to let a trick of the lighting dupe him into thinking otherwise. He dressed as usual, styled his hair as usual, and dabbed on the merest hint of Acqua di Gio, as usual. And he did his best to banish from his mind the ludicrous notion that he, Dominic Mann, had woken up gorgeous.

⚘ ⚘ ⚘

IT TOOK LONGER to get to Cypress Estate than usual—a lot longer. As Dominic idled behind the 5k charity walkathon that intersected Franklin Pike and cut him off from his destination, he struggled with the urge to flip down his visor and see if he was still good-looking. Then he mentally razzed himself for even entertaining the notion to begin with. Of course he wasn't. Never had been. Although, maybe a little peek wouldn't hur—

Damn. That was one handsome devil staring back at him from the visor mirror.

The car behind him leaned on its horn. There was a gap in the walkathon, and a traffic cop was herding the line forward. Dominic flipped the visor up and drove, profoundly disturbed that he'd been as smitten with his own reflection as Narcissus.

Dominic tried to remember how the story went, and although the specifics escaped him, he was pretty sure the guy hadn't lived happily ever after.

Since he'd been held up by the walkathon, every parking space near the Cypress was already taken by the time he arrived. He finally found a spot two blocks away and skirting the edge of a fire hydrant curb, and then he walk-jogged to the mansion with his camera bag pulling on his shoulder all the way there. A volunteer staffer in a Preservation Society polo shirt directed him to the backyard veranda, where clusters of genteel folks in their Sunday finery were just breaking up their conversations so they could be seated.

Mimi was a vision in lavender, with a sleek sheath dress, gloves, and a broad-brimmed hat atop a severe silver wig. "And there's Dominic Mann," she said. "Fetchingly disheveled and fashionably late. Come take your seat, darling. We almost started without you."

Dominic located his place card at a table in which three moneyed widows were seated. Odd. Mimi didn't seat people at random. He usually found himself among reporters, patrons of the arts, and if Mimi'd been in a generous mood while she put together her seating chart, other "bachelors."

Speaking of which…he scanned the crowd to see if Johnny Palomino was anywhere to be seen, and found the musician several tables away. His seat was facing the opposite direction, but he'd turned to watch as Dominic pulled out his chair. He caught Dominic's eye, and smiled. A very big smile. Dominic supposed he smiled back. Hard to say. He was so stunned he felt numb.

Conversation at Dominic's table was light. It centered on whose granddaughter was going to Vanderbilt and whose to Duke, up and coming fall design trends and colors, and the next fundraiser over at the humane society. Safe topics. Things he could talk about without allocating much thought to them—and that lack of depth turned out to be a good thing. Because every time he bent over the silver tea tray to serve another cucumber sandwich to one of his companions, he saw that bizarre, handsome face looking back at him from the polished surface. Even weirder, every time he looked up, he spotted Johnny Palomino making bedroom eyes at him from across the veranda.

Normally, he would have stopped and eaten something substantial before he showed up at a party where the refreshments were meant to be pretty rather than filling, but he'd barely made it on time as it was.

Too busy chimping his own reflection.

Now, he was paying for it. The sunlight peeking through the latticework column of the veranda played across the back of Dominic's neck, and he shifted in his seat, doing his best not to squirm. The heat, the anxiety, and the lack of real food hit him at the same time; he felt lightheaded. Best not to make a scene in front of the ladies. He excused himself from the table before sweat began to prickle at his upper lip, and he made his way toward the mansion.

Back in 1953, Mimi Van der Berg's grandfather Archie knocked a wall out of his study so he could expand it with a walk-in humidor. By all accounts, the humidor was a bad idea from its inception. One of the laborers was caught stealing silverware. Another eloped with Mimi's aunt Rose. Adding insult to injury, the construction itself was poorly executed. Within a year, moisture damage that crept into the study made that part of the mansion nearly unusable. The shoddy craftsmanship turned out to be a blessing in disguise some fifty years later when the addition was razed without qualms, and replaced with a handicap-accessible entrance and a bank of public restrooms.

Dominic burst into one of said restrooms, grasped the sturdy handrail mounted in the tasteful but utilitarian tile, and tried hard to catch his breath. His heavy Nikon dangled, casting a swaying shadow on the bathroom floor. He hoped that if he blacked out, he'd tip backwards so that the camera could land on him, and not the other way around.

Maybe, he decided, the fatality theory he'd cooked up back at his apartment wasn't too far off the mark. What if, at the wine reception, the twinge he'd felt in his arm had been a hell of a lot more than a weird torque of his funny bone?

He turned on one of the taps, in hopes that a little cool water across the insides of his wrists might set the world right. It was a high order for something as simple as water, but it was the only solution Dominic could come up with. Dimly, over the spray of the water and the thudding of his own pulse in his ears, Dominic became aware of footsteps out in the hallway. Someone must have seen how unsteady he was and called a paramedic. Or, if not, someone who needed to take a whiz would find him collapsed on the bathroom floor.

The door sighed open on its sturdy pneumatic hinge, and the bathroom mirrors filled with a half-dozen reflected reflections of a sharp-jawed man in dressy jeans and a white western shirt piped in black.

Or maybe Dominic would find himself alone again with Johnny Palomino.

Dominic grabbed a brown paper hand towel from the dispenser, touched it to the water stream and blotted his face. "I had to get out of the sun," he said, as if that would explain everything. "I'm too hot."

It made perfect sense to Johnny. "I'll say." He strode up to Dominic, grabbed him by the hips, and ground the flies of their pants together with as little hesitation as he would have offered a handshake. "I thought maybe you were puttin' me on last night about coming to this tea-thing."

Putting him on? The Texas drawl had evaporated from Johnny's voice, and left him sounding less like a ranch hand and more like a Red Sox fan.

Dominic tried to back away and get his bearings, but his shoulder blades were pressed into the tile wall and there was nowhere for him to go. Johnny pressed his thumbs hard into Dominic's pelvic curve, and rubbed up against his groin again. There was a distinct bulge now in the front of Johnny's jeans.

"What's a matter?" he said. "You pissed off I went home with Stan Beloit? Don't worry about it."

"No, I—"

"That was just business. You know how it is. Besides, I hardly even felt it." Johnny ground their crotches together so hard, Dominic was surprised he didn't wear a hole in the material. His bulging package caught Dominic's just so, and Dominic felt his body start to respond. Johnny felt it, too. He smiled—perfect dental work—and leaned in so he could whisper against Dominic's overheated neck. "But with you—I *know* I'm gonna feel it. 'Cos when you fuck me, I want you to pound my ass right through the mattress. Got it?"

If it weren't for the Nikon, Dominic suspected the scenario Johnny had in mind would spin out right there and then—but the massive DSLR was like a brick between them. A familiar and reassuring brick, Dominick realized… and then Johnny had the audacity to grab it.

"How'd those pictures we took last night come out?" He twisted the camera so the display faced him, and the lens cap prodded Dominic in the sternum. "I'll bet they're smokin'."

"I didn't get a chance to look."

An expression flickered over Johnny's face too fast for Dominic to follow without his finger on the shutter, and then those sultry bedroom eyes were back. "No prob'. You behind the camera, me in front of it, I'm sure they're good."

Dominic didn't know how to answer that. It had never occurred to him that they wouldn't be. "Listen." Dominic didn't want to seem ungrateful for the cheap thrill from the handsome cowboy, but he couldn't seem to keep his head in the game. "You maybe wanna meet up later on, go to—"

"I thought you'd never ask. Butch—my pain-in-the-ass manager—has me booked in meetings and socials practically back to back this weekend. I'm supposed to be talking to some recording engineers after this, but I could catch up with you around seven."

"Seven. Sure. We could grab a bite."

Johnny's free hand dropped to Dominic's crotch, cupped it, and squeezed.

"Here's the only thing I want to grab. I could give a rat's ass about dinner."

He flicked the camera on, and Dominic automatically thumbed off the lens cap. Johnny held it away from the two of them and snapped something that couldn't have been anything more than a blur.

"Make sure you call me. Not like last night, where you disappeared the second I told you I couldn't hook up."

"That's not what happened." Dominic didn't say it with much force, though, as he realized that he was no longer completely clear on what exactly *had* happened the night before.

Johnny squeezed the shutter as he dragged his teeth down the front of Dominic's shirt, over his chest and, crouching, his belly, in a promise of things to come.

He dropped to his knees and looked up at Dominic with sly eyes to make sure there was no mistake he was promising to make Dominic very happy indeed, then let go of the camera. It bounced against Dominic's chest. With his hands now free, Johnny pulled a card from his jeans pocket and tucked it into Dominic's waistband. "Call me. I mean it."

He stood, still smiling, and ambled out of the restroom. The door sighed shut behind him, and Dominic was alone.

Deep breath in, let it out….

Dominic slumped against the wall and stared at his Nikon's viewscreen. The shot on it was blurry—but not too blurry to tell it was Johnny Palomino biting one of the buttons on the front of Dominic's shirt like he was about to clip it off with his teeth and spit it out over his shoulder. Spooked, he hit the menu button and trashed the picture.

A few more deep breaths were in order. Dominic breathed, and did his best to clear his mind. Eventually the mental noise subsided, and he could focus on the reality around him. The tile wall. The air-freshener smell. The hiss of the running water. The moist feel of the air as it clung to his now-clammy skin.

Even though it would shatter his newfound calm, Dominic turned toward the mirror to seek out another glance at his own reflection with the hope that maybe now, after all that had happened, he could finally make sense of it. But the faucet was cranked on hot, and steam covered the mirror. Dominic looked, more or less, like himself again, but only because he was now mostly a silhouette.

He shut the tap off. Ghosts of fingerprints and smudges rose through the mirror's steam coat, where the public's idle hands had drawn words into prior generations of steam, and somehow the fastidious cleaning crew's washrags had passed them by.

"It's not the heat," Dominic's Hoboken relatives would remark every August, "it's the humidity." He now saw the wisdom in that statement, as the air in the Cypress public restroom suddenly felt wet enough to drown him. He adjusted the bulge in the front of his pants, plucked a dry paper towel from the dispenser, and gave his face a final swab before he headed back out to the veranda.

Even through the paper, it felt exactly like his own face.

Four

The hallway was dimmer and cooler than the bathroom, and less likely to stew Dominic in his own juices. He blotted his forehead again, then checked to be sure none of the teenaged gift shop volunteers would conclude he was having a stroke and call the paramedics. The gift shop area was deserted, as was the small foyer around the handicap entrance. Dominic was alone.

He thought so, anyway, until he saw a flutter of movement in his peripheral vision, and heard a snap. There was motion inside the newly-restored family dining room.

Dominic crept up to the doorway, and watched as a red tablecloth flared with a loud crack, then settled around a slim figure in black: Chance, who handled it like a matador. His chef's uniform was gone, but nonetheless he was all in black—black T-shirt, black alligator skin cowboy boots, black jeans.

He took his time folding the tablecloth, though he seemed more like he was being obstinate than careful, and finally, when he'd smoothed a dozen invisible wrinkles from the fabric, he turned to Dominic and said, "Well, what did you need?"

Dominic opened his mouth and almost answered *nothing*, but then he realized that would be answering the question he'd expected, *What do you want*, rather than the one he'd actually been asked. He closed his mouth again and considered. This pause seemed to please Chance, who finally turned toward him and actually graced him with more than just the dregs of his attention.

"I need to know what's going on."

Chance crossed his arms over his chest, cocked his hip and leaned against the buffet while he considered Dominic's words. "Do you really? What do you suppose will happen if you don't?"

"Well, I…" Dominic tried to imagine a catastrophic scenario that would result from him never understanding why, suddenly, he'd gone to bed a frog and woken up a handsome prince.

Would it really be so bad, not knowing how, not knowing why? Maybe not.

But the idea that someday the prince would turn back into a frog…that would eat at him, for sure.

"Tell me this," Dominic said. "Do I look the same to you I did last night, or not?"

Chance tilted his head and considered. "Different suit…."

"You know what I mean."

"I'm surprised you even noticed," Chance said, "given that beauty holds so little importance for you."

"What are you talking about?"

"Last night. You told me looks weren't everything—and it struck me as truthful, at least as far as anyone can tell the truth these days. So what is it? Does a person's physical appearance matter…or not?"

Dominic could think of dozens of reasons to reaffirm what he'd said at the wine reception, and just as many to contradict it. "It's not that easy."

"Undeniably so." Chance turned and began dropping trays onto a cart with crashes that reverberated through the room like cymbals. "And I assure you, there's nothing more tedious than an easy life."

Dominic felt an invisible wall slam down between them, and he sensed he'd been dismissed again. When he exited the Cypress into the oppressive early-afternoon heat, it was almost a relief.

The second half of the tea was more bearable than the first, since Dominic was able to retire from the peculiar approving gazes of the older ladies at his table and to circulate among the crowd, shooting photos in the dappled sunlight. There was an artlessness to the natural lighting that he enjoyed. It allowed him to concentrate on the composition of the shots, and the expressions on the subjects' faces.

Unfortunately, since he was going from table to table to ensure he got some shots of everybody, he couldn't avoid ending up face to face with Johnny Palomino. Johnny dropped a shoulder and leaned toward one of his tea companions to say something witty, and the woman laughed. It was a perfect shot—or it would have been, if Dominic hadn't been too distracted to take it. His finger lagged on the shutter, and caught the poor woman at the moment where her smile turned into a strange twist of her mouth. Johnny, of course, still looked good. He was very still; he'd seen the camera coming.

The guy across from Johnny stood and smoothed the front of his shirt. He was a tall, raw-boned man around fifty, with black hair touched at the temples with gray. He was dressed in black western wear, with a short black goatee—the living, breathing embodiment of the Renegade Sam Cobra action figure a 10-year-old Dominic had taken through its paces so many times, the joints had worn out.

"How d'you do, Mr. Mann. I'm Butch Arlen, Johnny's manager." His voice was deep, his accent was pure South Texas, and when he shook Dominic's hand his grip was like granite—and he held on for an extra beat. Did he know what they'd just been up to in the restroom? Was it written across Johnny's face…and did Dominic need to worry about getting his ass kicked? Dominic considered how fast he'd need to run to outstrip the aptly-named Butch. Pretty fast, judging by those long legs. Just as Dominic was angling for his escape, Butch added, "I'm a big fan of your work."

As Dominic stammered his thanks, Mimi cut in and saved the day. "There you are, darling. Such a social butterfly. Be a dear and get a shot of me with Mr. Wipperfurth. His angina is giving him a hard time, and he has to go home to his central air."

Dominic excused himself and offered his arm to Mimi. The lawn had been more of a slimy, wet sponge after the Cumberland flooded, but once the waters receded, the sun baked the soil beneath the turfgrass to its usual state of hardness in just a few weeks. Even so, Mimi needed to tiptoe in her stiletto heels to avoid aerating the lawn, and she seemed happy enough to lean on him. As she did so, she said in his ear, "You do realize there's a business card sticking out of your waistband, don't you?"

Dominic palmed the card and slipped it into his pocket. Hopefully anyone who noticed how red he was would attribute his color to the heat.

Mimi patted his arm as they walked. "I've never regretted aging—after all, what's the alternative? And as a woman, one finds there are certain perks associated with every passing decade one survives. But still…" she slowed and gazed up at Dominic for a moment, then smiled and led the way to the

Wipperfurth table. "Sometimes when I'm with you, I do miss being a young, ravishing creature with the world wrapped around my little finger."

Dominic laughed nervously. He himself felt neither young nor ravishing, but arguing about the finer points of Mimi's proclamation would only drag out the conversation and make whatever was going on that much more confusing.

He shot the photos quickly—Mr. Wipperfurth's complexion was a peculiar shade of aubergine—and wondered if he had a filter that would compensate for the flush. It felt good to work. If Dominic stayed behind the camera, there was no need to try to make sense out of what was going on with his own face, and to try to determine why the people who knew him were treating him differently now…as if there could be any doubt.

He moved through the crowd even as the tea came to an end and the wilted philanthropists began to filter back toward their air-conditioned sedans, hoping to capture one final candid shot in the challenging lighting conditions.

The human eye was more adept at making sense of what it saw than any camera. The eye was connected to the brain, and so it could compensate for things like color cast, contrast and backlighting. While the camera was, in Dominic's opinion, a miracle of modern invention—it took a lot more finessing to capture things the human eye saw with no effort at all.

He waited a moment until Mrs. Boyer-Brown stepped out of the sun-shade pattern that lay across her face like vitiligo, then shot a few frames that would hopefully be more flattering, though he did so with only a tiny fragment of his attention.

A plan had just occurred to him. Maybe the fact that he couldn't find any old photos of himself didn't matter. Maybe what he needed to know was what he really looked like right now. If the camera was too simple to tell the difference between a trick of the light and a skin condition, he reasoned, maybe it wouldn't fall for whatever glamour had been tricking not only his eyes, but the eyes of everyone else he knew.

He couldn't very well shoot a photo of himself out there on the veranda without coming off as a joke, but the thought of going back into the men's room for a little privacy spooked him. Ten, fifteen more minutes, he told himself, and he could go back to his car, snap on his macro lens, and get a good, *objective* look at that face of his.

When Dominic made one final circuit of the dissipating crowd, Johnny Palomino was facing the other direction, which was, in a way, a relief. It enabled Dominic to plant an air-kiss on Mimi, then sneak past the trellises and out to the sidewalk without another awkward encounter.

He was so eager to see, really *see* what was going on once and for all, that it took him a few moments to realize his car was no longer there. He stared at the spot where he could have sworn he'd left it, and then he marched up and down the block a few times. It was preferable to think he'd just forgotten where he parked—but the yellow-painted curb by the fire hydrant that he might have overlapped by a foot or so could hardly be ignored.

"Damn it." Stomping his foot didn't help any. It hardly even made him feel better—but he hadn't quite figured out his next course of action, so at least it was something to do.

"Is there a problem?"

Dominic spun and found tall, austere Butch Arlen witnessing his little snit. He straightened up and did his best to look dignified. "I think I just got towed."

Butch eyed the curb. "Probably so. Maybe you should take a picture of the spot…from an angle that makes it look bigger than it is. That way you can contest the ticket."

"I could give a rat's ass about the ticket. I just want my car back."

Butch shook his head and gave a rueful smile. "You won't get anywhere with the impound lot on a Sunday."

Dominic gave the empty parking space a few choice Hoboken hand gestures, but stopped short of stamping his foot again. He stepped around Butch and took a shot that made the parking spot look big enough to fit an extended cab pickup. It gave him some satisfaction, but not much. "I can't believe this would happen right when I needed to…" take a picture of himself? He could hardly go shooting his mouth off about that. A lightheaded wave of giddiness washed over him, and instead he said, "eat some real food."

"Cucumber sandwiches don't exactly stick to the ribs. I was about to offer you a ride home, but if you'd rather stop for something to eat…?"

Dominic was about to say no, and thanks, and never mind, I'll call a cab. He was hot, confused, and royally pissed off—and, frankly, things had been so far out of whack since the wine reception the night before, he was wondering if he'd sustained a head injury he hadn't happened to notice. But his favorite Wild West action figure incarnate had just invited him out to eat. How could he refuse?

⚘ ⚘ ⚘

If Butch Arlen had come into Dominic's life at any other time, Dominic would have been over the moon with delight. Judging by the looks Butch stole when he thought Dominic wasn't looking, he seemed interested in more than just a post-tea snack. His deep, easy Texas drawl was beyond charming. He'd ridden in and rescued Dominic from danger—or at the very least, the inconvenience of calling a cab. Most importantly, he had that whole Renegade Sam Cobra thing going on.

Circumstances being what they were, though, Dominic found himself dawdling in the restroom of the world's busiest barbecue joint, waiting for the guy in the stall get on with his dump, and the guy at the urinal to shake himself off and get out of there. Finally, after a long enough stretch that Dominic would have to invent an excuse that didn't make him sound like a candidate for an emergency colonoscopy, the door swung shut behind a well-dressed guy who hadn't washed his hands…and Dominic and his camera were alone.

He focused on a spot on the wall two feet away, just about the length of his arm, then turned the camera on himself. It would've been easier with a little point-and-shoot. The Nikon felt awkward in reverse, and it dragged his arm down. There was noise in the hall, dishes rattling in busboy trays, footsteps. Dominic held down the shutter and took a quick series, turning his face slowly in hopes of capturing some image he could make sense of, and then just as the door opened, he dropped his camera, the neck strap snapping taut.

Since he'd had his fill of restroom shenanigans for the day, he turned on the tap and pretended to be washing his hands so he didn't have to explain himself. It was awkward with the camera, which he would have normally put away for safe keeping rather than risk getting it wet. He clasped it to his chest with one hand and reached for the water with the other, figuring he only needed to look like he was actually doing something legitimate for maybe a second or two, and then he could crumple up a paper towel, throw it in the trashcan and get back to Butch.

The water was hot enough to brew tea.

"Sonofa—" he snatched his hand back and shook it. The large, trucker-looking guy in the greasy baseball cap heading for the stall was not impressed.

Now Dominic did actually want to run water over his hand. Cold water. He tilted the chrome lever toward the right, but the water only got hotter—hot enough to fog up the mirror.

Enough, already.

Dominic's hand was blotchy red, but he'd live. He pushed down on the tap so he could get back to the table before Butch sent in a search party....

The tap was stuck.

Of course it was. Dominic rolled his eyes. He considered leaving, but how could he? The guy in the stall had seen him in there. Another guy shuffled in and started to take a leak. Dominic shoved harder at the tap, but it wouldn't budge. He even tried opening it up farther so he could gain a little momentum before he pulled it down—but that only succeeded in making the hot water run faster.

"Okay," he said, loud, over the rush of water, since it seemed he'd have to own the situation. "This faucet's all screwed up. I'm getting the manager."

He looked over his shoulder at the pissing guy, who was too absorbed in what he was doing to acknowledge that Dominic had just spoken. Fine. Good. Dominic had done his part. He turned to head toward the door and get the manager...and found a word had appeared in the steamed-up mirror. One simple word.

Ugly.

Dominic jerked the tap and it snapped down, shutting off the flow. The oval of steam on the mirror began to shrink immediately, but that single word, *ugly*, hovered there just below the blurred reflection of Dominic's face. He smeared it away with his palm, and then lunged out the bathroom door and wiped his hands dry on his pants.

He fell into the seat opposite Butch, picked up his ice water, and held it against his cheek. "You all right?" Butch asked. "Maybe you're not used to the heat. Could be sunstroke."

"I've lived here four years. It's fine."

Butch eyed Dominic with the shrewdness of someone who was accustomed to spotting problems and then handling them…but he chose not to challenge Dominic's reassurance that he was "fine," even if it was obviously not the case.

The waitress hauled two heaping plates to the table. The platter groaned with pulled pork sandwiches the size of footballs. Smoky baked beans spread over the dishes, their brown sauce mingling with the creamy, white mayonnaise running from the coleslaw, and buttery roasted corn on the cob threatened to roll off the overstuffed plates. The hickory-sweet, buttery smell made Dominic's nearly empty stomach rumble, but the image of that word appearing in the steam—that single damn word that was the bane of his existence—made him doubt he could even swallow.

"Maybe a bite to eat would settle your stomach," Butch suggested. He took a forkful of coleslaw into his mouth, and his eyelids fluttered closed in rapture. He swallowed with a sip of sweet tea, and that, too, made him smile. Dominic could hardly sit there like a lump while his companion was having a religious experience with his food, and so he bit into his sandwich. Salty, spicy, hot and sweet.

"Now that's some fine barbecue," Butch said.

The need for conversation was suspended as they ate. Butch relished every bite, while Dominic struggled to even taste it. He was out with a smoking-hot, honest-to-goodness Texan, there was a hell of a spread on the table, and for the first time in his life, Dominic didn't have to worry about someone reassuring him that he had a very nice personality. But with the word *ugly* haunting him, how could he enjoy himself?

Once Butch's plate was clean, he sighed with contentment, and only then looked over at Dominic's picked-at plate. "You didn't like the food?" He seemed surprised, like he'd met someone who didn't like money, or maybe sex. Or chocolate.

Dominic stared at the cooling strings of pulled pork for a long moment, and without looking up so he didn't lose his courage, blurted out, "Were you at Cypress last night?"

Butch paused, then said, "I was."

They hadn't been personally introduced at any point—Dominic would have remembered—but he himself had been pointed out to the entire gathering. "Did you see me there?"

"I did."

Dominic forced himself to meet Butch's dark eyes. "What did I look like?"

Butch blinked as if Dominic's question had caught him off guard. "Well, you had this here camera with you. Your suit was black. Your tie was red." He shrugged. "Your hair was neater."

"And that's it. That's all you remember."

Butch turned his hands palm-up. They were big hands, with long fingers, squared-off fingertips and thick knuckles. Hands that could change a tire or saddle a horse. He wore a single, wide gold band—on his forefinger, of all places—inlaid with an onyx music note set between two small diamonds.

"You remember I had a red tie on?"

Butch tipped back his sweet tea, probably, Dominic thought, because he was acting like a freak and it was the easiest way to break eye contact. Butch put the tall, sweating glass back in its ring of condensation on the tablecloth, considered his words for a few seconds, looked Dominic in the eye and said, "Seems like there's something specific you want to know." He dropped his voice very low, and his accent took on a musical lilt. "You can tell me. Whatever it is."

"Yeah. Right."

Butch looked at Dominic harder. His eyes were piercing.

"It sounds crazy," Dominic whispered. "I can't say it. Not here, not in front of all these people."

Butch nodded, dropped his magnetic gaze, and signaled for the check. "I'll take you home. You decide you want to talk about it? We'll talk. If not, I drop you off without another word."

Five

Dominic regarded the numbered parking spot behind his apartment from the unusual perspective of the passenger seat. The silent drive from the barbecue joint had yielded up exactly zero ways for him to ask Butch whether or not he'd noticed Dominic was an ugly duckling at the wine gala, but a swan at the tea. He turned towards Butch to see if something in his face would help Dominic to find the right words…but the sight of him, framed and backlit by the truck window, the late afternoon light playing over the angular planes of his face, the type of face a real artist would want to shoot, not like those same-old, same-old models….

"You want me to stay, or go?"

Dominic had been quiet so long, his voice broke on the word. "Stay."

The walk up to the second-floor apartment seemed like it should have looked different, viewed, as it was, through Dominic's newly-attractive eyes. It didn't. It looked the same as it always had. Same popcorn-textured ceiling, same unassuming low-pile carpeting and classic woodwork, same quiet, understated utility. *Just say it,* he thought. *Ask him whether he noticed you were ugly last night and get it over with. The worst he can think is that you're screwed in the head. Heck, you probably are.*

He unlocked the door and led Butch into the open-plan living space that doubled as his personal gallery, and drew breath to speak. He lost his nerve, however, when Butch strode past him to the photographs like he'd been itching to see them all afternoon.

"There it is…." He'd stopped in front of the last shot ever taken of Carl Perkins, the image that had rocketed Dominic to fame on the cover of Rolling Stone after Perkins' death. Butch sighed like he was enjoying a sip of sweet tea, and inspected it from inches away, tilting his head this way and that, before he took a few steps back, crossed his arms over his chest and drank the whole photograph in. "This one's my favorite."

"So you weren't shittin' me when you said you were a big fan."

"That, I was not."

The most famous photos of the rockabilly legend were from the 1950's—but Dominic had captured some elusive quality that mild autumn day in Jackson, some play of the bluish Tennessee sunlight over the hard-earned creases of Carl's face that made the photograph not only compelling, but to a fan of the genre, iconic.

"It looks different like this than it did on the magazine," Butch decided. "Deeper, like." He shook his head. "Sorry. I'm no artist. I don't know how to put words to it."

"You're doing fine." Dominic approached. They stood shoulder to shoulder and gazed at the photo together for several minutes. When Butch was done looking he turned toward Dominic, and Dominic leaned in.

Butch eased into the kiss, as if he intended to savor it. There was a certainty to his lips that Dominic didn't find in younger men, an ease that spoke of many years of putting their paces through the eternal dance of seduction. Dominic's eyes had closed, some universal reflex, he supposed, but he forced them open to take in the harsh and wonderful lines of Butch's face.

As if he felt Dominic looking at him, Butch opened his eyes too, and paused. His black eyebrows screwed up in a silent question, and Dominic sensed that if he were to find the balls to ask about what he looked like, now was the time.

But with Butch looking at him like that, brow furrowed, jaw set, his stance practically trembling with raw need?

He couldn't.

He held a hand out instead—Butch took it, the gold ring a hard, heavy pressure as his big hand enveloped Dominic's—and led the way into the bedroom.

At that point, Dominic would normally have turned the lights off. Today, he couldn't. The room was filled with late-afternoon sunlight—gentle, diffuse, and a bit hazy. Even if he pulled the curtains from their tiebacks to cover the slats of the miniblinds, light would sneak in around the edges (as light had a tendency to do, both in a film canister, and in a darkroom) and reveal him in all his vulnerable glory.

Butch began to unbutton his own shirt.

Dominic pulled the camera strap over his head and set his Nikon on the dresser. There was no mirror there. Why start the day on a sour note, he'd always figured. But suddenly he wished he hadn't been so eager to avoid himself. If he'd had a mirror, he would have known whether he was still gorgeous, or whether it was all some sunstroke-induced fantasy.

Butch stepped up behind him and pressed his mouth to the back of Dominic's neck, right over the spot the camera strap usually covered. His lips pressed to the hot, smooth-rubbed flesh, and clung to Dominic's skin even as he dragged his mouth along the trail. More kisses, and then a trace of tongue. Gooseflesh danced over Dominic's forearms.

Butch reached around and began to unbutton Dominic's shirt. His big, strong hands worked the buttons with more precision than they seemed like they should have been capable of. His body was all hot, hard planes and angles against Dominic's back. No gym-sculpting there. Dominic turned in Butch's arms to face him. No spray-tan or dental veneers, either. Just a man in his late prime with all the character of Dominic's single most famous photograph.

Beautiful.

Dominic felt himself straining against his fly without even having been touched directly, like a horny teenager hoping to get some action under the old viaduct. Damn. Everywhere Butch's hands went, arms and chest, collarbones and stomach, Dominic's body sprang to attention. Tingling trails of aliveness followed his touch.

The deliciously squirmy anticipation verged on being uncomfortable, these intense sensations that surged beneath Dominic's skin—which had fit him as easily as his old, ugly wrapper earlier, but now seemed tense enough to split open and reveal him.

He fumbled with Butch's star-shaped belt buckle and dropped to his knees. If his real face did choose to make a reappearance, at least it would look better wrapped around a hard-on. So he'd been told. On more than one occasion.

Butch groaned, a mingle of relief and anticipation. His huge hands cradled Dominic's head as he planted his feet wide. His cock had already grown thick with anticipation, and it stiffened as Dominic took the musky saltiness into his mouth.

He grabbed onto Butch's hipbones as he picked up speed. He'd need to slow down if he wanted to make it last, but this new face of his seemed like it had something to prove. He took Butch's cock deep, over and over, so it butted against the back of his throat—and he sucked hard.

Panting, Butch caught Dominic by the wrists and took a step back. His stiff red cock, bulging with veins, bobbed at Dominic's eye-level. "Lay down with me," he said. "I want to get you off, too."

Dominic almost insisted on staying put, but he had the sense that Butch was accustomed to taking care of business rather than being waited on—and Dominic was so far out of his own comfort zone, he figured he shouldn't tempt fate. He stripped down. As he stepped out of his pants, he turned away from Butch and ran his fingertips across his forehead, down his cheeks and jaw. His face felt the same. But that had been how it felt that morning too, so that didn't mean anything.

Butch sat on the edge of the mattress and pulled off his cowboy boots and socks so he could push his jeans the rest of the way off. He tugged Dominic down beside him onto the bed, both of them profoundly naked in the late-afternoon sunlight that leaked in around the blinds, and cupped Dominic's face for a kiss. Dominic felt the brush of whiskers, then lips, then tongue. Butch slid one of his big hands between Dominic's thighs and began stroking his balls, trailing more kisses down his neck.

The kisses, the seductive, uneasy tension of them, made the question bubble to the surface before Dominic could stop himself. "Didn't you notice what I actually looked like last night?"

Butch paused with his goatee tickling Dominic's sternum. "Why's it eating at you so bad? I told you—I saw you. I got a look at you when Miz Van der Berg said you were the official photographer, but other than that, I reckon we were on opposite sides of the room. We must have been. You don't remember seeing *me…*do you?"

"I think I woulda noticed."

Butch straightened and looked deep into Dominic's eyes. "You got something to say, then say it. Whatever it is…it's all right."

Dominic searched Butch's face. His big, dark eyes were tender, and a bit sad. Dominic gazed into them and wished he could figure out the right words—or whether he should say anything at all.

Butch's eyebrows hitched with worry. He'd been at the party, too. What if, Dominic realized, he hadn't been the only one to wake up in a new skin? What if Butch had also gone from zero to hero overnight?

Did it matter?

Dominic leaned in for another kiss, lips parted, this time with his eyes closed. Butch's mouth was eager beneath his. Sure, Dominic decided, the Renegade Sam Cobra look made for a pretty package, but that only served to grab his attention initially. What held it was the quiet self-assuredness, the way Butch was unruffled by heatstroke and impound lots and crazy photographers who asked too many vague questions.

And, of course, the fact that he genuinely admired Dominic's work was probably the headiest turn-on of them all.

Butch stroked his thumb down the cleft of Dominic's balls as he took their kiss deeper, bolder, until Dominic's worry began to swirl away on the intoxicating waves of caresses and kisses.

Butch sank down on one elbow and nudged Dominic to mirror the position, head to groin. Butch was still hard and ready, and Dominic took him down deep just as Butch did the same, all heat and wetness, generous with his mouth, and bent on pleasing Dominic.

Technique? Sure, everyone had their little tricks—especially prettyboys whose main objective was to get you off and get on with their evenings. It wasn't that Butch went deeper or had a more skillful tongue. It was the noises he made, the guttural grunts of satisfaction like he'd never wanted anything in his mouth more—not even the pulled pork and sweet tea.

His enthusiasm was contagious.

Dominic abandoned his worries—and his reserve—and gave in to the moment, sucking cock, sucking balls, sneaking his tongue as far around into the ass crack as he could reach while he ran his hands over Butch's body—hips, ribs, spine, all hard-fleshed bone and sinew. He peaked first, with his cock squelched so far down Butch's throat he felt teeth and chin pressing into his pubic bone. He groaned against Butch's spit-wet taint, then turned onto his back and encouraged Butch to fuck his face. Butch's cock hammered into his mouth, straining his aching jaw, and he lay back and relinquished control, while Butch took him, and used him—and finally, with a gasp, shot a huge, hot load on his face that oozed from the corners of his mouth and down his cheeks and jaw to settle, sticky, in the crook of his neck.

Butch rolled off. Dominic stared at the ceiling fan in a daze. The light had dimmed. It was getting on toward dusk. He worked his sore jaw a few times, and then swallowed. Butch trailed his fingers along Dominic's arm. A little thrill shot down Dominic's spine and he wondered if he might even be up for a double-header—if he could manage to catch his breath again, first. He wiped his face on the top sheet and turned himself around. Butch wrapped strong arms around him, and they lay together, sweaty and content, while the light continued to fade.

"That was incredible," Butch said, so quietly the words were almost lost in the pillow.

"You should stay," Dominic added quickly—before he could convince himself that it wasn't the sort of thing a guy like him dared to say.

Butch squeezed him tighter. "I'd like that."

So, the new face was talking for him now? Dominic couldn't see any other way to explain it. Maybe, he figured, he could get used to it, as long as it meant he could look forward to someone like Butch in his bed.

Butch nuzzled him, scraping whiskers against Dominic's jaw. No, not someone *like* Butch Arlen. Just him. Butch.

Once the room was more dark than light, and both Dominic and Butch succumbed to the urge to move and stretch, and shake sensation back into the limbs that had fallen asleep beneath them, Butch rolled a crick out of his neck and said, "A shower would feel good right about now. You up for one?"

A stirring deep in Dominic's balls said yes, but a bright red 7:00 popped up on the clock radio, and he remembered he was supposed to be wining and dining Johnny Palomino at that very moment. Shit. "Yeah, sure. Through the kitchen. I'll, ah…I'll be right there."

Johnny fucking Palomino. The thought of that kid grinding against him in the restroom made his burgeoning hard-on wilt like a gelatin ring in the sun. Dominic would have blown him off in a heartbeat—Johnny didn't have *his* number, after all—if it weren't for the fact that Butch was Johnny's manager. If he wanted to keep seeing Butch, no doubt he'd cross paths with Johnny again. Better to call and own up to the fact that he was no longer interested in a rendezvous.

The phone only rang once. "It's Johnny," he said in a sultry voice with a fake southern twang. "Talk to me."

"Hey, pal, it's Dominic. Listen—"

"Do you realize what time it is, Mr. Mann? Y'all were supposed to be in my pants ten minutes ago."

"About that…."

"Don't tell me y'all need to postpone. I've been thinkin' about you so long my balls are aching."

"See, the thing is…." Dominic sighed. He always thought it would be easier being on this end of the brush-off. He'd been wrong. "I don't mean to be a jerk about it, but I gave it some thought, and I just don't think you're my type."

There was a long pause in which Dominic wondered if Johnny's cell had cut out, although he strongly suspected it hadn't. When he'd been in Johnny's shoes, practice had made him quick to say *yeah, sure, I understand*. But Johnny Palomino didn't know what to make of the word *no*.

Dominic attempted to spare him the discomfort of wrapping up the conversation. "So, anyways, I guess I'll see you ar—"

"Listen, you arrogant fuck."

It was Dominic's turn to sit in stunned silence.

"I guess 'cos you're some high-and-mighty hot shit New York photographer, some big *star*," the nasal Boston-r crept in, "that you can just toy with the heads of all the little peons scrabbling around at your feet."

"What? No, that's not—"

"I'm not what you're looking for? You're disappointed? You think I'm not good enough for you?"

"I never said that."

"Yeah, well, I get it. Take a good look in the mirror, 'pal.' The feeling's mutual."

Dominic stared at the phone for several long seconds after Johnny hung up on him. He considered calling back, apologizing—but what more was there to say? Initiating another conversation would only dig him in deeper.

He'd been honest with Johnny, he decided, and that was the important thing. But what if Johnny was pissed off enough to sabotage his relationship with Butch? What then? Dominic put his head in his hands and listened to the patter of the shower, and wondered if it hadn't just been easier being ugly, and have no one care what he did one way or the other.

Telling Butch was the logical next step—not that there was much to tell. Johnny was Butch's client, though, so Dominic would need to be careful not to badmouth him. Dominic pieced together the most neutral explanation he could come up with: that he'd stood up Johnny because he found he'd rather be with Butch. It didn't make him sound like the man of the year, but it shouldn't be the end of the world, either.

He grabbed an extra couple of clean towels from the linen closet and made his way, barefoot and naked, to the bathroom. Steam billowed out when he opened the door. Butch Arlen liked his showers hot.

He set the towels on the toilet tank and studied the lines of Butch's body through the dimpled texture of the shower door glass. When was the last time he'd showered with anyone? He couldn't remember. Couldn't remember the last time he'd been treated to a second round of the good stuff, either. Butch's silhouette soaped up its hair, then shook it out under the rushing showerhead, and Dominic felt a pang he hadn't felt in ages—hadn't let himself feel. Genuine affection.

All the more reason to come clean about Johnny. Get it out of the way so it didn't come back and bite him in the ass—because that kid had been beyond pissed-off. The crazy things he'd said. *You think you're better than me?* Then he'd called Dominic a *hot shit photographer*. And, what else? Oh, yeah, *take a look in the mirror....*

The mirror.

Dominic's gaze snapped to the medicine cabinet. The steam was so thick, his reflection was obscured as surely as the shower door hid Butch. He couldn't tell if he looked like a firecracker or a dud, but the warm, fuzzy feeling that the sight of Butch's outline behind the textured glass had brought on started draining away, replaced by the cold, certain dread that if Dominic wiped the steam off the mirror, he'd be stuck with his old appearance. His old love life.

He grabbed the sink with both hands and leaned in close, inches away, afraid both to wipe away the steam and reveal himself, and to climb in the shower with Butch not knowing if he still looked anything like the guy Butch thought he'd just spent the afternoon with.

Knowing was better than not knowing, but that didn't make it any easier. Dominic steeled himself, took a good, deep breath, and raised his hand to wipe away the steam.

And then it moved.

The steam moved.

It was as if a dozen invisible fingers wrote out a word all at once, each line of each letter being dragged through the steam at the same time. Whatever it was, back at the barbecue joint, that had called him out, seen him for what he was—that thing was back. In his own house. And it was going to tell Butch exactly what Dominic looked like.

Fat.

Dominic stared. Fat? It was in the same spot the word *ugly* had been in the restroom's mirror. He was no handwriting expert, so he couldn't say if it was the same hand—or hands—that had written it. But chances of it being anything else seemed awfully slim.

Still, he couldn't help but be puzzled. *Fat.* All his life, he'd been the homely guy, the backup date, the "let's be friends" fella. But…fat? Weight had never been a problem.

He mouthed the word, as it if might help him understand.

Fat.

It didn't. He looked down at himself. Same body he'd always had. Decent enough. Looked back at the mirror again. There it was, plain as his old face.

Fat?

"You gonna get in here while there's still hot water left?" Butch called over the hiss of the shower stream beating against the tile wall.

"Just a sec." Dominic looked at Butch through the shower door, and then at the sink, where he'd set a necklace and a ring—the gold ring with the music note he'd been wearing on his forefinger. Dominic picked up the heavy ring and slid it onto his ring finger. It was huge. Then he tried it on his forefinger. Still big, but it almost fit.

Maybe weight had never been a problem for Dominic. But Butch?

Dominic let his breath out slowly. It shook. He made a fist around the loose ring and held it against his chest, just over his pounding heart. Butch, with his big, dark eyes and his caring disposition…Butch, who'd actually meant it when he said he was a fan of Dominic's work—no way was Butch going to get taunted by his own personal demons here. Not on Dominic's watch.

As he raised his hand to wipe the word away, Dominic could practically see it reappearing the next time the mirror steamed up—he hoped there'd be a next time, anyway, and what if Dominic didn't catch the word's appearance in time to get rid of it?

He considered the letters. Instead of rubbing them out, he added a letter of his own. An "e."

Fate.

He took a step back and looked at it. Not bad. But even as he admired his own cleverness, the letters began to shrink in on themselves.

"Skootch over," Dominic called to Butch, "I'll soap up your back for you."

And if it sounded forced, like he was covering for his own nervousness, it wasn't terribly obvious over the sound of rushing water. He opened the shower door and a great cloud of steam rolled out, filling in the letters on the mirror, slowly, one by one…until in the space where the word *fate* had been written, nothing remained but a silvery haze.

About Pretty Ugly

I have an author friend from Tennessee who told me that most people seem to think everything set in Tennessee should have something to do with Graceland and the Grand Ole Opry. Evidently, my subconscious took that as a challenge.

Though I couldn't afford a scouting trip for the story, I did discover many historic Nashville houses and estates online—and I'm big into visiting historic houses, albeit closer to home. I've certainly found a number of places I can't wait to see when I do get to Nashville! Cypress Mansion isn't based on a particular mansion or plantation; it's a mash-up of Belle Meade and others—and its interior is heavily inspired by the Ruthven Mansion in Ontario.

This year I had the opportunity to attend Photoshop World, a massive photography and graphic design event, after the initial drafts of Pretty Ugly were written. I came back from all the professional photography workshops certain that I'd gotten all the photography details in the story wrong…but weirdly enough, I'd bluffed through all of them admirably and they didn't need much tweaking. I did end up editing in mention of the Nashville flood, which originally I hadn't done because I thought it would date the story. Once I read about all the residents who lost their homes or even their lives, and how the media downplayed it, I decided it wasn't right to blithely pretend the flood hadn't happened.

Since I did some photography in college, particularly my senior year when I needed to shoot a slide portfolio to get into grad school, I developed some serious camera-envy while I was picking out Dominic's camera! No doubt the mondo Nikon would be too much camera for me. I get the feeling I'd be overwhelmed by all the setting and controls on a DSLR and end up using it as a point-and-shoot.

(The Italian proverb Chance mangled was *col pane tutti i guai sono dolci,* which means that all troubles are sweet when there is bread. Chance is understandably more partial to chocolate than bread!)

Sort of Stranger Than Fiction
Josh Lanyon

His name was Michael.

Not Mike. Not Mikey. Certainly not Micky.

Michael.

Like the archangel.

Michael Milner of Milner's Martial Arts. Two doors down from Red Bird Books and Coffee in the self-consciously rustic Viento Square mini mall. He'd been in business six weeks, which was a long time given the economy—and a town the size of Peabody. That was two weeks longer than Paper Crane Stationery had lasted. He wasn't packing them in like the candy shop, but he seemed to be doing all right. He had students. Mostly skinny boys and girls needing to be kept busy during their summer vacation.

Michael looked like an archangel too. He was built like a runner or a knight of old. Tall, lean, wide shoulders and ropy muscles. His hair was nearly shoulder length—when he didn't have it tied back—and of the palest gold. Not that Ethan—who owned the book store half of Red Bird Books and Coffee and hoped to be a published author one day—would have normally used that kind of hyperbole to describe Michael, but *blond* just didn't seem to cover that particular shade which somehow brought to mind the gleaming tips of arrows or reverberating harp strings. Michael's eyes were blue, the blue of a cloudless sky or the color you believe water is when you're a little kid. His face was beautiful. Really beautiful. Elegant, almost exotic, bone structure—at least on the one side of his face.

The right half of his face had been destroyed at some point. Smashed and burned, it looked like, though Ethan was no expert—and he tried very hard not to stare. They—whoever *they* were—had tried to rebuild Michael and they'd saved his eye, but the skin looked like it had been stretched too tight over reconstructed bones. It had a stiff, shiny, inflexible quality. Since Michael was mostly expressionless, it wasn't as noticeable as it might have been if he'd been the smiley, chatty kind.

Ethan figured he'd had about thirty words out of Michael in the weeks since he'd opened the dojo. Actually it was more like one word thirty times—*Thanks* when Ethan handed him his change.

It was Chance from next door's Sweets to the Sweet who had told Ethan that Michael had been Special Ops in Afghanistan.

"How'd you find that out?" Ethan asked through a mouthful of divinity fudge. Chance was generous with his samples. Maybe that was why Sweets to the Sweet had been a hit practically from the moment the doors opened.

Chance raised a negligent shoulder. He reminded Ethan of a cat. Sleek and graceful and inscrutable. Chance and his boutique chocolates seemed even more out of place in Peabody than Michael Milner's kajukenbo lessons.

"Do you know what happened to his…?" Ethan put a hand to his own right cheekbone rather than complete the sentence. It was probably in bad taste to ask such a question but it wasn't possible to pretend he hadn't noticed. He found Michael fascinating. He wanted to know everything about him. He told himself it was his writer's imagination wanting fuel for the fire.

"Why don't you ask him?" Chance had returned too innocently.

Ethan had retreated instantly from the suggestion. Of course he would never ask—who the hell *would* ask that kind of question? Even if his previous attempts to be friendly to Michael hadn't fallen flat. Michael was unfailingly polite and unfailingly distant. On the rare occasion that he bothered to make eye contact with Ethan, he seemed to see something slightly off center that made him narrow his gaze.

Ethan swallowed the last heavenly bit of white fudge. How was it that everything in Sweets to the Sweet was *so* delicious? He half suspected Chance of adding addictive substances. It wouldn't surprise him. He made Ethan a little uncomfortable sometimes—like now when he was studying Ethan as though he could see right into the secret corners of his mind. The places Ethan himself was afraid to explore too closely.

"I should get back." Ethan rubbed his fingers, trying to remove the lingering sugary sweetness. He headed for the door.

"Ethan?"

Ethan glanced back.

Chance smiled that sly smile of his. "He's not married."

※ ※ ※

"What's the matter with you?" Erin asked when Ethan returned to the bookstore.

Ethan wiped his forehead. "Nothing."

"You look like you have sunstroke."

It was hot enough for sunstroke. Summers in Peabody were like vacationing in Hell. Minus the scenery.

"It's just…hot."

"Understatement. Here try this." Erin leaned across the counter and handed over a tiny paper cup with chilled pale green liquid.

Ethan took an incautious sip. He was still badly shaken by the encounter with Chance. It wasn't that he was closeted exactly. Being the only gay man in Peabody—the only gay *person* as far as he could tell—his sexuality was as irrelevant as if he'd taken a vow of chastity. Erin, his twin sister, was straight and had pretty much the same problem. With a population of 339, there were not many unmarried eligible people of their age in the little desert town.

No, it wasn't that Chance had correctly identified him as gay. Heck, Ethan had originally wondered if Chance might be gay. It was that Chance had correctly identified Ethan's interest in Michael. Ethan himself had strenuously avoided recognizing his interest for what it was, but he could no longer avoid the truth. The fact was he…well, he had a thing for Michael.

Had it bad. Bad enough that other people had noticed.

Had Michael noticed?

Ethan nearly choked as the mint green slime slid down his throat.

"What do you think?" Erin asked.

Frozen Nyquil? Chilled hemlock? One could never be sure with Erin. Ethan cleared his throat. "Uh…." He took another sip to avoid having to answer.

It seemed to be mostly ice, mint with perhaps a hint of coffee. Whatever it was, it wasn't very good. But then most of Erin's experiments weren't. She was a passionate and spectacularly ungifted barista. Luckily for everyone in Peabody—and the financial stability of Red Bird Books and Coffee—she stuck mostly to the premixed recipes.

"Hmm. I don't know."

"What do you think it needs?"

"Chocolate?"

Erin brightened, looking past Ethan. "Here comes Michael."

Ethan stiffened. A hasty glance over his shoulder offered a view of Michael pushing through the front door of Red Bird Books and Coffee. As usual, when he spotted Ethan, Michael's face grew more impassive than ever and he got that squint like Ethan was a foreign particle that had flown into his eye.

If Chance had so easily recognized Ethan's attraction to Michael, it was more than probable that so had Michael. No wonder he looked pained every time he spotted Ethan.

Ethan mumbled an inarticulate hello and retreated hastily for the back of the store and the comfort of the stock room.

Michael usually came in twice a day. In the morning he ordered a medium house blend. In the afternoon he ordered a fruit smoothie. Sometimes the mixed berry with acacia and sometimes the citrus cooler with passion fruit. Once a week, usually on Friday, he'd buy a book. Those brief Friday encounters had been the high point of Ethan's week for the last month and a half.

He lurked in the back for a few minutes waiting miserably for the coast to clear. He could hear Erin's cheerful voice and a lot less frequently, the dark, blurred tones of Michael, and then Erin called, "Ethan, what are you *doing* back there? You've got a customer."

Ethan groaned silently and walked out to the front.

"Were you working on your book?" Erin teased.

Ethan scowled at her. Erin found the idea that Ethan was seriously trying to write a book endlessly entertaining. She'd told everyone they knew that Ethan was working on A Novel. He could see their customers laboring over some polite question to ask—besides *how's it coming?* Except Michael. He had greeted the intelligence of Ethan's literary aspiration with raised eyebrows and a reminder of no strawberry in his mixed berry smoothie.

Now he stood at the book counter holding a copy of *History Man: The Life of R. G. Collingwood.* He looked up at Ethan's approach.

Usually Ethan couldn't shut up around Michael, chattering away about a lot of stuff Michael obviously didn't give a shit about. Today he took the hardcover Michael handed him, rang it up quickly.

"Twelve seventy-three." He stared determinedly down at the cover photograph of the English countryside.

Michael got out his wallet and selected the bills. A ten and three ones.

Ethan took the bills, made change, and handed the coins over, trying to avoid physical contact. He was horribly, painfully conscious of how transparent he'd been all these weeks. God. Like a teenager with a crush. No wonder Michael made a point of being as standoffish as possible.

Michael dropped the coins in the Jerry's Kids container on the desk next to the cash register.

Ethan realized he hadn't bagged the book. He grabbed a bag, shoved the book inside, and handed the bag to Michael, who took it unhurriedly.

"You didn't read this one?"

Ethan's head jerked up. He stared at Michael. He couldn't have been more startled if the bonsai tree on his counter had addressed him. As far as he could recall, it was the first time in six weeks Michael had initiated conversation between them.

"Who, me?" Ethan said brilliantly.

"You've always got something to say about the books. You didn't read this one?"

The books were all mostly used at Red Bird Books and Coffee. Ethan ordered a few paperback bestsellers, but he actually preferred the old books. According to Erin, the bookstore was just Ethan's excuse for buying and reading all the books he wanted. She wasn't far wrong.

"I read it. It's good." Ethan made an effort. "You'll enjoy it."

Michael nodded politely. He turned and left the store.

"Bye, Michael!" Erin called as the door swung shut him. She looked across the floor. "What's the matter with you?"

"Nothing."

"Did something happen?"

"No."

"You acted like you were mad at being disturbed. *Were* you working on your book?"

"No I didn't and no I wasn't."

"I thought you liked him?"

"I don't like him!"

"Come off it. If you were a puppy, you'd be on your back and wriggling every time he walks in here."

Ethan's temper, generally mild, shot up like the red strip of fake mercury in the giant thermometer outside the Bun Baby Restaurant. His voice rose with it. "*Like* him? I'm so sure!"

The door to the shop swung open. Ethan registered the chirping bird, saw out of the corner of his eye that the door was moving, but it was too late to stop the angry words already spilling out. "I think I can do better than the Phantom of the Dojo."

Erin's stricken expression told him what he needed to know. He turned to the front of the shop expecting to see Michael, and sure enough Michael stood in the doorway, frozen in place—just as the scarred half of his face was frozen.

Ethan swallowed. Even as he was trying to tell himself that Michael could only have heard half of that outburst and no way could connect it to himself— and that "Phantom of the Dojo" could mean anything, didn't have to be a reference to a scarred and tragic monster—he knew he was sunk. If Michael *hadn't* heard enough, Erin's patent horror filled in the necessary blanks.

The longest two seconds of Ethan's life dragged with agonizing slowness. Neither he, Erin, nor Michael moved. Neither he, Erin, nor Michael spoke. Ethan's fervent prayers for the earth to open up and swallow him went unanswered.

If he'd been the one to overhear that ugly comment, he'd have backed up, closed the door, and never returned to Red Bird Books and Coffee. Michael stepped inside, closing the door after him, and crossed to Erin's counter. The wooden floorboards squeaked ominously beneath his measured footsteps. Ethan's heart thudded heavily in time to the thump, creak.

"I'm working late tonight. I thought I'd get one of your sandwiches." Michael's voice was even, without any inflection at all.

It was the bravest thing Ethan had ever seen.

"Sure!" Erin said brightly. Too brightly. "What kind did you want? Tuna fish on whole wheat, chicken salad on sourdough…." She babbled out the options.

"Tuna on wheat."

Ethan couldn't stop staring at the uncompromising set of Michael's wide shoulders, the straight way he held himself. His throat felt too tight to speak, practically too tight to breathe. He'd have felt sick about anyone hearing him say something that stupid and cruel, but for Michael to have heard it….

Erin was still gabbling away as she got Michael's sandwich.

Shut up, Ethan willed her. *You're making it worse.* But silence would've probably been worse. It would have been a dead silence. Michael hadn't said a word since he'd requested his sandwich. The back of his neck was red. It probably matched Ethan's face, which felt hot enough to burst into flame. Now there was a solution to his problems. Spontaneous combustion.

As though feeling the weight of Ethan's gaze, Michael turned and gave him a long, direct look.

That look reduced Ethan to the size of something that could have taken refuge beneath the bonsai tree. After an excruciating moment, his gaze dropped to the counter. He scrutinized the schedule of California sales tax beneath the clear plastic desk blotter as though he was about to be tested on it.

When he looked up again, Michael had his wallet out.

Erin waved his money away. "Oh, no. On the house!"

Ethan could have put his head in his hands and howled. Why didn't she just sign a confession in blood? Couldn't she see that undid all Michael's efforts to put things back on a normal track?

Her eyes guiltily met his own across the floor. Had she been a mime making sad eyes and upside-down smiles she couldn't have more clearly conveyed distress.

"Thanks," Michael said. "But no thanks." He handed her a bill and Erin, her face now the shade of her hair, quickly made change.

Michael unhurriedly took his change and his sandwich. He nodded to Erin.

The bird-bell cheeped cheerfully as the door swung shut behind him.

TWO

"Oh my God, I think he heard you," Erin gasped as soon as the door was safely closed.

"Ya think?" Ethan wavered, undecided, then darted out behind the counter and headed after Michael.

The dusty heat of the afternoon hit him like a thousand needles. His skin prickled. Sweat broke out over his body.

Michael was already at the dojo entrance, keys in hand. His profile, the good side of his face, was stern and beautiful.

"Michael?"

He turned at Ethan's call, but his expression didn't change. Ethan forced himself to continue down the wooden walkway, past Sweets to the Sweet. It was a bad idea to pursue this, of course, but not doing anything was equally bad—and gutless.

He stopped about a foot from Michael and said, "I want to apologize."

Michael shrugged. His eyes held Ethan's levelly. Ethan had never seen eyes so fiercely blue. "Why? It wasn't meant for me to hear."

It was a relief that he didn't pretend not to know what Ethan was talking about. Ethan was grateful for that courtesy—and mortified all over again. He got out, "It was a stupid thing to say."

Michael shrugged. "Yeah. Well, I know how I look, but I'm grateful to be alive. I'm not ashamed of my face."

Ethan said painfully, "I am, too. Grateful you're alive, I mean."

Michael made a sound somewhere between a laugh and a snort. Not unkindly but as though Ethan were a harmless kook. He nodded, the conversation clearly at an end, and went inside the dojo, closing the door after him.

Ethan walked slowly back to the Red Bird.

"What happened?" Erin demanded.

"Nothing. I apologized."

"Jeez. What did he say?"

"He said he knew how he looked but he was glad to be alive."

Erin winced. "He was in Afghanistan. Did you know that?"

Ethan nodded. "Chance told me. He said Michael was Special Ops."

"He was part of some hush-hush mission to stop the Taliban kidnapping the Pakistani ambassador. His team's truck hit an IED."

"Did he tell you that?"

"Eventually. In drips and drabs. He's not much of a talker." Erin made a face. "But I am."

The door opened and they both jumped as guiltily as if they'd been planning the overthrow of the town council. It was just Beth Miller and her three monsters. Ethan and Erin hurried to fill orders for comic books and fruit smoothies.

The remainder of the day passed without incident.

At five o'clock, Erin grabbed her Peanuts lunch box from the back room.

"Is your serial killer stopping by tonight?"

"Don't joke about that." Ethan glanced uneasily at the door. He didn't want to take a chance on being overheard again. Speculating aloud on this particular topic could put them out of business. If Peabody could be said to have a first family, it was the Hagars of Hagar's Truck and Tractor Equipment. Karl Hagar was the scion of the dynasty.

"I'm just saying what you think."

"I don't think Karl is a serial killer. I mean, yes, he is a little…weird."

"I'll say." Erin shivered. "I don't know how you can all stand to read those gory stories of his."

"You could say that about half the bestselling crime writers out there."

"Well, who knows what those people would do if they couldn't get it all out in their writing."

Ethan rolled his eyes. He did find Karl's writing disturbing—as did the other four members of the group—but there was no doubt Karl was very talented. Even gifted. He was probably the best writer in the group. Even better than Ethan, as much as Ethan hated to admit it.

"Well, but he does have that outlet," he pointed out.

"Maybe it's not enough."

"This is a creepy conversation," Ethan protested, laughingly.

"I haven't been able to get that story out of my head. The one about the young guy who poisons all the patients in the nursing home where he works."

That *had* been a disturbing story. Not least because it was so sympathetic to both the victims and the murderer.

Erin added, "You know, the Hagar ranch isn't far from where those men were found."

"Oh, come on. You can't go by that. If you want to get technical, their bodies were found closer to Lena's property."

Lena Montero was another member of Ethan's writing group. She was in her seventies now, but she lived way out in the boonies.

"You just don't want to consider the possibility because he's a Hagar."

"No shit. That's one household we don't want to go to war with. Anyway, Karl doesn't strike me as the serial killer type."

"How do you know? Serial killers look just like you and me."

"They have red hair?"

"Ha ha."

Actually, Ethan's hair wasn't red. It was brown with reddish highlights. Erin had the red hair. Red hair and green eyes. Ethan's eyes were hazel. He knew himself to be reasonably attractive, but Erin was beautiful. Everyone always said she could have been a model or an actress—usually after they'd sampled one of her original coffee drink recipes.

"Seriously," Erin said. "I was reading an article in *Reader's Digest* and most serial killers are not the dysfunctional weirdoes you see on TV. A lot of them can pass as perfectly normal."

"That leaves Karl out."

She laughed, and Ethan reflected that he probably shouldn't encourage her. She was liable to slip and say something in front of Karl.

"Anyway, be careful tonight and have fun!"

Erin went out into the sunny evening, and the door swung shut with a friendly chirp behind her.

Ethan got his copies of the group stories out and began to browse through them. This was always their quiet time of day. He and Erin took turns manning the shop for the three hours between five until closing. An occasional customer might wander in from the Interstate, but the good citizens of Peabody were generally having dinner and settling down to a night of reality TV.

He made a few notes on three of the stories, and then he started reading Karl's. It was the first in a new novel, and, yes, it did seem to be about a serial killer. This time the serial killer was a sweet little boy with a twin sister.

The further Ethan read, the more unhappy he was. Not that he and Erin were ringers for the kids in Karl's book, but they were the only fraternal twins in Peabody and Karl's physical descriptions hit too close to home. Jeez, Erin had her faults, but she wasn't a sociopath, and far from exhibiting serial killer tendencies, Ethan got lightheaded at the sight of blood.

There was a great deal of blood in the first of Karl's novel as little Iain Dearie dispatched the family cat and then went after the neighbor's baby. Happily the chapter ended with dear little Iain stuck in the shrubbery. Maybe he would stay there for the next seventy thousand words.

Ethan shuddered, drew a happy face on the first page, and went next door to visit with Chance.

He nearly bumped into Pete McCarty on his way out of the candy shop.

"Hi, Pete," he said tentatively.

Pete looked straight through him and walked away toward the parking lot.

Anna McCarty, Pete's wife, had stepped out onto the wooden walk behind him. She hesitated, then said uncomfortably, "Why hello, Ethan. How are you these days?"

"Hi, Anna. I'm good. How are you and...."

It was unexpectedly hard to finish it. He and Erin had grown up next door to the McCartys. Up until last year they had looked upon Pete and Anna as an informal aunt and uncle, but now everything had changed.

Anna ignored his swallow. She said brightly, "How's Erin? Is she seeing anyone?"

Ethan shook his head.

"No? Well, you tell her I said hi."

Ethan nodded.

Anna hesitated for a fraction of second. "I'd better skedaddle. You know how Pete hates to be kept waiting."

Ethan nodded again.

Anna bit her lip. She patted his arm and hurried off, clutching her box of candy.

Ethan watched her go, watched her plump figure cross the parking lot, watched her climb into the SUV beside Pete. He appeared to give Anna a piece of his mind. And from the look of things Anna was returning it with interest. A few seconds later, the SUV roared past Ethan and out of the parking lot.

He gritted his teeth as the SUV disappeared down the road, and pushed through the door to Sweets to the Sweet.

The usual heady fragrance greeted him, a warm blend of cocoa, butter, and citrus. Somewhere Ethan had read that just the scent of chocolate acted as a male aphrodisiac and he could totally believe it when he walked into Sweets for the Sweet. It didn't hurt that Chance was the guy behind the counter.

"Just in time," Chance greeted him. "Try this."

Ethan came forward and took a tiny bite of a dark chocolate flower. He blinked at the unique flavor, the bite of spice and dark chocolate. "What is it?"

"Ginger, wasabi, and black sesame seeds."

"It's great. Unusual."

Chance smiled that enigmatic smile of his, and tucked back a silky strand of dark hair that had worked loose. "What happened between you and Michael?"

"Er, nothing," Ethan said guiltily. "Why?"

Chance nodded at the glass window. "I saw you tearing after him when he left your shop. I wondered what you'd said."

That was just…uncanny. How could Chance have guessed that Ethan had said anything?

"I—"

"Did you decide to ask him about his scars after all?"

"Of course not!"

Chance studied him as though making his mind up as to whether that was true or not. He smiled lazily. "Just wondered. I could see Michael was upset."

"You…could?" Ethan couldn't imagine how that would be. He found Michael as unreadable as the sandstone bluffs that overlooked the valley.

"I know Michael pretty well by now." Chance seemed to watch Ethan. What was he looking for? Signs that Ethan was jealous? He was, a little.

"Erin was teasing me and I said something stupid."

Chance's eyebrows angled up. "What did you say?"

"I…it doesn't matter."

"I didn't realize you had such a terrible temper." Ethan could hear the mockery in Chance's voice, but it was friendly mockery. At least, Ethan hoped it was. It was hard to tell with Chance.

"I don't. I just…I think it's the heat. I haven't been sleeping well."

Chance continued to regard him as though he could see right past that lame excuse, see right into the Ethan's heart. He murmured something that could have been commiseration or amusement. "Well, I wouldn't worry. It'll work itself out."

Would it? It seemed unlikely. To keep himself from saying anything else, Ethan popped the last bit of dark chocolate flower into his mouth. The spices stung his tongue, and then melted into sweetness.

❁ ❁ ❁

"It's all these people who want something for nothing. Illegal aliens. They're the ones bringing the rest of us down."

They're not the only ones, Ethan thought.

John Dylan was fifty and heavy-set. He wore his dishwater blond hair pulled back in a ponytail. His day job was "postal delivery specialist," but he had dreams of being a paperback writer.

Then again, so did everyone else in the Coffee Clutch writing group.

"I don't like your racist remarks," Lena Montero said. She was small and brown and as tough as a rusty nail.

"I'm not a racist," Dylan said. "I'm not just broken up over some wetbacks dying in the desert when they shouldn't have been here to start with."

Uneasily recollecting Erin's theories on how the vagrants had died, Ethan looked sideways at Karl.

Karl's gaze slid to meet Ethan's. His mouth quirked into a faint smile.

Karl was two years younger than Ethan. He was blond and tanned and handsome. He looked like a police cadet or the poster boy for Hitler Youth. In school, Karl had been a star athlete but a loner. Ethan had been aware of him, but had zero contact. Karl moved in a very different crowd from Ethan. He'd been surprised when Karl had shown up two months ago asking to join the Coffee Clutch.

Surprised, but pleased to gain another member. Especially one who could really write. Greater familiarity with Karl's work had spoiled some of the pleasure. It wasn't easy reading the violent and gruesome fantasies that poured out of Karl's brain.

Studying the stark perfection of Karl's face, Ethan couldn't help thinking that in a movie or a book Karl would always be cast as the cold-blooded killer. Real life generally wasn't so tidy.

The group ended. Everyone said goodnight. Ethan locked the rear door. He turned the OPEN sign to CLOSED, emptied the register, deposited the day's take in the floor safe in the back office, and dragged the trash bags to the front.

The trash dumpsters were at the far end of the parking lot.

As Ethan dragged the trash bags over to the dumpster, he noticed that Michael's pickup was still parked in front of the dojo. Another car was parked on the far side of Michael's truck. Was he giving someone a private lesson that evening?

Ethan raised the lid on the dumpster, swung the first trash bag, and tossed it over the rim. It landed with a dull thud.

He turned to grab the second bag and realized someone was standing behind him. Right behind him. Ethan hadn't heard footsteps, had no warning, but there he stood, fair hair gleaming in the silvery, summer moonlight.

Three

"Jee-zus!" Ethan jumped back, knocking into the dumpster. The lid banged down. "What are you doing, Karl?"

Karl didn't say anything.

The hair stood up on the back of Ethan's neck.

"What do you want?"

By moonlight, Karl's expression was frightening. His eyes looked black.

There was nowhere for Ethan to run. He was already backed against the dumpster. *This can't be happening*, he thought, and just as the disbelieving words took shape in his mind, he spied movement behind Karl. A pale figure strode toward them through the darkness.

Ethan's heart leaped with relief even before Michael called crisply, "Is there a problem?"

Karl spun with a kind of wary precision.

"Everything okay, Ethan?" Michael asked, still in that hard voice. He sounded more than ready to deal with it, if everything wasn't okay.

"Everything's fine," Karl answered.

"Ethan?"

Ethan got out, "Yes. Everything's fine. I was just...." He grabbed the remaining trash bag, heaved it into the dumpster, and turning back to Karl said with an effort at normality, "What did you need, Karl?"

Karl seemed to have forgotten about him. He was still staring at Michael. Ethan took advantage of that distraction to scoot past him, walking toward Michael. Michael, too, ignored him, staring at Karl. Did they know each other?

If so, neither was saying anything.

Karl said, "It'll keep," and for a second, Ethan couldn't even remember what the question had been.

Karl walked past Michael to his car. He didn't say goodnight, he didn't say anything at all. He went to his black TR7 sports car, and got in. The engine started, a hornet's buzz in the warm night.

"What was that about?" Michael asked. He was still watching Karl as he backed up the car, swung around, and sped out of the parking lot.

"I don't know," Ethan admitted. "He just freaked me out popping out of nowhere like that. But I probably freaked him out reacting like I thought he was a...."

Serial killer.

Damn Erin for planting that thought in his mind. He gave Michael a sheepish smile.

"He was waiting for you in his car. I noticed him when I was closing up the dojo. I wondered why he was just sitting there, and when you came outside, he got out of his car to follow you. I could see you weren't expecting him."

Ethan had jumped so high it was a miracle he hadn't knocked himself out on the moon. It would have been hard to miss that panicked reaction—even in the dark.

He firmly put aside the knowledge of what Michael must think of him—after the "Phantom of the Dojo" remark he probably couldn't get a lot lower in his estimation. "It was probably nothing, but thanks for coming out here."

That would have been kind and conscientious anytime, let alone after the afternoon they'd had.

Michael nodded curtly.

"I should probably take some kind of self-defense course."

Michael made a *yeah right* sound. "What you should do is take a minute or two to check your surroundings before you walk out here late at night. Erin too. You both usually close up after the rest of us have gone. We're not that far from the freeway."

Right, that never-ending conveyor belt of potential customers and crazies, also known as the Interstate. From where they stood they could see the constant moving flash of lights coming and going through the scrubby barrier trees.

"Chance is usually here," Ethan said.

Even now the windows of Sweets for the Sweet were cheerfully shining like a beacon in the night.

"Yeah, he is," Michael said thoughtfully. "But somehow I don't see Chance running to your rescue."

Ethan laughed. "Probably not." Chance would probably be too busy in his kitchen cooking up more amazing addictive confections to notice if all of Viento Square burned down around him.

Michael was turning away, crisis averted, conversation over.

Without giving himself time to think, Ethan blurted, "Michael, you want to go grab a drink somewhere?"

His face burned in anticipation of the imminent rejection. He meant it simply as a friendly gesture, but Michael would almost certainly misread it, and even if he didn't, he'd shown zero interest in forming any friendships. Or even acquaintanceships.

To Ethan's surprise, Michael hesitated. "Where?"

Good question. Ethan had thrown the offer out there; he hadn't actually expected to be taken up on it. Options in Peabody were limited, and he knew with certainty that Michael would not be up to driving any distance to one of the other little towns along the Interstate. Denny's served wine and beer, but it would be full of noisy—and nosey—high school kids at this time of night.

"The Drifters?"

"*The Drifters?*"

Michael's astonishment was understandable. The Drifters was a grubby hole-in-the-wall mostly patronized by Peabody's redneck career drinkers—and the occasional biker gang.

Ethan had been there twice in his entire life, and he had no particular desire to go back, but he thought Michael could tolerate the toxic testosterone levels.

"Sure. They've got a good selection of import beers."

"The Drifters it is." Michael turned away.

They were going to the Drifters. It took Ethan a second to register it. They were actually *going*. "Okay, I'll…see you over there." He was equal parts excited and alarmed as he jogged back to the store and finished closing up. Why on earth had Michael agreed? What the hell would they talk about? Could Michael possibly be—no. But at least it seemed unlikely he knew Ethan was attracted to him. That was a huge relief. It was like having his ego handed back to him on a platter.

By the time he got back outside, Michael's pickup was already waiting in the driveway, exhaust drifting in the summer night, and again Ethan felt a surge of gratitude that Michael hadn't just driven off. Not that there could be any real threat to him, but the bracket of shops that made up Viento Square was eerily empty at night, store windows lit like museum exhibits.

He followed Michael's red tail lights down the highway, turning left before the railroad crossing, and then down the narrow road that led to a small white building between the feed store and the Mobil station. A blue neon cocktail glass poured its winking green bubbles into the starry night.

Michael parked at the back of the lot. Ethan edged his prim Toyota in between a row of gleaming motorcycles knowing if he happened to scrape one he would die before the night was over.

By the time he'd finished parking, Michael was out of his truck and waiting for him at the door of the bar. He was dressed like Ethan, jeans and a T-shirt, but somehow he looked like he belonged at the Drifters—or at least like no one would challenge his right to be there.

The two previous times Ethan had been to the Drifters he'd been carded even though he'd been at school with George, the bartender, who knew full well Ethan was twenty-eight.

Michael didn't say anything as Ethan joined him. In fact, he seemed a little distant, but maybe that was Ethan projecting. He pushed open the door and the sound of country music flooded the night. Garth Brooks.

Inside the bar it was dark and smoky. The greatest source of light in the room was the jukebox. No one was smoking, so it was probably twenty years' worth of accumulated tar and nicotine haunting the structure. The bar was lined with men in cowboy hats and baseball caps hunched over bottles of beer. A few heads turned their way and then turned back. It wasn't exactly a warm welcome but no one actually hissed at them.

In the farthest and darkest corner of the room was a crowded table. Ethan had an impression of beards, shades, and a lot of leather.

"Grab a table, I'll get this round," Michael said. "What did you want?"

"Pauli Girl." Ethan didn't particularly care for beer, but his father had always drunk St. Pauli Girl, so when he did have beer, he always picked that.

Michael headed for the bar.

There were a number of small, empty tables. Ethan picked one well away from the biker corner. He sat down and folded his arms, trying to find some place to stare that wouldn't seem rude. He felt awkward and conspicuous. He reminded himself that this wasn't a date.

Michael came back with two bottles—no glasses, and Ethan made a mental note not to identify himself as a candy ass by asking for glasses when his turn came to get the next round.

Michael hooked a foot around the chair leg, dragged it out, sat down and placed the open bottles on the table.

"Thanks," Ethan said, reaching for his bottle and automatically wiping the mouth.

"Come here often, do you?" Michael inquired gravely, and as Ethan found the gleam of his eyes in the gloom, it occurred to him that Michael might actually have a sense of humor. That was dangerous. It not only made Michael more real, it made him a lot more appealing.

"Er, no."

Michael's teeth flashed in a white, very brief smile. He was sitting slightly angled toward Ethan so Ethan couldn't see the scarred half of his face. What would it be like to be that handsome, to have that power, and then lose it? Not naturally fade away with age, but have half your face torn off.

The jukebox started up again with the same Garth Brooks song that had been playing when they walked in. "Standing Outside the Fire."

Michael put the bottle to his mouth and drank. Ethan followed suit and stared at the large girly calendar on the wall behind Michael. What *was* the appeal of naked girls on tractors? It just looked…uncomfortable. He glanced at Michael again. Michael was staring into space.

There were a lot of things Ethan wanted to ask him, but he wasn't sure if they'd be viewed as intrusive or not. Michael seemed so private.

Ethan looked around the bar. He recognized a couple of faces. Dave Wilton fleetingly met Ethan's eyes, before turning away. Of course, Ethan had never had much in common with Dave, but it was easy these days to put that coolness down to Pete McCarty and the Starbucks thing.

Did Michael know about that? Ethan glanced back at Michael who was looking more tuned out and distant with each passing moment. If there was going to be any conversation, Ethan was going to have to initiate it.

"So," Ethan said, and Michael's eyes jerked his way. "What made you settle in Peabody? You're not from around here." No way could Ethan have missed Michael Milner while he was growing up.

"No." Michael set his bottle on the table.

Ethan waited. Michael said reluctantly, "After I got out of the service—the hospital—I was trying to figure out what to do with the rest of my life."

"Were you career military before…?" Ethan stopped awkwardly, but Michael didn't seem offended.

"That wasn't the original plan, but I enjoyed the military." He lifted a shoulder. "I could have stayed in after I got this, but I felt like it was time to do something else."

Ethan nodded. There couldn't be that much of an age difference between them, but every time he was around Michael he became conscious of his lack of life experience. All Ethan had ever really wanted was to sell books at his mom and dad's store. That, or be a librarian, but Peabody didn't have a library of its own.

"Some friends of mine wanted me to go into their sailboat rental business. I was on my way up north to check it out when I got off the freeway to buy gas."

"And you decided to stay?"

"This place appealed to me. I liked that it was quiet and out in the middle of nowhere."

"It's a long way from the ocean, that's for sure."

"The boat business wasn't my idea. It was just…something to focus on when I needed it."

Ethan nodded. He could understand that only too well.

Michael said with sudden curiosity, "When I was looking at rental spaces for the dojo, the realtor was badmouthing you because you'd refused to be bought out by Starbucks."

Ethan's heart sank, though maybe it shouldn't have come as a surprise.

"Mr. McCarty. He's still upset."

"Yeah, he did seem irate."

Ethan tried to smile. It wasn't exactly cheering to hear Pete went around badmouthing them to anyone who would listen—including people who might just be passing through town.

"Pete wanted us to let our lease expire so that Starbucks could buy out the Red Bird."

"Why would you?"

"A Starbucks would attract freeway business to Peabody."

The scarred half of Michael's mouth curled. "And it'd mean a big fat commission for Pete?"

"Yeah, but I guess you could argue—Pete did—that it would be good for everyone in Peabody. It would mean jobs."

"What about your job? And Erin's?"

Ethan nodded. It would have cost them their livelihood and perhaps eventually their home. But it just hadn't seemed to matter to Pete. Then Ethan had compounded that sin by getting 215 signatures on a petition to stop Starbucks from moving into Peabody at all. Ethan had taken the petition to the town council and the town council had agreed that Peabody was not large enough to support two coffee houses. Pete had been furious. He had still not forgiven Ethan and apparently never would.

"I liked that about you," Michael said, as though reading his mind. "It was one reason I settled on Viento Square."

Ethan hoped the poor lighting concealed his blush. Before he knew it, he was telling Michael all about how he and Erin had grown up thinking of the McCartys as extended family and how hard it had been since the falling out over Starbucks. That had been a real eye-opener. Ethan still couldn't get over the fact that Pete and his business cronies were honestly outraged that he had fought for his survival. The fact that Pete and the others had been outvoted and overruled didn't alter their resentment an iota.

"That's human nature." Michael took a pull of his beer.

"I guess." Ethan brooded for an instant. "It's when I realized what greed could do to people like Pete that I decided to write *Death in a Very Small*

Town."

"Yeah, your sister mentioned you're writing a book. That title sounds familiar."

"*Death in a Small Town* has been used a few times. But not *Death in a Very Small Town*."

"Hm." Michael's gaze seemed to weigh him. "Are you sorry you fought McCarty on it?"

Ethan shook his head. "No. We couldn't give up the Red Bird. It's not just our livelihood, it's our…inheritance." Then he had to explain about how his parents had been killed four years ago coming back from the first vacation they'd taken on their own in twenty-five years.

By the time he finished bringing Michael up to date on his entire history, it was last call. Embarrassingly, Ethan, who really wasn't much of a drinker, had forgotten all about getting the second round. Worse, he'd been so busy telling his life story, he'd barely let Michael get a word in edgewise. Not that Michael had tried to get a word in, but it would have been nice to throw the occasional question his way. If only in an effort not to look like a total egomaniac.

"I've got this. What did you want?" Ethan rose belatedly.

But Michael was rising too, shaking his head. "Thanks, but I've got an early start tomorrow. I need to get going."

Ethan looked at the Budweiser clock on the wall. He'd been talking for nearly three hours straight. No wonder Michael couldn't wait to escape.

"Oh my God," he said, and it was truly heartfelt. "Why didn't you tell me to shut up an hour ago?"

Michael had a nice laugh. It was the first time Ethan had heard it and he seemed to feel it in his solar plexus. "Nah. You were fine." But Michael didn't deny that Ethan was a blabbermouth and Ethan blushed again. The worst part was he'd spent three hours with Michael and basically didn't know anything more about him than he had that morning—and it was totally his own fault.

He followed Michael outside. The stars were brilliant in the black sky.

The bikers had vanished at some point during the evening and Ethan's Toyota sat by itself next to the chain link fence.

"Night," Ethan called as Michael walked back to his truck.

"Night, Ethan."

Just hearing Michael say his name made his heart skip. *Oh you have it bad*, Ethan told himself once he was in his car and buckling his seatbelt. *He probably thinks you're…*but there his imagination gave out. It was very hard to know what Michael thought about anything.

He watched Michael's pickup trundle slowly past his rear window, bump onto the paved highway and disappear into the night.

Four

"Listen to this." Erin read from the paper, "Kern County investigators are trying to determine the identity of a man whose body was found Thursday in the desert eight miles from the town of Peabody. The man was found just before 7 a.m. north of Highway 19, according to a release from the sheriff's department. Deputies at the scene were unable to determine the cause of death and requested homicide investigators. The identity of the deceased has not been confirmed and an investigation is ongoing. An autopsy will be conducted. This is the third body to be discovered in the vicinity of Peabody over the past six weeks. Anyone with information regarding the incident can contact Det. Ricardo Cabot or Sgt. Tony Guinn at 999-313-3859. Tips can also be left anonymously at 1-800-712-7123." She looked up from the paper. "That makes three. Three in six weeks. It says so right here."

Ethan, busy changing out the fragile vintage paperbacks in the swivel bookcase, replied, "That doesn't mean a serial killer is at large."

"What *does* it mean, then?"

"How should I know? It doesn't even say how he died. It could have been heat exposure. It's 114 out there right now."

"All *three* of them?"

"Where does it say that all three of them died from the same cause?"

"It doesn't have to. This is obviously more than a coincidence. You have to call the sheriff's department and tell them about Karl."

Ethan stood up. His sister was starting to make him nervous. "Tell them *what* about Karl?"

There was a belated cheeped warning and the door swung open as Erin said in clear, carrying tones, "That he's a serial killer."

Ethan turned to face his doom, but it was only Chance.

"Who's a serial killer?" Chance inquired with great interest.

"No one," Ethan insisted. He glared at Erin. "*No one.*"

"Karl Hagar," Erin told Chance. "He writes all these creepy, gory stories about murdering people for Ethan's writing group."

"Murdering people for Ethan's writing group? Is that one of the requirements?"

Erin laughed. Ethan couldn't see the humor. "She doesn't know what she's talking about." To Erin, he said, "You're going to get us sued."

"By who?"

"By the Hagars, if they find out you're going around accusing Karl of being a serial killer."

"You should see the stuff he writes," Erin told Chance. "It's sick."

"Ethan?"

"*Karl.*" Erin was laughing again.

"It doesn't work like that," Ethan tried to explain. "That's just imagination. Writers…they make stuff up."

Erin quoted wisely, "Write what you know."

"Yeah, but that's what I'm saying. It doesn't work like that. You don't have to be a detective to write mysteries, and you sure don't have to be a murderer. Most writers don't live what they write. Most writers are like…me. They don't get out a lot. They make stuff up. It's all imagination and—and the creative process."

Erin seemed to have her heart set on Karl being a psycho. "He couldn't write like that if he didn't have firsthand experience."

"That's research. That's imagination. That's what being a writer is all about."

"When did these killings start?" Chance selected a variety of Pez candies. Why, when he surely had access to all the candy he could ever desire?

"Six weeks ago."

"*Ah.* So I could be the killer. Or maybe Michael. We've both only been here about six weeks."

"Michael is *not* a killer," Ethan said.

Hot embarrassment flooded him as both Erin and Chance laughed in response to his vehemence.

IN THE AFTERNOON Michael came in for his usual fruit smoothie. Ethan had missed him earlier as Erin had run out of milk and he'd needed to make an emergency trip to pick up a couple of gallons to tide her over until the next delivery.

His stomach did its usual nervous belly flop at the sight of Michael. It was worse today because he was very conscious of what a lousy impression he must have made the night before. Thank God, it *hadn't* been a date. Michael would judge him less severely as a neighbor and potential friend. Hopefully Michael thought of him as a potential friend. It was hard to know since Ethan hadn't let him get more than a few words in all night.

"What do you think about Karl?" Erin asked, after Michael placed his order for a citrus cooler.

"What about Karl?" Michael shot Ethan a wary look as though he was unsure of what stories Ethan might be telling.

"Nothing about Karl," Ethan said. "Erin is convinced Karl is...."

"A serial killer," Erin finished.

"You *can't* keep saying that," Ethan warned her. "We don't need any more enemies in this town."

"We don't have any enemies."

Michael, not easily detoured, asked, "Why do you think Karl is a serial killer?"

"You should see the stuff he writes for Ethan's group. It's sick."

Ethan was miserably aware he should never have let Erin look at Karl's stories. He'd gotten in the habit, when they were bored and the customers were few and far between, of reading stories from the group to her. She often had good insights. But her dislike of Karl's writing, and her suspicion of him personally, was beginning to be a liability.

Now she was describing the story about the nursing home poisoner to Michael. What Michael made of it was impossible to know. The scarred, frozen side of his face was turned Ethan's way.

Erin finished up with, "And *why* would he be waiting for Ethan in the parking lot after the Coffee Clutch group?"

At that, Michael's expression did change. He gave Ethan a funny look.

Ethan didn't know what to make of it.

A few hours' distance had already given the bizarre encounter with Karl an unreal aura. Ethan said, "He could have been out there for a lot of reasons. Maybe he thought he forgot something inside the shop."

"Why didn't he come to the door, then?"

"He could have had some question he didn't want everyone to hear. He's very reticent in the group. He knows the rest of them don't like his stories."

"The rest of *them?* You hate his stories too."

"I know, but I can't say that. I'm the moderator."

"Chance thinks it's all a big joke," Erin complained. "What do you think, Michael?"

"I think Chance isn't in any position to point fingers."

Ethan said curiously, "He says you two know each other pretty well."

"Chance and me? No way. Not my type."

Not my type? It seemed a funny way of putting it. Of course, people used that phrase all the time and didn't mean it literally. Ethan really needed to stop trying to find signals where none existed.

"I think you should go to the police," Erin said.

"With *what?* The fact that he writes weird stories? The fact that he surprised me in the parking lot?" He realized he was looking at Michael, waiting for Michael to weigh in on this. Poor Michael. Why was any of this his problem?

Michael said, "What's your instinct tell you?"

Ethan frowned, consulting his inner oracle. "I don't know that I have instinct. I think civilization has bred it all out of me."

Michael made a sound that fell somewhere between amusement and impatience. "You were scared last night."

Funny that he didn't mind Michael knowing he had been scared. Not that Ethan could have hidden it. "Yeah, but I think that was mostly because Erin put the idea in my head. That and then reading the start of Karl's new novel."

"Chance said that we'd have all the same doubts whether Karl was a serial killer or not."

"If we're wrong and we accuse Karl of *anything*, the Hagars will ruin us. We couldn't survive a lawsuit."

Erin handed Michael his drink. Michael sipped from the straw with the good side of his mouth. Not looking at Ethan, he said, "If I were you, I'd just ask him what he wants."

⚘ ⚘ ⚘

It was Erin's night to stay late. Ethan left her with warnings to take the trash out while it was still daylight and to make sure no one was lurking in the parking lot.

"Don't worry. It's only men being killed," she told him cheerfully.

Ethan sighed and left her to it.

Michael's truck was already gone for the day. Ethan noted its absence with an internal sag of disappointment. Which made no sense at all. All day he'd been hoping for some sign that…well, what? He was impatient with himself for wishing whatever it was he wished: that last night would be a turning point in his relationship with Michael? It had been. But of course, he wanted more. He wanted Michael to feel the same way he did, and that was ridiculous.

There was no reason to think—hope—

Just because someone wasn't married didn't mean they were gay. Look at Erin. Beautiful, smart, fun, straight…and not a single marital prospect on the horizon. For all Ethan knew, Michael could have been married. Maybe his wife had left him after his face was destroyed. He absently embroidered this sad scenario as he drove home. By the time Ethan reached the big old comfortable two-story house he'd grown up in, he'd saddled Michael with a faithless prom queen high school sweetheart and two point three children now being raised by their grandparents.

He made Fritos casserole for himself and Erin, put hers in the fridge, and ate his standing over the sink. He rinsed his plate. Taking out the pot of iced coffee they always kept chilling, he poured a glass and carried it out to the aboveground swimming pool in the backyard.

He plugged in the cord to the little plastic Chinese lanterns that hung in a large square around the yard. They glowed cheerfully as he skimmed the glassy water, removing the dead bees and moths. The black cloud-shaped shadows cast by the tall apple trees gradually dissolved into the deepening dusk.

For a time Ethan swam in the shady water. The evening was still very warm and the water pleasantly tepid. A bat twittered overhead.

He had stopped to drink his now-watery coffee when he spotted headlights moving slowly through the trees, coming up the road to the house.

His spirits soared even as he warned himself that this could be a belated UPS delivery or someone asking for directions. He climbed out of the pool and dried hastily, pulling on his jeans over his damp trunks. He finger-combed his hair out of his face as he walked down the gardenia-lined path along the side of the house.

He was rounding the corner when he spotted the car parked in the sandy circle in front of the lawn. A black TR7.

Ethan froze.

Karl.

He drew back and leaned against the side of the house, thinking rapidly. What on earth could Karl want? Why was he there?

If I were you, I'd just ask him what he wants.

No kidding. It was ridiculous to be skulking around like this just because Erin had a vivid imagination and Karl was maybe too effective a writer. But nothing Ethan could think of would entail Karl driving all the way out to Ethan's home.

Then again, the idea that Karl might intend him harm was preposterous.

For one thing, why pick Ethan? If, by some weird chance, Karl did have something to do with those transients dying in the desert, it still didn't make sense that he would suddenly focus his homicidal interest on Ethan.

Ethan was being a tool, and he knew it. In fact, if anyone was behaving suspiciously, it was Ethan. Karl had walked up to the porch and was politely ringing the doorbell. Ethan was the one skulking in the bushes and gawking.

There was no reason to react like this. None. Which didn't change the fact that he would've preferred not to be on his own for this meeting.

"Were you looking for me?" he asked, coming up behind the porch.

Karl jumped—much as Ethan had the night before—and turned as Ethan reached the steps. He looked yellow in the porch light.

"Ethan. Hi."

Was it Ethan's imagination, or did Karl sound strained?

"Hi." Ethan gestured vaguely. "I was swimming out back."

"You have a pool?"

"Yeah. It's just one of those aboveground deals," Ethan hurriedly qualified. Safe to say their venerable Doughboy was probably not Karl's idea of a real swimming pool given the in-ground pool on the Hagar property. "We've had it for years."

"I guess that's why you're tanned even though you're inside all day."

Ethan didn't really think of himself as tanned. He rarely got in the pool before five-thirty in the evening. It was an odd thing for Karl to comment on, wasn't it?

Neither of them spoke

"Would you like an iced coffee?" Ethan really couldn't think of anything else to say other than *what are you doing here?* and that felt too blunt.

"Coffee?" Karl's pale brows rose.

"Iced coffee."

"Sure."

Ethan led the way around the back—the front of the house was locked—and Karl followed him inside after briefly checking out the pool.

Karl prowled around the kitchen while Ethan got a clean glass out. The sound of crickets was loud through the open windows.

"When does your sister come home?"

Ethan glanced at the clock. "She has her scrapbooking class tonight. She'll be home around nine." Belatedly, he realized he should have said Erin was due home any minute. But that was only if he believed himself in danger, right? And he didn't. Karl was acting perfectly normal—within the parameters of the oddness of his visiting Ethan.

Karl said nothing.

Ethan opened the fridge and pulled out the jug of cold brewed coffee. "How's business?"

Karl began to give him a precise accounting of how business was. The Hagar controller probably couldn't have been more accurate as far as facts and figures. It was kind of surprising in someone who was as imaginative and descriptive as Karl, but people's contradictions were often the most interesting thing about them.

"That sounds interesting," Ethan said politely, when there was finally a pause. He handed a glass to Karl.

Karl took his iced coffee and sipped it. Ethan became conscious of the wet trunks beneath his jeans and how close and confined it felt in the shabby, over-warm kitchen. The smell of Fritos casserole was overpowered by Karl's aftershave.

"We can talk out back," he said.

Karl followed him outside. Through the distant trees Ethan could see the lights of the McCarty house. He wondered if the McCartys would help him if he came pounding on their door. Once he would have taken that for granted.

"It's quiet out here," Karl observed.

"Yeah." A mosquito buzzed past his ear and Ethan slapped at it.

Karl cleared his throat.

Ethan glanced his way. Karl stared straight ahead at the pool, which now looked black as an oil well.

"Was there something you wanted to ask me?"

"I…" Karl's voice gave out in a squawk that in other circumstances might have been funny. Whatever this was, it was obviously awkward.

Ethan waited nervously.

"I wanted to hire you," Karl said at last.

"*Hire* me?"

Karl nodded. "As a writing coach. I was hoping you'd work with me one on one."

This was so far removed from Ethan's uneasy, anxious speculations, it was almost surreal. "But I'm not a writing coach."

"You run the critique group. You sell books."

"But that's not like being a writing coach. Anyone in the group could give you as good, or better, feedback as me."

"I don't think so. I don't care what Lena Montero or any of the rest of them have to say. They don't know anything."

"Neither do I, really," honesty compelled Ethan to say.

"You know more than the rest of us. Anyway, I'd pay you."

Money always being an issue, Ethan asked, "How much were you thinking?"

"I don't know. What do you think is fair?"

"I have no idea." Ethan sipped his coffee to give himself time to think. "I guess I could look it up, but what you ought to do is see about enrolling in the junior college in Modesto. You could work with actual writing instructors."

Karl said decisively, "I don't want anything that formal. I don't have time to take a bunch of classes."

It wasn't that Ethan couldn't use the money, but the idea of tutoring Karl made him uncomfortable even without analyzing why. He was trying to formulate some diplomatic but convincing reason for why he couldn't accept the job, when the glide of headlights through the trees down the lane caught his eye.

It was still too early for Erin, so who the heck was this?

His heart did another hopeful leap, like a goldfish in a too-small bowl. If nothing else, this interruption would give him a chance to postpone answering Karl.

"Hey, look, here's someone else." He rose, feeling like someone in an amateur theater production. God knows, he'd sat through enough performances of *Our Town* and *Oklahoma* in support of Erin.

Karl didn't move.

"I'll be right back," Ethan said as it became clear Karl wasn't going to budge.

Karl took a long swallow of his drink and didn't reply.

So…okay. Ethan left him and padded barefoot around the side of the house again. He stepped out of the trees as Michael's white pickup pulled neatly up beside Karl's TR7.

Five

Ethan's heart thumped. He couldn't think of a single reason Michael would come to see him other than Michael *wanted* to see him, and that was the best news he'd had all evening.

"Hi," he called as soon as Michael climbed out of his pickup.

Michael glanced around, spotted Ethan walking toward him. "Hi." He nodded at Karl's TR7. "I guess you've got company."

"Not exactly. Karl dropped by." Ethan wanted to make it very clear that he had not invited Karl.

"Ah." Well, it wasn't exactly *ah*. It was more or less a grunt, but the impression was the same.

Whatever it was, it didn't sound promising. Ethan said quickly, "You want to come around to the back?"

Michael hesitated. "Please?" Ethan added. "We're having iced coffee and talking."

"Iced coffee?" It was polite if doubtful.

"I could fix you something else." He wasn't exactly sure what. Crystal Light? Warm milk? The never-opened twenty-year-old cognac that had belonged to his father?

"I brought you Pauli Girl." Michael leaned back in the truck and lifted out a brown paper bag.

Ethan's spirits shot up still higher. Michael was definitely paying a social call. He hadn't blown it the night before. "Thanks!"

Somehow he was going to have to get rid of Karl without insulting him, because Ethan needed this time with Michael. He just…did.

He led the way to the back where Karl was still sipping his iced coffee. The little lanterns bobbed gently in the night breeze like colored moths. At the sight of Michael, Karl put his glass down and stood up.

"I don't know if you two have officially met." Ethan started off cheerfully enough, but even in the shadowy light he could see that Karl was not thrilled. "Karl, this is Michael Milner. He owns Milner's Martial Arts."

"I know who he is." Karl's voice was tight.

Ethan finished lamely, "And Karl is one of the Hagar boys. From, you know, Hagar's Truck and Tractor Equipment."

"Hi," Michael said.

"I need to get going." Karl was looking at Ethan as if Michael was invisible. "Thanks for the coffee."

"You're welcome." Something was obviously wrong. Ethan didn't really think Karl was disappointed he'd missed an opportunity to kill him, so what was his problem?

"I'll just—" He intended to walk Karl to his car, but Karl went striding off into the darkness, leaving him standing there.

"That was weird," Ethan said, turning to Michael.

"What was weird?" The scarred half of Michael's face looked mutable and unworldly in the uncertain light.

Ethan explained about Karl trying to hire him as a writing tutor, his gaze following the disappearing tail lights as the TR7 hurtled down the dusty road like a rocket.

"On the bright side, I don't think he's planning to kill me." He was kidding, of course.

"Do you really not see what's going on here?"

At the sharpness of Michael's tone, Ethan stared at him.

"No. What's going on?"

Michael expelled an impatient breath. "The guy is trying to ask you out."

"Ask *me* out?"

"You're not going to pretend you're in the closet?"

Ethan's mouth moved, but no sound came out. That was probably just as well since it wouldn't have been anything very intelligent. He was astonished on so many levels. Astonished that Michael *was* aware that he was gay. Astonished that Karl was apparently gay. Astonished that Michael must be gay too—mustn't he?—to have realized that Karl was interested in Ethan? And most of all astonished that he had missed all of that.

"You honestly didn't see it?" Michael asked while Ethan was still floundering.

Ethan shook his head. "Karl Hagar is *gay*? Somehow it was easier to imagine him as a serial killer. How do you know?"

"How do you *not* know?" Michael retorted.

"I guess I just never thought about it."

"Really?" The disbelief wasn't polite. "Because from the way you look at me, I'd say you've thought about it a lot."

Instantly Ethan felt as though he'd been dipped in boiling water. "Sorry," he mumbled.

After a second or two, Michael relented. "If it was a problem, I wouldn't be here."

"Oh. Right."

Well, that was the good news, wasn't it? Michael knew he was interested and here Michael was. All these highs and lows in the space of minutes; Ethan was beginning to feel like he was suffering from emotional whiplash. He looked at the paper bag Michael held, and said, "I've got a bottle opener inside."

"I've got a bottle opener."

Michael reached in his pocket, pulled out a Swiss army knife and sat down in the Adirondack chair vacated by Karl. He opened the sack, pulled out a bottle, opened it and handed it to Ethan.

"This is where you grew up?"

Ethan nodded. He sat down in the other chair and put the bottle to his lips. The beer was cold and fizzy. It tasted crisp and slightly hoppy. He thought he could get to like it.

"And you've lived all your life in Peabody." It wasn't a question so much as Michael arranging the facts in his mind, perhaps determining why Ethan was apparently so blank on the finer points of romance.

Ethan made a face. "I know. Pathetic, right?"

"Not if you're happy here."

Ethan considered that as he drank his beer. He was not *un*happy, but he was lonely. Oh, he was friendly with a lot of people, but he wasn't really close to them. It had been the same in school. Erin was better at forming friendships.

She belonged to a lot of clubs and social groups. She always had something going. Ethan didn't think she had time to be lonely. He hoped not, anyway.

He knew enough not to talk about loneliness to the guy he was hoping to spend the night with, and he made a determined effort to turn the conversation back to Michael.

"Where did you grow up?"

"La Crescenta. It's in L.A. County."

Ethan had never heard of it. It sounded…affluent.

He dropped his empty to the grass and took the second beer Michael handed him. "Where'd you go to college?"

"UCLA. You?"

"Bakersfield Junior College. I always planned on going to a real university, but after Mom and Dad…."

"Sure. You and Erin had to keep the Red Bird running." Michael had no doubt heard all he wanted on that subject.

"Yeah. Well, no. We could have sold out then, and I guess we would have gotten an okay price for it. Enough for each of us to go off and start someplace new. But we didn't want to. We grew up thinking this would all be ours one day."

Michael glanced around the large yard, the old house, and the open fields that stretched beyond.

"It probably doesn't look like much, but—"

"It looks like a home," Michael said. "It looks like a place where people have lived for a long time and been happy."

"That's exactly right." Ethan smiled, pleased that Michael recognized what had always seemed obvious to him. This was home and worth fighting for. He finished his beer and said tentatively, "Would you want to swim?"

Michael's eyes seemed to shine in the gloom. "Among other things."

Ethan laughed. It was probably a nervous-sounding laugh, but he was happy and excited. More happy and excited than he'd been in a long time. He pulled off his jeans and tossed them to the back of the lawn chair. He tried not to stare as Michael rose and stepped out of his Levi's in three quick moves.

Even without staring he could see that Michael's body was silvered with scars. He was still beautiful though, and the fact that he seemed unselfconscious about the scars made him even more beautiful in Ethan's opinion.

Anyway, it wasn't Michael's scars he couldn't keep his eyes off. His gaze naturally gravitated to the neat bulge beneath Michael's white briefs. How big was Michael? There was one way to find out, of course.

Emboldened by curiosity or maybe more alcohol than he was used to, Ethan shucked his swim trunks and then levered himself up over the side of the pool. The water was cooler now—though not cold—and silky soft. The moon drifted across the black surface like a giant lily pad.

"Skinny dipping in the moonlight?" Michael sounded amused.

"Sounds like a song." Sounded like a dream come true, in fact. Ethan watched while trying to appear not to be looking as Michael peeled off his briefs and dropped them on top of Ethan's trunks before splashing down beside him in the water.

Broad shoulders, narrow hips, long legs…and Michael had looked perfectly well-endowed in the glimpse Ethan'd had. Nothing missing or damaged structurally, thank God.

Michael struck off toward the opposite side of the pool in clean, long strokes. He surfaced, shook his wet hair back. "This is great."

He did a couple of brisk laps across the broad diameter of the pool while Ethan floated and simply enjoyed Michael's open pleasure. When Michael changed direction and swam toward him he felt a momentary unease. His memories of high school swim class weren't fond ones. He'd been in a class with Dave Wilton and Kurt Hagar, Karl's older brother, and he'd always taken the brunt of the inevitable roughhousing. He didn't doubt he'd take the brunt in any wrestling match with Michael.

But when Michael's arms closed around him, it was playful and easy. He didn't drag Ethan beneath the water before he had time to catch his breath, he didn't accidentally-on-purpose bang his elbows or knees into any soft parts of Ethan's anatomy. He wasn't trying to overpower Ethan, and Ethan stopped wrestling and wrapped his arms around Michael's shoulders.

He could see the glimmer of Michael's smile as Michael hoisted him up, and he could feel the prod of Michael's erection against his thigh. It was kind of a turn-on to know Michael could feel him as well, although the thought was immediately followed by uncertainty over how he compared with other guys Michael had been with.

Michael fell back in the water, dragging Ethan with him. As they sank down, Michael's mouth closed on Ethan's. It was too fast and too wet and too bubbly to be romantic, exactly, but Ethan was vividly conscious of Michael's warmth and strength. The next moment they were laughing and splashing away from each other.

ж ж ж

Though it was still in the high eighties, it felt cold by the time they climbed out of the pool. They toweled off and pulled on their jeans and shirts. They picked up the empty beer bottles and went inside. The house, by comparison, still felt warm and a little stuffy.

"When does your sister get home?" Michael asked as they went through the living room with its overstuffed plaid chairs and sofas, and pseudo Duncan Phyfe tables.

It seemed to be the question on everyone's mind. Ethan looked at the clock over the bookshelf. "We've got the house to ourselves for about an hour."

He led the way upstairs to his bedroom. Michael said nothing as he followed Ethan down the hall with its threadbare carpet and gallery of family photos.

Ethan felt for the light switch and the room was illuminated. It was almost disorienting, this sudden merging of his old dreams with his new. Until he saw the room through Michael's eyes, it hadn't occurred to Ethan that maybe it was time to start living in the present. Not that it was a child's room. Even when Ethan had been a little kid, he had not been particularly childish. The shelves were full of books. Travel posters and maps of places he had never been to—and probably never would now—adorned the walls.

His boyhood had been spent planning for a future and his adulthood had been spent in the trappings of his past. He had never really considered it before.

Michael moved slowly around the room lifting a model airplane, examining a map of the Sahara. Ethan sat down on the edge of the bed—it seemed newly, embarrassingly prominent as though positioned to be front and center stage—watching, waiting for the moment when Michael would finish exploring.

As though reading his thoughts, Michael came toward the bed. "So have you ever...?"

Ethan shook his head.

"*Never?*"

"There wasn't anyone around to practice with."

"But when you went to college?"

Ethan could feel his face getting red, but it was better if they just got this out of the way. "I didn't know how to...." *Ask.* Nor did he know *who* to ask, as should have been obvious from his inability to read what was happening with Karl. "Sorry."

"Don't apologize."

Michael climbed onto the bed beside him and Ethan let himself fall back. It almost felt like he was moving in slow motion, he was so aware of every movement, every look between them.

Michael leaned over him, his hands slid beneath Ethan's T-shirt, raising it, and Ethan obediently raised his arms to let it be pulled off. He should probably be reciprocating, right? He reached up to slide the open shirt off Michael's broad shoulders. He liked the feel of Michael's skin, smooth and still cool beneath the warm cotton from their swim. Even the touch of Michael's scars was not displeasing to him, and he hoped he was communicating that as he gently traced the cobwebbed lines.

Michael's eyes lingered on the pulse beating at the base of Ethan's throat. He brushed it with his fingertips and smiled faintly.

"I feel like I'm dreaming. I didn't even think you liked me," Ethan admitted. As he said it, he realized it was a stupid comment. Maybe he had grown up in the boonies, but he wasn't so naïve that he didn't know you didn't have to like someone to have sex with them. Michael's options were as limited as his own—as were Karl's—so assuming that this was the start of anything, except maybe an occasional roll in the hay, was a good way to get his heart broken.

"You're not very good at reading people."

Was that true? Ethan wasn't sure. He'd always thought himself a reasonable judge of character. "Well, in fairness, you don't give a lot of clues."

Michael's mouth quirked, the scarred half, lopsided.

"*Do* you like me?" He couldn't help that asking probably made him sound insecure. He preferred knowing upfront.

"I like you." Michael's voice was low. "I liked you the first day I saw you. You were sitting on the floor surrounded by books, and you looked up when I opened the door and smiled right at me. It felt like you had been waiting for me, like you were welcoming me home."

Ethan sucked in a breath. Just *that* was so much more than he'd hoped for.

Michael added, "And I've got a perfectly good coffee maker at the dojo."

Ethan started to laugh. "Do you?"

Michael nodded, shrugging the rest of the way out of his shirt. He gathered Ethan into his arms. It was better than Ethan had imagined, and he had a vivid imagination. The startling, solid human reality of skin and hair and breath as they held each other, pressed closer was better. One of Ethan's flip flops fell to the floor, the other bent back and sprang free.

"Boing," gasped Ethan.

Michael laughed against his mouth. His weight pressed Ethan into the pillows, but it was reassuring, not threatening. Ethan could feel Michael's heart pounding—nearly as hard as his own. He lifted his head from the pillow, kissing Michael deeply, partly as a distraction from his own lack of technique, partly because he couldn't get enough of kissing Michael.

God. To finally kiss a man. To finally kiss *this* man.

Michael's mouth opened to his kiss, hot and wet, Ethan drank him in, submerging himself in the kiss as they had submerged in each other's arms in the night-cooled water of the pool. Michael's mouth was bigger than a woman's, a suggestion of bristle around the softness of his lips. He met Ethan's kiss with an openness, a hunger that seemed distinctly unfeminine—not that Ethan had a lot of experience kissing women either. He was surprised to hear Michael making little sounds again: not moaning, exactly, but a roughened breathing. He realized that he was the one making those excited sounds and promptly shut up.

Michael shifted sideways so that he wasn't crushing Ethan, his thigh no longer nudging aggressively into Ethan's crotch. Ethan wanted to touch him, but he felt uncertain as to what Michael would permit. Not that he seemed standoffish. His hand stroked Ethan's chest, his fingers trailing over Ethan's nipple. That wasn't something that had ever figured into Ethan's fantasies, but it felt nice. Startling, but nice. He copied the motion, pressing Michael's right nipple between his thumb and forefinger. Michael sucked in a breath.

It felt good to be able to deliver pleasure as well as receive, nice to control some of what was happening, because the jolts of sensation going through him every time Michael scratched his thumbnail against the sensitive tip of Ethan's nipple was cutting the current between his brain.

"Michael. God…."

Michael squeezed the little nub, and Ethan could feel it stiffen into a hard point. "You like that?" His breath was warm against Ethan's damp skin.

Ethan made an inarticulate response, feeling blindly for the back of Michael's neck, pulling his head down. He could feel Michael's smile against his chest and then Michael's tongue flicked out. Ethan gasped and arched up. That wet rasp of tongue on him…it was like all his nerve endings were exposed.

When Michael's teeth closed on his nipple, raw sound tore out of Ethan's throat. It sounded like protest and Michael raised his head.

"No?"

"No. I mean, *yes. Please* yes."

Michael's teeth clamped with peculiar delicacy on the tiny peak and he bit down. Ethan moaned and tried not to thrash as he wordlessly urged him on.

Thank God he didn't have to say it aloud. Michael seemed to translate his little gasps and moans with no trouble. He ground his teeth very gently on Ethan's nipple and then he transferred his attentions to Ethan's other nipple.

Ethan's fingers wound in the long hair at Michael's nape, soft as silk, still damp from their swim. He wasn't guiding Michael, he was hanging on for dear life beneath that intense pleasure.

Finally, Michael's mouth worked its way up to Ethan's again, and Ethan let his hand drop to absently massage his deliciously abused nipple, savoring the kiss.

"What would you like?" Michael asked. The warm words were murmured against his flushed skin. "Tell me."

Despite the cooling night air stirring the curtains, Ethan's skin felt hot, especially through his jeans where their lower bodies touched; the brush of Michael's hand through denim felt like a brand.

Michael lightly stroked his thigh, waiting perhaps for some signal—beyond the obvious signals Ethan's body was sending for him.

"Anything."

"*Anything*?" Michael repeated gently. "We can do better than that."

Ethan was willing, though "anything" sounded pretty good to him at the moment. His groin felt heavy and hot, his jeans increasingly restrictive. He could feel Michael was hard. No question there. Ethan slipped his hand between the join of their bodies to stroke the shape he could feel within the soft denim. Michael's eyelashes flickered, watching him. He made an encouraging sound as Ethan traced the length of his cock, trying once again to judge how big he was.

Michael's fingers worked the rivets of Ethan's Levi's. Ethan closed his eyes, focusing helplessly on the lovely moment when Michael opened his fly and slipped his hand inside. *Oh God. Yes.* That was what he'd wanted, needed, longed for—for what felt like his entire life. Instinctively Ethan pushed up into Michael's hand.

"Yes?" Michael murmured.

Ethan nodded. Talk about rhetorical questions. Michael sat up and divested himself of his own jeans in a couple of strong kicks. They landed beside the bed with the rest of their clothes as Ethan awkwardly followed suit—awkwardly because his cock was now so stiff it was presenting logistical problems.

He stared down and blinked. He'd never been this close to another man's erect penis in his life. Michael's cock slanted up from the soft dark tangle of pubic hair to brush the smooth, brown skin below his navel. It looked sleek, and hard, indefinably weapon-like—and about the size Ethan had guessed. Michael's balls were shadowed in the lamplight.

"Did you want to fuck me?" he asked. It took nerve because Michael's cock looked the size of a cruise missile. But Michael had been patient so far, putting a lot of effort into pleasuring Ethan. He'd like to do that for Michael. It couldn't be as impossible and painful as it looked or no one would do it.

"Would you like to fuck me?" Michael countered.

"Are you—?" Ethan's voice cracked like the teenager he'd once been. "Seriously?"

"Yep." It was terse but Michael gave one of those brief, crooked curves of his mouth.

"How?" It came out baldly. He thought he'd die if Michael laughed, but Michael showed no sign that Ethan had said anything stupid.

"Do you have a condom?"

Ethan nodded, scrambling to the side of the bed and rifling through the odds and ends there. He pulled out a foil-wrapped packet and handed it to Michael.

Michael took it without expression. "Actually, I've got one in my wallet. Why don't you find something we can use as lube?"

"Lotion? Suntan lotion?"

"Sometimes that stings. Do you have any cooking oil? Preferably not something currently being used for french fries."

Michael was teasing him, getting him past the embarrassed moment of realization that the condom was past its safe use date. Ethan nodded and headed downstairs, trying to tell himself it was no big deal. Michael already knew he wasn't getting any.

He went through the cupboards, found the olive oil, and started upstairs again. He glanced down at the green and gold label and had to bite back a laugh at the words *Extra Virgin*.

That about summed it up.

SIX

It was a relief when Ethan got back to the bedroom to find that Michael seemed content merely to kiss and caress. He didn't seem to be in a huge rush and that eased some of Ethan's performance anxieties. He could see why Michael was probably a good martial arts teacher.

After a time when Ethan was enjoying himself again, aroused and no longer self-conscious, Michael pulled a little away and said, "Do you still want to?"

Ethan nodded. He couldn't believe Michael was really going to let him do this, but Michael rolled onto his stomach, cradling his head on his arms. "Okay. Just be sure to use plenty of oil. Inside and out."

Inside and out. The thought of that seemed to stop Ethan's heart in his chest. He put the condom on. Once upon a time a long time ago he had practiced this very thing, and he still remembered how—although it was too painful to recall all that fruitless preparation. As he poured the oil into his palm, he could see that his hands weren't steady. He stroked the one firm, white globe of Michael's ass and left it glistening. There were scars on Michael's back, but his butt was as soft and innocent looking as a baby's.

"Nice. Go on," Michael encouraged.

Ethan leaned forward and very carefully parted Michael's buttocks with his free hand until he could see the rose brown entrance of his anus. He swallowed hard as Michael drew one knee up slightly, giving him better access. Ethan touched a tentative, slick finger to the clenched muscle. Michael's skin was warm, damp beneath the muscular curve of his ass, but dry between his cheeks. Ethan smoothed the oil over him, and then recalling Michael's instructions and his own youthful lurid reading, pressed a cautious fingertip inside.

He closed his eyes at the startling heat. He could feel Michael's sphincter muscle gripping on. He twisted his finger experimentally, and Michael made a sound.

"Am I hurting?"

He could see the beautiful half of Michael's face. Michael gave a small shake of his head. "No way. Feels good."

How could this part feel good? Ethan always thought it only felt good if you hit the prostate gland—which had to be here somewhere—but Michael was smiling and drawing his leg up higher, so Ethan must be doing something right.

"How many fingers…?"

"Hmm? Oh. One is fine. Even though it's been a while, I'm…" Michael didn't finish the thought, but Ethan inferred that Michael's level of experience meant he didn't require the same preparation Ethan might.

The idea that one day Michael might be doing this to him sent a little shudder of delighted apprehension through Ethan.

Michael's breath caught. "That's nice."

Ethan touched the firm little lump again and Michael jerked and moaned. God, Michael's body was so hot and tight around his finger. Ethan was suddenly desperate to feel that grip on his cock, aching with need.

He drew his finger out, wiped it on the sheet and applied more oil to himself. Michael was panting softly, watching him out of one blue eye. He blinked.

"Listen," Michael said, and Ethan eyed him attentively. "We're okay here, but if you were to do this with someone else…don't use olive oil. It breaks down latex."

"Oh." That put a little damper on Ethan's enthusiasm. He didn't want to think about doing this with anyone else. He didn't want to think about anything but this moment. And Michael didn't give him time to consider it, lifting up and repositioning so that Ethan could kneel between his legs. Ethan absently stroked his rubber-coated cock with one hand, hesitantly reaching out with the other to touch Michael's taut buttock.

"Is there anything in particular…?"

Michael gave a breathless laugh. "Take your time. You're a big boy."

He was?

Gratified, Ethan inched forward and began to guide himself into the narrow entrance of Michael's ass. It was tight, deliciously so, like nothing he'd ever felt. A couple of inches in, Michael grunted. Ethan felt the unmistakable feeling of muscle clenching around his cock. He stilled, waiting. Michael let out a breath and relaxed.

"We're good. It's just been a while. Go on."

Ethan shoved in farther. In fact, it would have been nearly impossible not to. His balls touched Michael's flesh, Michael's thighs pressed against his, Michael's smooth naked skin rested against his crotch. Ethan could feel the blood beating in his cock, feel each pulse.

He *had* to move. He was going to go crazy if he didn't.

Michael made it simple by pushing back against him and wriggling his hips. The grip of his body felt like a living glove around Ethan. Cautiously, Ethan pulled out and thrust in again, and the intensity of that set his nerves on fire. Little sparks skipped and danced from the top of his scalp to the tip of his cock.

He had to steady himself, hands on Michael's hips as he thrust into him. Michael pushed back and they were starting to find a rhythm to it, a sensual sawing, swaying into it, swinging back….

Vaguely he was aware of Michael, balancing on knees and one hand, reaching beneath himself to stroke his cock. That was probably something Ethan should be attending to, but it was hard to think past the incredible sensation of that tight, slick dragging caress. Sparks flared behind his eyes—and in his groin. God, it wasn't taking long at all.

He would've liked to kiss Michael again, liked to be held in his arms, but that wasn't possible in this position, and no other position would be possible because it was happening now. He wrapped his arms around Michael, holding him tight, wanting to feel his heart beating against Michael's own. He jerked his hips frantically, crying out against Michael's scarred skin as he came.

✼ ✼ ✼

ETHAN OPENED HIS eyes. Moonlight illuminated the map of the Sahara, angled the planes of Michael's sleeping face.

A wave of happiness flooded him. For a few contented moments he simply enjoyed *being*. Michael's arm was looped casually about his waist, Michael's breath warm against his forehead. Ethan listened to the crickets chirping merrily, the night sounds, the feel of Michael's heart beating against his own.

They hadn't been dozing long. Ethan realized he hadn't heard Erin come home. He glanced at the clock beside the bed. She was nearly two hours late. Worry flickered into life. They made it a rule to let each other know if they were going to be late.

Ethan eased out from beneath Michael's arm and went downstairs to get a glass of water.

He was leaning against the sink, gazing out at the moon, when he heard Erin's car coming down the lane.

He emptied his glass and waited. In a little while he heard her key in the front door. When she walked into the kitchen her cheeks were flushed and her eyes shone brightly.

"Do you know what time it is? Where were you?"

He wasn't sure she even heard him because she said at the same time, "Is that Michael's truck out front?"

Ethan nodded.

"That's great!" She walked straight through to the living room, leaving Ethan no choice but to follow her.

"Why didn't you call?"

Erin blinked at this uncharacteristic heat. "You know it's my scrapbooking night."

"You're two hours late!"

"So? I went out for coffee afterwards." She was looking around the living room obviously expecting to see Michael, and clearly puzzled to find the lights turned down low.

"With who?"

Erin threw him a mildly exasperated look. "Tony Guinn."

"Isn't he married?"

"Divorced. Where's Michael?"

"Oh. Well…" Ethan rubbed the back of his neck. "I have to tell you something."

Erin's brows rose at his tone. "What?"

"I...."

"What?"

"It's about Michael."

"What about him?"

"It's just…we've never talked about this stuff."

"You and Michael? What stuff?"

"You and me. Well…about me and…."

"For God's sake, Ethan!"

Ethan drew in a long breath. "About me being gay."

Erin was staring at him as though she'd never seen him before. "Oh for—! Is that supposed to be a news bulletin? What did you imagine I thought was going on with you?"

He relaxed. "I wasn't sure you knew. I mean, it's never really been an issue."

"Well, I should hope not. You're my brother. It was kind of hard to miss the fact you never went out with any of my friends no matter how much they hinted." Her face changed. "Wait a minute. You mean, it *is* an issue? You and Michael are…?"

Ethan nodded. "At least I think so," he qualified quickly.

Erin's face broke into a huge smile. "Ethan, that's wonderful!"

"Shhh." He looked uneasily over his shoulder at the staircase.

"Is it a secret?"

"I don't know what it is yet. At least…I know what I *think* it is, but I don't want to scare him off."

"Aw." She squeezed his arm. "You won't scare him off. It's going to work out. I thought from the first there was something there. Chance knew it too."

"Chance?"

Erin nodded. "He's very observant." Her expression changed. "Erm, listen, Ethan. You're not going to like this, but I told Tony about Karl."

Tony Guinn had been Erin's boyfriend in high school. Ethan had never quite understood why they'd broken up, but Tony had gone on to marry Petra Walsh, who had been prom queen their senior year.

"*Why*? I told you not to spread that around."

"Because Tony's now a sergeant at the sheriff's department. If you'd been listening to me this morning you'd know that he's working the case of those men they found in the desert."

"Please tell me you didn't." Ethan closed his eyes. "Please tell me you did *not* do that."

"Ethan...."

Ethan opened his eyes and glared at her. "Did you tell Tony you thought Karl was a serial killer?"

Erin's chin rose. "I just told him that Karl might bear watching. That's all. I told him about Karl's stories—"

Ethan moaned and put his face in his hands.

"—and I told him that Karl cornered you in the parking lot last night."

Ethan dropped his hands. "He didn't. He was...what did he say?"

"Who?"

"Tony."

"He said it was interesting and he'd look into it."

Ethan moaned again.

Watching him, Erin said, "Well, Chance thought it was a good idea."

"Chance? How did Chance get involved in all this?"

Erin shrugged. "I don't know. He just...does."

"And Chance told you to go to the police?"

"Yes. Well, no. I happened to mention Tony, and Chance suggested that talking to someone informally about Karl might be the way to go. It made sense. Tony will be discreet. I told him you were afraid of Karl retaliating."

"Oh. My. God."

"What?"

Ethan shook his head. "I can't deal with this right now. I can't. I'll talk to you in the morning."

"Okay. Good night." Erin sounded maddeningly untroubled. In fact, there was a lilt of laughter in her voice as she called, "Sweet dreams."

❦ ❦ ❦

A LONELY TUMBLEWEED bounced across the parking lot at Viento Square and rolled off into the desert as Ethan pulled in.

Michael had left him early that morning with a kiss but not offering plans of a future get together. He had yet not arrived at Viento Square, but Karl's TR7 was parked outside the bookstore.

Ethan winced, seeing it. He thought of Erin going to Tony Guinn with her suspicions. Well, he knew who was to blame for that.

The lights to Sweets for the Sweet were on, and though it was only seven in the morning, the sign in the window read OPEN.

Karl got out of the car as Ethan came down the wooden walkway. Karl looked as pale and sleepless as Ethan felt, although in Karl's case the cause was probably not nearly as pleasant.

A few feet from Ethan, Karl said brusquely, "I wanted to talk to you."

Ethan squared his shoulders. "Karl, I thought about it and I really don't believe I'm the right person to try and tutor you." He added honestly, "Whether it's instinct or what, you already know more about writing than I do."

Karl threw an uneasy look around the empty parking lot. "That isn't what I wanted to talk to you about. Can we go inside?"

"Okay." Ethan hesitated before unlocking the door and leading the way into Red Bird Books and Coffee. The smell of coffee beans and paperback books greeted them. "What's wrong?" He was very much afraid he already knew what was wrong. He wished he could spare both of them this.

"Nothing's wrong. I just wanted to…." Karl's voice faded out. He swallowed, said, "I'm gay."

"Oh." Ethan knew Karl deserved more, but he also knew Karl was probably going to bitterly regret this revelation in a couple of minutes.

"And you're gay. I *know* you are."

"Yes." Ethan thought about Michael. He smiled. "True."

"And I thought maybe we could…I mean, it makes sense." Ethan opened his mouth but Karl rushed ahead, "We're the only two queers in five hundred miles."

"That's not a good enough reason for…whatever it is you're thinking. Besides, it's not true."

Karl's face seemed to flatten. "If you mean Milner, forget it."

"I just mean roughly ten percent of the population —"

Karl burst out, "I've heard all that bullshit about same-sex attraction in heterosexuals. The only thing that matters to us is where we live, and where we live we're the only two of our kind. We're the only two that matter."

That was a warped view on so many levels that Ethan hardly knew where to start. And what was the point of getting into a debate when the simple truth was even if he and Karl were the last two gays on the planet, he didn't like Karl enough to spend any more time with him than he had to?

He tried to say kindly, "Karl, thank you for trusting me enough to come out to me. I appreciate what you're saying, what you're offering, but that's not what I want."

"If you're thinking Milner, you're way off base. All he'll want is a quick fuck."

It hurt. How could it not since it was exactly what Ethan feared? But he knew firsthand where Karl's anger came from. He kept his tone steady. "What happens with me and Michael doesn't have anything to do with what happens between you and me. I see you as a friend."

"That's not how I see you."

"But wouldn't that be the place to start?"

"No."

"Well, I'm sorry, but—"

Karl turned on his heel and walked out without another word, slamming the door shut behind him and cutting off the bird chirp.

It felt like a very bad start to the day.

Michael's truck pulled into the lot half an hour later. He got out, walked toward the dojo. He was looking at the windows of Red Bird Books and Coffee. Catching sight of Ethan, he gave that broken grin. Ethan smiled in response and lifted his hand. Michael lifted his hand too.

Ethan's heart lightened once more. It didn't matter what Karl or anyone thought or didn't think. It was going to be okay. It was going to be terrific.

At ten Erin breezed in, humming a little tune. She went straight to her counter and began mixing her caffeinated potions.

"You're in a good mood," Ethan told her over the whir of the blender.

She grinned at him. "Then I guess it's catching."

He grinned back, nodding.

He was rearranging the vintage Harlequin Romances when she brought him a small paper cup. "I think I've got it now."

Ethan studied the pale green liquid doubtfully and tossed it back.

"What do you think?"

"What is that? Absinthe mocha?"

She giggled. "It's mint chip surprise."

"What's the surprise? Wormwood?"

"What do you think it needs?"

"Chocolate." He couldn't help adding tartly, "Maybe you should ask your pal Chance for more advice."

The door chirped and Michael walked in right on time for his morning medium house blend.

He looked straight at Ethan and nodded politely.

Remembering the "perfectly good coffee maker in the dojo," Ethan smiled widely back.

"Oh. My. God."

Ethan looked up from the crossword puzzle. "What?"

Erin raised her head. Although she was staring straight at him, she appeared to be seeing someone else.

"*What?*" Ethan asked again. He was on the verge of figuring out a nine-letter word for "love."

"The sheriffs made an arrest in the deaths of those men they found in the desert."

"They actually *were* murdered?"

Erin's gaze slid away from his. "Erm, not exactly."

"What exactly?"

"They've arrested Dave Wilton and his brother for toxic dumping."

"Do I want to know the rest of this?"

"No, seriously. They've been dumping waste from their disposal units in the desert and it sounds like it's poisoned the water hole near the Hagar property. The coroner thinks the three men who died might have drunk or bathed in the water."

"That's horrible."

She nodded, still reading and frowning.

"So Karl didn't have anything to do with it."

She continued to read. "Probably not."

"And you'll make sure your ex-boyfriend doesn't say anything to Karl?"

"Yep."

"Erin."

She looked up. "Yes. I'll make sure." She looked down again, but she was smiling. "It'll give me a good reason to see him again."

Nine-letter word starting with an "A"...

Erin gasped, once more breaking Ethan's concentration. "But he must have known all along!"

"Who?"

Erin's cheeks were pink. "If the coroner reached his findings yesterday, Tony must have known the whole time we were talking last night. He was just…just…."

"Wanting to have coffee with you." Ethan laughed at Erin's face. "Or maybe just trying to keep you from making it!"

About Sort of Stranger than Fiction

We used to take a lot of long drives when I was a kid, and as we'd pass those little population-one-thousand towns off the freeway I used to wonder what it would be like growing up in a place like that. Even today some people spend their whole lives in the same place with a lot of the same people. I think there might be some comfort to that—assuming you like those people.

Ethan has spent his entire life in Peabody, California, but until Michael Milner opens up a martial arts studio next door to the Red Bird Books and Coffee it never occurred to him the greatest adventure might be in his own backyard.

One Less Stiff at the Funeral
Sean Kennedy

Jason tried to stifle the yawn that threatened to burst from him without any deference to social or professional etiquette at all. He attempted to cover it up further by taking a sip from his lukewarm coffee, but he almost ended up choking. He set the mug down with an unintentionally heavy blow, making the woman sitting across from him jump.

"Is there a problem?" she asked.

Adele Conway was a strange fish. Most people would have asked *Are you okay?* but she was too formal for that. She sat rigidly on the chair with a perfectly ironed handkerchief held in one hand. One perfectly ironed, perfectly dry handkerchief. Jason had seen many people sitting across from him in what passed as his poor excuse of an office, and none of them were this composed. Usually he was exposed to raw emotional displays every day, but Adele was sizing him up instead, and obviously waiting for him to say something.

"Please continue, Ms. Conway," Jason managed to choke out. His face was burning from trying to suppress the cough. He wondered how red he looked.

"Miss," she corrected him. "I never married."

She didn't look old enough to be from that generation that cared about such precise gender pronouns, as if using *Ms* was the equivalent of burning your boyfriend's draft card along with your bra, but Jason decided not to fight it. "Miss Conway, sorry."

"We were talking about Mother's chocolates."

"Of course." And that was weird as well. *Mother.* Not *Mum.* Or *Ma.* Or anything that could be seen as even remotely affectionate. But Adele was no different from any of the other Conways; at least those that Jason had met so far. It was a strange mix of disdain and reserve that seemed to hold them upright. "You want some kind of display?"

"I'm not certain I would say *I* want it particularly," Adele said. "But appearances must be maintained. And people always seem to appreciate spectacle. I'm sure that's probably why she had it written into the will, as just one more thing to have people running around doing for her!"

Jason wasn't exactly sure what she meant, but he nodded, hoping he had his suitably concerned mask on. Adele was the kind of person who seemed to want you to know exactly how busy she was, how much of her time she spent on other people, and how she never got any thanks for it in the end.

Adele gave a hearty sniff, and wiped at her eyes with her handkerchief. Jason couldn't help but notice yet again that the eyes and the handkerchief remained entirely dry. Yet he couldn't silently accuse her of crocodile tears; it just didn't seem to be her way. He had been waiting throughout their whole appointment for the dam to break, but there must have been some hardy beavers keeping watch over it in her brain. "Mother always liked her chocolates."

"Don't we all?" was what he said, and immediately regretted it. It was so easy to overstep the mark with some clients, even with the lightest tone. Most of them wanted you to be as sombre as they were in their darkest moment, and that was what Jason often had trouble with. In fact, he had had trouble with it ever since he started with the Newlin Funeral Parlour.

And Adele Conway was one of those clients. She straightened up, if it was even possible for her to get any straighter, and looked down at her dry handkerchief. Sighing, she closed it away in her handbag, obviously deciding it was going to remain that way and its presence was therefore useless.

"Of course, what I meant to say—"

She waved him off. "May I be blunt with you, Mr. Harvey?"

Jason had been Mr. Harvey to her from the very first moment they had met, even though he had stressed he would prefer to be called by his first name. That had been ignored immediately. "Go ahead."

"The Conways are *not* known for their…I guess it would be…emotional displays?"

Jason nodded, even though he had to bite his tongue rather viciously.

"Frankly, when they said it was part of the service here at Newlin's to deal with a counsellor when making the arrangements for my mother's funeral, I almost decided to go elsewhere. If I wanted to see a therapist, I would most certainly pay for one who possessed comfortable furniture and didn't look as if he just graduated from high school."

Feeling as if he was withering beneath her steady, unflinching gaze, Jason didn't even really feel like he could argue the point—after all, didn't he think exactly the same thing himself? He felt like a fraud every time he met with a grieving family member. This hadn't turned out to be exactly the job he envisioned when he stepped off the stage at graduation with his psychology degree in hand. Jobs were hard to get at a clinic in Melbourne at that point of time, so the advert in the paper calling for a combined counsellor/funeral arrangement assistant had seemed pretty grim, and he'd been sure that the competition wouldn't be that fierce given the work involved. After all, who really *wanted* to work in a funeral parlour? It wasn't exactly every kid's dream job. At the very least it would be good enough to tide him over until he decided what it was he actually wanted to do with his life, and then figured out exactly how he was going to achieve it.

Hell, he had even gotten used to the bodies, once he started seeing them as bizarrely life-like wax dummies that smelled a bit too much of cleaning chemicals.

"I may look young—"

"You look fifteen. I don't know what on earth they're thinking putting a child in such a position—"

A *child*? "Ms. Conway—"

"*Miss!*"

"*Miss* Conway, I assure you my age has nothing to do with my ability to plan your mother's wedding—"

"*Funeral!*" she barked.

Jason could feel his face burning again. "That's what I meant." He wished the recent sinkhole in Guatemala had a cousin that would open up beneath his feet and swallow him whole. "Anyway, this is my job, Miss Conway, and I aim to do it satisfactorily—"

Her eyes were lasers that could have destroyed planets.

"*Beyond* satisfactorily. I will do an *exemplary* job with your mother's wed—funeral. I promise you that. Now, let's get back to the chocolates." *Oh, please, God, or whatever god may be out there listening to me, let's get back to the chocolates!*

Adele sighed again. "Chocolate. Mother loved it. And even though she wasn't prone to emotional displays in life, she specified in her will that she would like us to have some at the service to share around. Personally, I think it's a bit bizarre, and I'm not sure if everyone at the service will even participate. Perhaps those people can just take some home—I suppose with your obsession with weddings you would probably think of them as bonbonniere, Mr. Harvey?"

Jason smiled weakly, and accepted his public flogging. "It's a nice idea."

"So you think you'll be able to arrange this?"

Pick up some chocolates? Yeah, I think I'm capable of that. But Jason would have laid money on the fact that Adele would think he wasn't. She probably had visions of him turning up at the service with a couple of Freddo Frogs and a carton of Cadbury Favourites.

The thought of chocolate made his stomach start to rumble. He hoped Adele couldn't hear it; it would be another black mark against him. His lunch break wasn't that far away, and he was looking forward to getting out of the office. Now he was dreaming of Caramello Koalas, and the crispness of the chocolate shell breaking beneath his teeth and the smooth caramel flowing out onto his tongue.

Not right now, though. He could never eat at work. He knew it was stupid, but the proximity of the bodies always made food seem tainted. Some mornings he could swear he tasted embalming fluid in his coffee.

Thankfully, Adele was now on her feet—she had decided their meeting was at an end.

"I'll investigate the chocolates," Jason said, "and present you with some options tomorrow."

She shook his hand. Her grip was firm and unrelenting. "Until tomorrow."

Jason resisted locking the door behind her.

※ ※ ※

FREE FOR AN hour—sixty glorious minutes on his own. Jason took a deep breath as he headed outdoors. Sure, he was sucking in a huge lungful of exhaust fumes from the passing traffic and the smell of burning rubber from the nearby tyre factory, but it still seemed better than the chemical-with-an-undertone-of-rotting-flesh that permeated his workspace. Locating a funeral parlour in the 'industrial' part of Moonee Ponds should have affected business, but as the saying went, people always wanted alcohol, and people always died. Pubs and funeral homes were the only businesses that would never go out of business.

Perhaps he was exaggerating about the smell, as he knew it was more of a psychological force than a physical one, but he was always relieved when he got to escape it.

Jason diced with death to get to the other side of the road, lunch weighing heavily on his mind (but not in his stomach) when he tripped over the metal A-frame sign in the street. He threw out a hand, slamming it against the store window to balance himself. The glass shuddered beneath the force of his touch; for one brief moment he had a vision of it shattering and was already figuring out what the cost of replacing it could be, but it calmed itself like a ripple on the water that spreads outward and is seen no more.

Breathing heavily, embarrassed, and just a tad angry, Jason stared at the sign that had almost caused him to crash through plate glass.

It read *Sweets to the Sweet*, and before Jason could even guess the obvious, the sweet, rich and familiar aroma of chocolate wafted out of the door.

He was still hanging on to the window when a face loomed out of the darkness on the other side and stared at him. Jason jumped back, his heart racing. His heart raced even harder when he took in the finely chiselled features and dark hair of the man looking at him, but this time for another reason entirely. The guy was *hot*. The face disappeared, and Jason watched it move towards the door.

No longer obscured by glass, it was even handsomer than it first seemed.

"Are you okay?" the young man asked. He was dressed in a red and black chef's apron with a nametag pinned to his chest, but Jason couldn't make it out.

Jason could only gape, though finally he remembered to nod. This was not your run-of-the-mill chocolatier. It wasn't even Willy Wonka, unless it was

Willy Wonka by way of the annual Rugby League nude calendar.

"Thanks for not breaking my window. It would be annoying and time-consuming to have to get it replaced. Not to mention expensive."

Indignation replaced the fire of attraction in Jason's belly. "I only almost broke it because I tripped over *your* shitty sign!"

Unperturbed, the chocolatier looked down at the offending article. "It's in plain sight. Were you daydreaming?"

Jason continued to sputter, but was unable to form coherent sentences.

"Come inside," the other man said, although he seemed less than happy about it. "The least I can do is buy you a drink."

That scent of chocolate hit Jason again, and that made it impossible to refuse despite the clerk's demeanour. "I guess it's the least you can do," he grumbled.

The smell of the shop was even better once he was inside. Jason found himself feeling envious, reminded of the reason why he often fled his own workplace. You would never go home at the end of the day from here thinking that you smelled like death. It just increased his resentment of the spunky chocolatier. In any romantic possibility, who would choose the undertaker over the Adonis with the chocolate shop?

"I'm Chance, by the way," said the chocolatier over his shoulder as he moved behind the counter and set the fold back down into place.

"Jason," he replied, his attention now captured by the symmetrical rows of chocolate lined up behind the cool glass beneath the counter.

"Is coffee, tea or chocolate your poison of choice?" Chance asked, busying himself behind a coffee machine, which looked slightly outdated in comparison to the modern trappings throughout the store itself. Before Jason could even answer, Chance frowned as he looked him over and nodded to himself. "Scratch that, I have just the thing. Sit down."

Jason did so, and just as his butt hit the seat his mobile rang. He groaned when he saw Adele's name flash up. "Jason Harvey," he said wearily.

"I've been thinking about the service," Adele said, without any pleasantries. "Quite frankly, I think it would be better if you worked with another member of the family. One who is perhaps more amenable to your suggestions."

From the way she had started, Jason was expecting to be fired. So it was a surprise to discover Adele was actually firing herself.

"Mr. Harvey, are you there?"

Chance was watching him from across the store. Jason expected him to look away, but his gaze remained fixed upon Jason as he continued frothing milk at the counter. "Yes, I'm here. Have I done something wrong, Miss Conway?"

"We just think it might be easier on everybody if Frederick deals with this."

"Frederick?"

Chance grinned as he began pouring from a metal jug, using a spoon to keep the froth at bay. Jason wondered if he should take his call outside, but stayed put.

"My nephew. I've given him your cell number, and you can expect a call from him presently. Goodbye, Mr. Harvey."

She disconnected the call before he could even reply. Formal to the end, Miss Adele Conway.

Jason stuck his mobile back in his jacket pocket. Chance was now carrying a glass on an elegant silver tray to his table. He placed the glass before Jason, who took an appreciative sniff and was calmed by the rich chocolate perfume that managed to overpower even the rest of the fragrances within the store.

"Xocolatl," Chance announced. "Although it's a bastardised version of the original drink that was consumed in the time of Montezuma. *¡Ese sí era un hombre!*"

Jason was about to ask him what he had just said, but Chance didn't even seem to realise he had lapsed into another language. He opened a small silver box on the tray and sprinkled a pinch of blood-red powder over the top of the beverage. "Chilli flakes," he continued. "They give it the hit you need. Probably the best kick you can get out of a non-alcoholic drink. You looked like you needed it, especially after that call."

"Difficult client," Jason murmured, while wondering how on Earth chilli and chocolate would taste combined.

"I get a few of those," Chance said.

"Here?" Jason asked, his eyebrow raised.

"My customers often aren't as sweet as my wares." Chance lifted the tray and disappeared back behind the counter.

Try working in a funeral home, Jason thought. *Your clients are either dead, or you wish they were.*

He knew that was harsh. It was just that Adele was getting to him. He took a sip of the Mexican hot chocolate. It was rich and velvety, but tasted just like an exceptionally good cocoa.

Then the chilli hit. He felt it on his lips first, and it spread from there throughout his body, coursing through his veins, warming him from within. If Jason could have looked at himself in a mirror, he would have expected to see his body glow from the diffused heat. A contented sigh escaped him.

"Good?" Chance asked. He had poured himself a cup, and sipped it while standing by the register. Jason thought Chance was undoubtedly experiencing the same burning-lip sensation, but he remained cool and collected. He was obviously used to it; Jason couldn't even formulate a response, other than a nod.

"Good," Chance said. "I can tell you're impressed."

After his second mouthful, Jason found he could speak again. "I don't know why this place isn't filled with customers, if your chocolates are as good as this."

Chance shrugged. "I haven't been open that long. Besides, you could say I deal with a specialised clientele."

Jason had no idea what he meant, and couldn't press him any further as his mobile rang again. The number was unfamiliar. "Excuse me," he said to Chance, and hit the screen to answer it. "Hello?"

"Hi," came a light, breezy voice. "Is this Jason Harvey?"

"Speaking."

"My aunt Adele gave me your number. I'm Frederick Conway."

Great. He couldn't even have a Mexican hot chocolate in peace without a damn Conway spoiling the moment. However, Jason turned on his best dealing-with-Adele tone. "Hello, Mr. Conway."

"Oh God, don't. Call me Fred."

Jason almost replied with *Your aunt wouldn't like that*, but he stopped himself in time. This Fred person was a Conway. He would probably report back to Adele, and then Jason would *really* be in trouble. In fact, the whole of Newlin Funeral Parlour would be fired this time. And good old Grace Conway would never get her arse in the ground. "Uh, okay, *Fred*. I take it your aunt told you about our…" he faltered for an appropriate word, "…difficulties?"

Fred laughed, so loud that Jason was sure even Chance would be able to hear it. "I'm surprised you lasted so long with the old chook. The only difficulty in that equation would be her."

It wouldn't be right for Jason to join in the laughter, so he gave a sort of uneasy chuckle. "Your aunt suggested that she would like some chocolates to be distributed at the service."

"Yeah, they're telling each other some sort of fairytale about my grandmother being a chocolate fiend. If she was, she never let any of us grandkids get a glimpse of her secret stash. The only biscuits she ever had on hand were Milk Arrowroots, and she never even let us butter them because we would enjoy them too much."

Biting at his nail, Jason could only imagine. Something had to make Adele turn out the way she did. And it obviously skipped a generation, at least judging by the limited interaction he had with Fred so far. "Are you available to come in for a meeting after you finish work tomorrow?"

"I'm actually on bereavement leave, so I'm entirely at your disposal."

He did not sound like Adele at all—where her voice was crisp and officious, his was honeyed and languorous. Maybe he was adopted. "Is ten o'clock too early?"

"I'll be there with bells on."

Distracted by Chance moving behind the counter, Jason closed his eyes with pleasure as another wave of chocolate scent washed over him. "About the chocolate, I may already have something in mind."

"That'll make it easier, then."

"Actually, maybe you should meet me there. It's a shop called Sweets to the Sweet, and it's just around the corner from the funeral home."

"I'll Googlemap it. See you at ten, Jason."

Jason said his goodbyes, and pocketed his mobile again just as Chance came up to him with a small plate on which a perfectly formed chocolate lay on a square of shiny black paper. "Try this," he said.

"I couldn't," Jason said. "You already gave me a drink, and really, it was my fault with the sign."

"Just try it."

Jason did as he was told. The thin shell of chocolate broke easily upon his tongue, and rich cherry and coconut spilled across each and every tastebud. He moaned, unable to stop himself. He had often heard people joke that chocolate was better than sex, and truth be told it *had* been some time since Jason had gotten laid—but right now, he could believe it. He would pass up an offer of sex for a box of these gastronomic orgasms.

"So good," he said, pretty sure that Chance could only make out half of it as it was so muffled.

But Chance seemed pretty pleased with himself. "I know they're good. And it seems your new client sounds much easier to deal with than Adele."

It was only as he was walking back to the funeral home, that Jason remembered Chance had called Adele by her name. And Jason was sure that he had never once said it in his presence.

But he must have, surely. There could be no other explanation. Jason shrugged it off, and had forgotten about it by the time he sat back down at his desk.

TWO

It was back up to thirty-nine degrees by ten o'clock the next morning, and Jason was thankful for the fact that he worked in what was basically a giant fridge. If it weren't for all the dead roommates, he could seriously consider moving into the Newlin Funeral Parlour. But even that surely wouldn't be so bad, as at least those roommates wouldn't bitch about phone and power bills.

He didn't want to leave the air-conditioning, but he had that meeting with Fred. And Sweets to the Sweet was also chillingly cool, so he would only suffer on the short walk there.

Which felt like several kilometres. Even the tram passing him seemed sluggish. The soles of his shoes seemed to melt on the footpath, making every step longer and his feet increasingly difficult to lift. He took care not to collide with the chocolate shop's sign again, and breathed more easily when the refrigerated air within hit him.

Once again, Sweets to the Sweet was practically deserted, except for Chance in his regular position by the counter, and a young guy sitting expectantly at a table to the side.

"That's him," Chance said to the guy, nodding towards Jason.

Jason approached the stranger with his hand outstretched. "You must be Mr. Conway."

"I told you over the phone. Call me Fred."

His voice was just as seductive as it was over the phone line. And the face attached to it wasn't too bad either. Fred hadn't just skipped his aunt's brittle manner; he had also escaped her pinched, bird-like features. In fact, he was more like a koala—with a broad, pleasant face and a slight paunch that strained comfortably against the waist of his pants.

Did I really just compare him to a koala? Jason released Fred's hand. They sat down again, and before they could start speaking Chance appeared at their side. He held a small plate upon which a sole chocolate sat, gleaming against the silver paper.

"This is for you." He picked up the chocolate and offered it to Fred, as if they had stepped back in time and Fred was now a Roman being fed grapes upon a chaise by a solicitous slave.

An irrational jealousy flared within Jason. As ridiculous as it was to feel jealous, it felt even worse when Fred, turning crimson, took it on his tongue as it was presented. Jason watched Chance's fingertips brush against Fred's lips and glowered in silence. Was Jason really that lonely? Or worse, that horny?

Fred moaned appreciatively. "Ooh, that's good."

Chance grinned. "My version of a Caramello Koala."

On the last word he looked at Jason, who stiffened at the word.

"I love Caramello Koalas," Fred said. "But that…well, if that was the way Caramello Koalas tasted they would be sold out of the stores as soon as they were on the shelf."

"Glad you like it. Now, what can I get you guys?"

Fred motioned towards Jason. "You've been here before. What would you get?"

"Jason likes the xocolatl," Chance said, before Jason could even open his mouth. "He likes it spicy."

Now Jason was sure *he* was starting to blush. If his boss could witness what was going on in this store, Jason was sure he would feel it was against company etiquette. Bizarre flirting threeways with a client? That could be against Occupational Health and Safety Standards. "Mexican hot chocolate," he explained to Fred.

"Two xocolatls, then!" Fred said, looking rather pleased with himself even though he mangled the word beyond all recognition.

As Chance left to prepare the drinks, Fred leaned in to Jason as if sharing an extravagant confidence, and whispered, "He is *fucking* hot, don't you think?"

Jason was captivated by how open Fred was about his sexuality, and how quickly. Or maybe he just had exceptional gaydar. Jason decided that he wouldn't mess around either. "Chance?" he asked, with faux indifference. "Hadn't really noticed." *Fucking liar,* he admonished himself. *You sure as hell did yesterday, you just don't want to look as stupid as you feel right now.*

Fred wasn't convinced. "Bullshit." His laugh bounced off the walls.

"Okay, he's hot," Jason admitted. "But he knows it, which makes him less hot. If you know what I mean."

"Nothing wrong with a bit of confidence." Fred swivelled around slightly to look at Chance, who in Jason's eyes seemed to be manhandling the coffee machine with an indecent swagger.

The ease with which they were being, well, *themselves*, so quickly certainly made things different. Jason wasn't used to getting through that stage of *is-he-isn't-he* so quickly. It was actually quite refreshing. But the thing was, what to do now?

So he fell back upon business. "What do you think of the shop?"

Fred settled back into his chair. "Well, if we want fabulous chocolates, we came to the right place. They're probably *too* good for my family."

Jason found it interesting that Fred was being so forthright about his family's quirks. It seemed he was pretty forthright about everything, but Jason felt he still had to tread carefully. "Yes, I found your aunt Adele quite… interesting."

"*Interesting* is rather a polite word for it. I'd suggest *difficult* and *insufferable*."

Jason tried not to smile, but the damn thing escaped its shackles and danced across his face.

"Ha!" Fred laughed. "I knew she would be giving you a hard time. So, is it normal, this thing of assigning counsellors to funeral clients?"

"Not really," Jason admitted. "I think the Newlins just wanted to do something that would set them apart. To tell you the truth, this is the first time I've dealt with a client by myself. I mean, without direct supervision."

"And you had to land my crazy-arse family."

Jason laughed along with him. "I'd be lying if I said I wasn't relieved when Adele suggested I start working with you instead."

"Yeah, I'm easy," Fred said.

Chance chose that moment to arrive with the hot chocolates. "That's what I like to hear! Drink up, boys."

Jason was thankful that he left them without any further provocative comments.

Fred was still slightly crimson as he stared at the beverage in front of him. "I'm a bit worried about hot chocolate with chilli in it."

"It's good," Jason reassured him as he took a tentative sip.

"Oh. Wow. That's some hit."

Fred fell back against his chair, fanning his lips with his hand.

Jason tried not to observe how Fred's lips had reddened even further, and he could have sworn that they were slightly puffed. Kissing lips. Or as some of his friends might have suggested, lips that had done…other things….

"That's good," Fred said. "Really good."

Jason made some form of agreement, and distracted himself by drinking from his own cup.

"Seriously, how does this shop not have more customers?"

Jason leaned forward so Chance wouldn't overhear him. "I know! It's weird, right?"

"It's chocolate. I mean, everybody likes chocolate! This place should be *packed*."

"This is the second time I've been in here," Jason said. "And you're the only other customer I've seen. And I had to bring you here myself."

"I have a very select clientele," rang the clear voice of Chance, across the room.

Both men seated at the table laughed guiltily, having been caught out like kids talking in a classroom.

"Why is that?" Jason asked of the chocolatier.

Chance shrugged. "Who knows anything? Why bother asking? Just leave it up to the gods."

"I hope the gods take that into account when you want to buy food or pay your rent," Fred said.

Chance rolled his eyes, and disappeared into the back of the store.

"He's a strange one," Fred mused.

"Who cares if he makes stuff as good as this?"

"Like I said, too good for my family. But I see why you made me meet you here. How pricey do you think he is?"

"We can only ask."

Fred nodded. "Let's do it."

As if he had been eavesdropping on them via hidden microphone, Chance appeared again with a large book in his hands. He placed it before the two men, and flicked it open to the first page. "Chocolate portraits. They can be very tasteful, and very photo-realistic. You can display it and then break it up to divide amongst the guests."

"Looks good," Fred said, meeting Jason's eyes to get his reaction on it.

Jason nodded, wishing that he could be more proactive about it all. After all, he was meant to be the funeral co-ordinator.

"I'm very talented," Chance said. "In many ways." He let that sink in, and when he didn't get the reaction he seemed to be hoping for, he sighed. "Bring me a photo of the deceased. I can make her look like Marilyn Monroe."

"I thought you said photo-realistic?" Fred asked.

Jason snorted, and regretted it immediately. Fred just grinned at him, and Jason felt that warm feeling in his stomach that could be dangerous at times in any semblance of personal life. And it wasn't because of the Mexican hot chocolate.

"Price?" he asked Chance, trying to concentrate on the business at hand again.

"Cheaper than you think," Chance replied.

Jason hated vagueness, especially when he was meant to be working the best possible deal for his client. But Fred seemed pretty happy, and after all, wasn't that what he was meant to do? "Can I e-mail you the photo?" It would save him having to bring the photo back, or worse, having Fred deliver an alternate. For some reason he didn't want Fred to be around Chance without himself acting as a buffer. Okay, he had *a* reason. He wasn't going to lie to himself. He was attracted to Fred, and there was maybe a spark coming from Fred's side as well. But Chance was like the chocolates he sold—too much of a good thing, and Jason was scared he would never compare if Fred went *there* first.

"Sure thing," Chance replied. "I'm not a complete Luddite, although my register may say otherwise." He winked at Fred, and sashayed back behind the counter.

Jason resisted rolling his eyes, and turned back to Fred. "I'll email him the photo Adele gave me. And then we'll be cooking with gas."

Fred nodded, and an awkward silence fell.

"I guess…I better get back to work," Jason said.

"Oh," Fred sounded disappointed.

Or am I just hoping he does?

"But I'll see you tomorrow," Jason said quickly.

"Good," Fred said, just as quickly.

They shook hands, and Jason wanted to hold on just a little longer than societal expectations would allow. It felt good to feel the touch of another man again, even if it was just a handshake. But Fred dropped his hand, gave a little wave, and walked back into the world.

"He's cute," Chance called out.

Jason tried to think of a pithy comeback, but it came out sounding like a growl. He heard Chance laughing at him as he left the store.

❈ ❈ ❈

THAT NIGHT, AS Jason was trying to get to sleep, he couldn't help but keep thinking of Fred. He could have sworn that he still tasted the heat of chilli on his tongue, infused with the rich aroma of chocolate. Maybe those taste sensations would be so inextricably linked in his own mind that it would be something he would forever associate with Fred even if he never saw him again after the funeral service. Jason found himself wondering whether Fred's kiss would taste the same, then just as quickly dismissed it. Kisses didn't taste of anything but saliva—all the rest was sheer romanticism.

But maybe—just *maybe*—it wouldn't hurt to let yourself be seduced by the idea of something rather than succumb to the logic of reality.

Take Chance for example. The chocolatier, not the concept. Chance seemed the very embodiment of fantasy. Fred, in comparison, was refreshing reality. And in this example, for once, Jason was dreaming of the romanticism that could be found in reality. These things *could* merge, these *incompatible* things—just like chilli and chocolate.

Jason fell asleep with a smile on his face.

Three

Waiting for the guests to arrive at a funeral was always the worst part of the service. Especially when it was an open casket, which the Conways had insisted on. Jason had been unnerved when he first entered with the programmes and found himself alone with the body of Grace Conway looking for all the world like she was about to sit up and chastise the flower arrangement. Frankly, it had been a relief when Adele had arrived, although it meant that he was forced to endure her frequent complaints about the 'tardiness' of the rest of the family. Jason assured her that it was quite normal, and she reminded him curtly that she *had* been to many a funeral and knew how they worked. Jason had then excused himself to bring out the chocolate portrait that Chance had delivered an hour before. Jason had been impressed with the professionalism of the piece, and even more impressed with the price.

"I'm happy you're happy," Chance had replied, although his smile bordered on a sneer. "I live to serve."

Maybe he wasn't so much of a fantasy after all, Jason conceded. The moment just served to remind him of Fred's open, pleasant, smile and how it was so much more genuine in comparison.

Adele hadn't been as impressed by her mother being etched in chocolate. "Seems a bit showy. She would have hated it. This was Fred's doing, I suppose."

Jason had started to defend Fred, but Adele wasn't interested.

Families getting together for some sort of social occasion could always cause trouble, no matter how innocuous it might be. But a wedding or a funeral? Jason thought transporting nitrate over a rickety rope bridge would be less explosive. Adele was already on edge as she sat in the front row, having fussed over the flowers and barked orders down her mobile phone about the refreshments at the wake to follow. She sat in front of the casket, her mother's head perfectly parallel with her own.

Under her mother's eye, right to the bitter end, Jason thought uncharitably.

Or maybe she's just making sure she stays dead.

Adele kept fussing around in her seat, scrutinising each arrival, seeing if they passed muster. By now, any new guest had the added bonus of being late to be tallied against their other sins. Jason hated latecomers as well. It wasn't like a funeral service was something most people wanted to be at anyway, and latecomers only made it run longer than it should.

Fred still hadn't turned up yet; Jason fidgeted with the programmes he was holding. Mrs. Grace Conway stared dourly from the front cover, as if daring the photographer to tell her to smile. Jason could just imagine what would happen to the poor person behind the camera if they did.

Adele suddenly appeared before him, Nosferatu-like, only less charming. One minute she had been in her seat, and the next…well, she was just there. "Did you put the correct time on the brochure?"

Brochure. As if her dead mother was an ad for the Greek Isles. "You have one in your hand," Jason said in a controlled tone. "You can see that it's right."

"I don't understand people," Adele said. "It's not like this is the cinema, and people think if they're late they'll just miss the previews!"

What would previews for a funeral service be like? Jason wondered. *Coming soon…from the people who brought you The Death of Suzy Saunders…the tale of a woman who struck fear in the heart of everyone she met—The Tale of Grace Conway!*

"Would you like a cup of tea?" he suggested.

Adele sniffed; once again, with no tears. "No, but if this is the way it is going to be, I'll put in my order for a choc top and a packet of Twisties to go with the main feature!" She clomped back down the aisle to take her seat again—although it wasn't like anybody else was rushing to grab it. Jason sagged against the wall. When was the last time she had been to a movie anyway? There were no supporting features anymore. You were lucky if you even got a cartoon before a kid's flick nowadays.

Maybe the chocolates would sweeten her up a little bit, even if she did think they were a waste of time. Chance certainly lived up to the sterling recommendations he gave himself. Despite Adele's claims of inappropriate showiness, Jason didn't think Chance had jazzed up Mrs. Conway's portrait *too* much. He had just given her a smile that did not seem out of place or even out of character for her—it just seemed natural, even if it was rendered on a large block of chocolate propped up on an easel and surrounded by flowers.

"Ooh, lovely," said an old duck sidling up next to him. The absurdly large daisy on her hat bobbed along with the rhythm of her conversation. "It makes her look almost human."

That hadn't been what Jason expected to hear—even though he had heard the same sentiment from almost every guest at the service who was under fifty.

"Whoever did that had talent," the woman continued. "I look forward to eating the old bitch later on."

"Would you like a programme?" Jason asked, hoping it would make her move on.

"Thank you, love. Seems a bit of a waste to have to eat such a work of art, but I suppose it will be like an Easter egg and if you try to keep it, it'll turn white after a couple of months and you'll regret having kept it. Seems unfair that chocolate should only last so long, and yet people who don't deserve it live for decades."

"Do you want me to show you to your seat?" Jason asked desperately.

"I'm just going in the back row. Makes it easier to leave early."

"Oh. Good." Jason didn't know how else to respond. He hoped one day that he, or his likeness, would be spoken of as fondly at his service. With a reception like this, was anybody actually going to turn up at the wake?

He could have cried out with relief when Fred finally showed up at his side and grabbed a programme out of his hand. At least Fred could help try and keep his relations in line—and really, so far that only meant Adele.

Fred, distracted by the display of the chocolate, turned to Jason and said, "If it wasn't for the fact you were here, and I can smell fire and brimstone in the air meaning that people I'm related to are in the vicinity, I'd swear I was at the wrong funeral." He then looked pointedly down at the programme and did a double take. "Oh, wait, there she is."

Jason hid his smile behind the palm of his hand. "Chance did a good job."

Fred gave the chocolate portrait a critical eye. "Yeah, if the aim was to make her look completely different to the way she did in real life. By which, I mean *pleasant*. I mean, he might as well have done Marilyn Monroe if he was going to go out on a limb."

"You're okay with not really showing any respect to the dead, aren't you?"

"She never showed me any respect when she was alive, so it would be hypocritical for me to turn around and show her some now she's dead."

Jason felt uncomfortable with where this conversation was going—after all, this was what his entire profession was based on at the moment. But no amount of study on the human psyche, or even the limited training from his boss Mr. Newlin about how to handle the myriad of emotions experienced at a funeral service, had prepared him for the Conways. "Then why are you here? You obviously needed some sense of closure."

Fred stared down at his feet. "Closure, huh? Maybe that's it. I'm not even sure, to be honest. A sense of duty, I guess would be the closest to what I feel right now."

Jason found himself feeling sorry for Mrs. Conway. It seemed that not one person was here today because they truly loved her, or wanted to mourn her passing. In fact, it felt like if Jason were to lower a disco ball from the ceiling everybody would start doing a conga around the casket. The thought of it made his nose itch, and his mouth felt very dry. The hot burn of tears began to form, and he took a deep breath. He was *not* going to cry. Why was *he* even crying?

"Maybe," Fred continued, still staring at his shoes, "I'm here because I wanted to see you again."

The threat of tears instantly cooled, replaced by warmth spreading throughout Jason's body. However, that uncomfortable feeling remained. Jason was never good at this kind of thing, even when it was reciprocal.

"Oh," was his response. "Well."

Fred smiled. "Is that a good 'well'?"

"Um, yes," Jason told him. "It's a good well."

"The kind that Timmy doesn't fall down?"

"Exactly. No need for Lassie to mount a rescue."

"I never liked Lassie," Fred admitted. "I liked *The Littlest Hobo*, myself."

"Me too!" Jason laughed. Maybe that feeling was fading now….

All mirth was dispelled when Adele snapped, "Fred! There you are!"

Ahh, there was that *other* uncomfortable feeling again. Neither of them had even noticed Adele leaving her seat.

"What on Earth are you laughing about? Show some respect!"

Jason instantly began offering apologies; Adele waved him off, and turned to her nephew. Fred was still trying to gain his breath.

"Are we ready to start now or not?"

Fred acknowledged Jason graciously. "I think it's up to Jason to say when, don't you agree, Aunt Adele?"

Adele didn't look as if she even thought Jason was capable of making his own toast in the morning.

"I think it's time, yes, probably," Jason said, sure he was confirming everything Adele suspected of him. But what else could he say? *Yes, we'd better get a move on, because otherwise we'll still be here tomorrow morning for the next service, and people tend to freak out when they turn up and they find a different corpse in the coffin to the one they're expecting.*

"A stunning display of leadership," Adele said. "Anyway, I hope you both proceed with a little more decorum from now on instead of how I found you a moment ago."

"Shut up, Aunt Adele," Fred said, pushing her back down the aisle. "Go claim your spotlight."

Jason waited for Adele to explode, but Fred delivered it all in a tone of civil neutrality. What surprised Jason the most was how Adele simply accepted it and allowed herself to be steered away. It seemed that relationships in families never had a simple formula, no matter whose family it was.

Silence fell over the small gathering as Adele took to the small raised stage behind the coffin. "Good afternoon, those of you who made it on time," she began, and Jason anxiously watched the faces of the guests for those who could take offence. Luckily there were no walkouts.

Adele continued. "We are here to say goodbye to my mother. Now, nobody here will disagree with me when I say she wasn't the easiest woman in the world to get along with. Her husband, my father, would have been the first to say so. Her children would have seconded that motion." There were nods from those assembled at this point. "And if it had been put to a vote amongst the rest of those related to her, and those who simply strayed across her path during her life, then it would have been a landslide that only politicians can dream of. I like to think she loved us, but *love* was never a word that was spoken by her, unless it was about the Sunday roast." Adele's lip curled. "Cooked hunks of cow received more affection from her."

Jason wished that time would speed up, or that a small aneurysm would occur to take away his memory of this part of the service. Above all, he hoped his boss wasn't anywhere in the vicinity to hear what he would undoubtedly claim to be a travesty of the type of the funeral services that the Newlin Funeral Parlour normally provided.

"So, let's keep this short," Adele concluded. "Is there anybody else who would like to speak?"

The general consensus seemed to be *no*, until Fred cleared his throat. Adele stared at him, her brow furrowed, as if astounded that anybody else would want to follow her sterling example of speechifying.

Fred ignored her, and jumped up to the lectern. He had to briefly wrestle with Adele for control over the small microphone but she finally conceded and took her seat. Fred dazzled the audience with his broad grin. Or at least, he dazzled Jason. Everybody else seemed to be mentally calculating how much longer they would have to be here.

"Hey, everyone," Fred said. "You know me as Fred. To Gran, though, I was known as *the gay boy*, or *the nancy boy*, or *the poof*."

There was a rustle among the mourners, although Jason found it hard to think of them as such because none of them were particularly mournful. There were also a few suppressed sniggers—obviously Gran's views had filtered throughout some of the family.

"But you know what?" Fred asked, although his question was obviously rhetorical. "You'd think that would make me glad she's gone. But I'm not. I don't really care one way or the other. But there is one reason why I'm thankful for having had her in my life."

Jason became aware that Fred was now staring at him, seeking him out against everyone else.

"Because she was the first person to teach me that I had to stick up for myself—because if I couldn't rely upon family, then who would I be able to rely upon? She taught me family could be people you chose for yourself. People who love you for what you are, not despite what you are. So, thanks, Gran. Maybe you'll still get your Sunday roast, wherever you are."

There was a flutter of excitement from the assorted Conways as Fred jumped down from the stage and wiped the sheen of sweat from his forehead as he bounded over to Jason. "Wow. I wasn't really expecting to say all that!"

"You weren't? You sounded as polished as if you were standing for election."

"I wasn't even sure *what* I was going to say. But when I got up there, it all made sense."

"It was definitely…interesting."

"I have a confession to make, though. I stole some of Gran to steel myself for it."

"Gran?" Jason asked in horror, his line of sight immediately being drawn to the body in the casket.

"Gross!" Fred cried, grabbing him by the head and twisting it around so that he was now looking at the chocolate portrait. "Cadbury Gran!"

"*Chance* Gran," Jason reminded him. Sure enough, there was a corner missing at the bottom of the block. "You couldn't have waited?"

"I doubt anyone noticed."

Jason had already anticipated the screech from Adele when it sounded behind him.

"Who's been at it already?"

"I'm not sure, Adele," Jason said, not even daring to look at Fred in case he gave him away.

"Honestly! You can't trust anyone! Do people have no respect?"

"I'm as shocked as you are," Fred agreed, and Jason stood with mouth agape at his smooth audacity.

"I don't think anybody will really see it," Jason said in an effort to cover up for the criminal.

"Nobody needs to know, Aunt Adele," Fred agreed.

"Everybody saw the portrait when they walked in!"

"True," Jason said quickly, "so they don't need to see it again. Fred and I will cut it up now and put it in a basket to pass around for everyone to take a piece."

Adele nodded slowly, taking it all in. "I suppose that'll be fine. I'll go and update them all."

Fred waited until she was out of earshot, and leaned in to Jason. "Thanks for covering for me."

"No offence, but believe me when I say I don't want to do *another* Conway family funeral quite so soon."

"Would you miss me if my aunt killed me in a fit of rage?" Fred asked with a cheeky grin that once again made Jason's belly warm with affection.

But his response was, "I don't know you well enough yet." After all, he had to make Fred suffer a *little* bit for starting to eat his Gran before everybody else.

"Ouch!"

"But…I would feel that I am missing something I was starting to be intrigued by."

Fred's lip twitched. "I think that was a compliment."

"It is, believe me."

"Okay."

They were leaning in close enough now that Jason could feel Fred's breath warming the side of his cheek. He wanted to close his eyes and fully experience the sensation, but this wasn't the time. "So…don't get killed."

"I'll try not to," Fred said. His lips almost brushed against Jason's ear as he asked, "But if my aunt *does* off me, will you avenge my death at least?"

Jason laughed. "You want me to do a *third* Conway funeral service? You're asking too fucking much. Besides, how can you guys top this one in which everyone indulges in a metaphorical cannibalistic ritual?"

Fred leaned back, and Jason was disappointed by the greater distance now between them. "You're right. And I guess it's a lot to expect of you when you barely know me."

Feeling emboldened, Jason said, "I didn't say I wouldn't."

Fred grinned, and was about to reply when Adele yelled from across the room again.

"Frederick Conway!"

The man in question rolled his eyes. "I'm in trouble. She used the full name."

"Maybe not that much trouble. She didn't say your middle name. If you have one. Do you?"

Fred blanched. "I better go before she *does* use it."

"Hey!" Jason cried as Fred turned and ran down the aisle towards his aunt. He laughed at Fred's dodge of the name bullet, and then inwardly groaned as he realised he now had to carve the chocolate up by himself.

It didn't turn out to be that much of a chore. The chocolate was so creamy that the knife slid through the block as if it was butter. He was slightly creeped out when it came to cutting up the face, and made sure that somebody didn't end up with a piece that would disturb them too much, such as an eyeball or a recognisable curl of a lip.

"As I don't know you, Mrs. Conway," he murmured as he cut into her earlobe, "I can't say whether this whole damn thing was too good for you. I do know that its beauty may be lost on your daughter. But it won't be on your grandson."

That would make her roll in her grave, having another man speak in such a fashion about the grandson she had so cruelly dismissed throughout her life. And Jason knew he didn't know Fred well enough yet, but he was pretty sure that such a thought would probably make Fred happy.

Adele had already addressed the guests and was waiting for him by the coffin as he walked down the aisle with the basket of chocolate pieces. She gave her thanks, rather graciously in comparison to her normal behaviour, and took it from him. Fred was back in his seat, his face flushed, although wearing a grin somewhat inappropriate for the occasion.

"Please take a piece of my mother and think of her," Adele said, taking a piece herself and then passing the basket to those sitting in the front row.

Jason watched as she hesitated, the chocolate at her lips. What was she thinking about? Was the mere association of her mother with chocolate making the sweet too bitter to taste?

Adele closed her eyes, and the chocolate disappeared into her mouth.

Her eyes suddenly flew open again, and a barely audible moan escaped from between her lips. She immediately coloured, and looked over at Jason. He gave her a weak smile, and she covered her mouth like a kid being caught out at doing something naughty. She swallowed heavily, and then raised her middle finger at him.

It was as if a church statue of Mary had flashed him. In fact, he would have been less shocked had *that* happened.

Adele glowered at him, and turned her back. Jason looked at Fred to see if he had caught it, but he was eating what was now his second piece of chocolate and seemed to be lost in his own thoughts.

And it was at that point that everything seemed to go *really* crazy.

Four

Adele leapt onto the stage and hovered over the microphone, gripping the lectern with both hands. She looked like a fire and brimstone preacher, ready to deliver her audience the summation of their sins. "I know it's customary to be all decorous and prim and respectful at any funeral service…but *fuck* that!"

A hubbub began to arise among the guests, but it wasn't one of condemnation.

They were agreeing. One man, chocolate smeared around his mouth, actually stood and applauded.

"No one tells the truth at a funeral!" Adele sneered. "But let me break that tradition! Let me *really* tell you about my mother!"

Jason ran over to Fred and yanked him out of his seat, retreating to a more secluded corner. "Uh, should we be stopping this?"

Through a mouthful of chocolate, Fred said, "Can you believe that? I can't believe she said that! Did she not hear *me* when I was talking about Gran?"

The point had obviously flown over his head.

"No," Jason said patiently, "I'm talking about your aunt wrecking the funeral."

"This funeral's already ruined. Don't sweat it."

Fred *was*, though. Sweating, that is. Jason felt his forehead, and it was warm to the touch but not feverish.

"You know what?" Fred asked. "You're cute when you're stressed."

"Uh, thanks? But I have a lot to stress about at the minute."

"But you know what?" Fred continued as if he hadn't heard him. "You're cute when you're not stressed as well. I thought that the first time I saw you. In fact, it was the first thought I had the minute I saw you."

Momentarily distracted from Adele ranting at the microphone, where she seemed to be listing all of her mother's faults in chronological order, Jason smiled at Fred. "Yeah?"

"Yeah. So stop stressing. Have some chocolate."

Jason hadn't even realised that Fred had stuffed his pockets with Chance's wares until a piece was being thrust into his mouth. Fred watched him with twinkling eyes, as Jason was instantly taken by the taste washing over his tongue. It was like that instant jolt of caffeine in the morning when your brain and heart needed a boost to get moving—Jason could feel his blood roar through his body, causing sweat to break out on his temple and his brain to go haywire. He reached down and took Fred's hand, licking the finger clean of the chocolate it had just offered him.

"Wow," was all Fred could say as he stared down at Jason's hand.

"I feel weird," Jason replied.

"Good weird, right?"

"*Very* good weird."

Adele had begun to cry, and a line was forming next to her filled with other guests eager to have their say about Mrs. Conway. Jason didn't even really care anymore; he was focused on Fred, before him, flushed, and standing far too close for normal personal space parameters. If anybody had even been paying any attention to them it would have been obvious that they were more than funeral director and client. Living client, not dead one. Then that would have been disturbing, not the vaguely hot it seemed to be despite the surroundings.

Jason knew that his thoughts were racing as hard as his blood, and his blood wasn't racing only to his heart. He grabbed Fred by the collar and brought him in even closer.

"Very good weird," he repeated.

"Are you thinking what I'm thinking?" Fred asked.

"Seeing what I have of your family, I can honestly say I can't tell what any of you think on an hourly basis."

Fred rubbed up against him, and Jason was now more than aware of what he was thinking.

"Is there somewhere we can go?" Fred asked.

No words were necessary; Jason dragged him away from the service, as Adele wrestled for control of the microphone with another guest. The sounds of the ruckus in the service room became muffled as Jason led Fred down a long hallway and into a large room that was noticeably colder as soon as they entered it.

As soon as Jason closed the door behind them, his back was immediately pressed against it with the handle digging into his back and Fred's tongue digging into his mouth. One sensation was understandably more pleasant than the other, but Jason just went with it as Fred's hands began to fumble with his belt. One part of his brain wondered if this was all just going too fast, and whether this was something that would also be against the occupational health and safety regulations of the business, but Fred's tongue tasted so good despite the fact that he was starting to feel lightheaded from lack of breath and *oh God* Fred's hand felt so good sliding beneath his jockey briefs and brushing against his aching cock that—

—*oh God*.

Fred now had him completely in hand and was teasing him with slow little rubs, his thumb passing over the most sensitive part of all and Jason was torn between wanting to come right there and then or prolonging the pleasure until his brain melted out his ears.

"You like that?" Fred asked. His breath was still perfumed with chocolate.

Jason hadn't even realised Fred's tongue had left his mouth—it seemed like he could still taste him. He couldn't even reply; he just nodded.

"Let's get more comfortable," Fred said, turning away. "OH JESUS FUCK!"

His back slammed against Jason's chest as he backed into him, and Jason's pants fell fully to the floor. "What is it?" he asked. "Oh—"

"Oh?" Fred demanded. "Oh?"

In his haste to get them to privacy, Jason hadn't really thought about where he was dragging Fred. It just so happened they had stumbled into the reposing room, where the body for the next service was laid out in its coffin, waiting to be transferred to the service room in the morning.

"Yeah, that's Mr. Hazelhurst," Jason explained.

"Oh, I can *see* that's Mr. Hazelhurst." Fred didn't sound that happy.

Jason grabbed him, and turned him around. "Sorry, I wasn't thinking."

He kissed him, but Fred resisted.

"I can't do this…with *that* there."

"It's Mr. Hazelhurst, not a *that*. And really, you get used to it."

"What, you do this often with your clients?" Fred asked. "I hope you mean the live ones. Although I hope you don't do *this* that often."

Jason whacked him on the chest. "I meant you get used to the remains, you idiot! And no, I haven't done *this* before. This is my first time funeral sluttiness."

"Well, that's good, but no offense, *I* haven't been here long enough to get used to the fact that there's *remains* staring at me."

"They're not staring at you," Jason reminded him. "His eyes are closed. And you have your back to him."

"You think *that's* the logical point to be made here?" Fred asked.

"Oh, all right, you big baby."

Fred made a half-hearted thrust at him. "My cock is rapidly wilting here."

Jason laughed, his eyes inadvertently drawn down below.

"Don't look at it, you'll make it feel worse!"

"Well, I guess I don't want that happening."

"Neither do I," Fred agreed.

"You're not the one hanging out in the wind here, though," Jason pointed out.

Fred looked down, and raised an eyebrow. "I haven't heard Mr. Hazelhurst complain."

"Luckily. Because that would really make your cock wilt if he did."

"Yeah. I prefer my men to be living."

"Picky, aren't you?" Jason asked, pulling his pants back up.

Fred sighed. "That's a sad sight."

"You'll be seeing it again, don't worry."

"Soon, right?"

With a sense of déjà vu as he began pulling Fred along again, Jason said, "Sooner than you think."

He counted off the doors, looking for sanctuary. The urn room—no, if Fred was creeped out by corpses he would probably be freaked out by ashes. His boss's office—no, on so many levels. The next door he knew would have to do, and he shoved Fred within it. Jason slammed the door behind them, and fumbled for the light.

"No, don't," Fred said.

"Why?"

"I don't want to kill the romance. The last room had a corpse in it. And judging by the size and smell, I think we're in a cleaner's closet."

"Standing room only," Jason said, pressing up against him.

"Like I said, don't kill the romance. And to think I told my family when I first came out that I would never go back into the closet for anybody or anyone."

Jason snorted affectionately into Fred's chest, even as he was busy unbuttoning his shirt. "Shut up, and kiss me. And then you can…do other things."

Fred did as he was told and took Jason by surprise with the intensity of his kisses. Now Jason found himself up against the wall, and their clothes came off with an efficiency that would probably never be equalled again. Jason was thankful that the lights were out, as he hadn't been to the gym for a while and was sure every fault of his body would be on display—and for fuck's sake *what was he thinking?* He had never been to a gym in his life. And suddenly all thoughts of the gym were erased from his mind because Fred was sucking on his left nipple and the air was cold against it as it was released and oh god now Fred's tongue was tracing down his stomach and circling his belly button—

The sound of a zipper being pulled down echoed in the small space, followed by Jason's groan of anticipation and encouragement. He thought he would come right there and then when Fred took Jason into his mouth and chuckled, the reverberations travelling as far as the length of his spine and causing sensory overload. Jason's fingers curled into Fred's hair and, overcome and frenetic, he began to pump away. Fred didn't miss a beat, allowing himself to be taken in the mouth, pulling Jason in and encouraging him by wrapping his hands around his arse.

Jason wanted to howl as he came, especially as Fred proved merciless, continuing to work on him until the strength left his legs and he sagged against his new lover. Finally Fred let him go and Jason fell to his knees, panting heavily and struggling for breath as he kissed him. Insanely, Fred still tasted like chocolate, even after everything that had just happened. Jason's hand snaked downwards, until he held Fred's length and began stroking him off. Thanks to a shaft of light coming from under the door Jason could tell that Fred was watching him, unwilling to look away or even close his eyes and lose himself in his own sensations. Neither could break the stare, opening themselves up to each other, not even when Fred grunted and Jason felt the warm splash of release against his hand and belly.

But as the afterglow left them, the silence between them now was awkward, to say the least.

"What the hell just happened?" Fred asked.

"You gave me the best blowjob of my life," Jason replied.

"What you did to me wasn't that bad either," Fred said with a sheepish grin. "But we lost our heads a little here."

"We're in the cleaner's closet of a funeral home, having just done naughty things to each other. We definitely lost our heads." Jason reached above him and pulled a box of wipes free to begin cleaning himself.

"Need a hand?" Fred asked.

He looked very happy with himself, and Jason threw a wipe at him. "You've done enough."

"Not yet," Fred said in all seriousness.

Jason found himself being kissed again, and he didn't mind at all as they sank down to the floor in the most uncomfortable position he had ever been in. In fact, it barely registered at all.

Five

When Jason woke, he knew it was late. He just had that feeling, even though the windowless closet gave no indication of light or dark outside. Plus, he was cold. Being naked, even with another naked body draped over you, would do that to you. He fumbled in the dark, and pulled Fred's wrist close to his face so he could read his watch—6:24.

Fred mumbled something, halfway between asleep and awake.

"Get up," Jason said.

"Too tired," Fred replied.

"No, really, get up. This is not the way I want to get fired."

Fred yawned, and sat up. "I guess you wouldn't get a reference, huh?"

"That would probably be the least of my worries."

After Jason discovered that the light in the closet actually didn't work, they dressed with some difficulty in the near dark. Jason was swimming in his shirt until he realised it was actually Fred's. Once they were decent they unlocked the door and cautiously stepped out into the hall.

It was as quiet as a morgue, which made sense as it technically was. Jason hoped that as it was now so late the shenanigans at the Conway funeral must have ended. The silence seemed to indicate that.

The viewing room was destroyed. Pews were overturned. The floor was littered with flowers, some of which had been ripped apart. It could have been from the result of a zombie uprising, but in the middle of it all, pristine and untouched, was the body of Mrs. Conway, still in her coffin. Jason breathed with relief, and it was only then that he realised he had been holding it in.

"Some party we missed," Fred said. "Although what we did was fun."

"Fun?" Jason asked. "Fun?"

"What?"

"Look at this place! This is meant to be a room of respect! What the hell happened here?"

"What the hell happened everywhere," Fred said. "Including *us*. But they've moved on now. Let's get it cleaned up before your boss finds out."

"There's no way he couldn't have found out about this," Jason said, but he followed Fred's lead.

Despite the chaos, it only took them about an hour of steady work to clear up all the rubbish, stack the chairs up and drag the vacuum cleaner out of the closet they had so recently shared to clean the floors. Jason lifted his shirt to wipe the sweat from his forehead and caught Fred watching him appreciatively.

"Still liking what you see?" he asked.

Fred reached out and ran his finger along the strip of exposed skin. "It's gotten even better with the passing of time."

Jason decided that Fred needed to be kissed again, right there and then, but was rudely interrupted by the large floral arrangement behind the stage swaying dangerously and threatening to crash into the coffin. As he ran over to right it before it fell, he was surprised by his boss staggering to his feet from behind it. Normally Mr. Newlin was dressed impeccably, maybe to account for his short stature. But his tie was hanging loosely and his hair was mussed on one side only.

"Aah, Jason," Mr. Newlin said, still unsteady on his feet. "Good afternoon." He looked at his watch. "I mean, evening! Good evening, Jason!"

"Are you all right, Mr. Newlin?"

"Fine, perfectly fine! I just wanted to congratulate you on the success of your first service."

Jason looked back at Fred for confirmation that he wasn't imagining this exchange. Fred shrugged.

"Congratulations? Mr. Newlin, did you see the room before I cleaned it?"

He felt Fred come up behind him, and the warmth of his breath as he whispered, "Don't dig yourself into a hole, let it go."

"Oh, that!" Mr. Newlin replied. "Bit of biffo at the funeral!" He ran his hands over his hair, and reddened as he realised it was out of place in about six different directions. "Happens all the time!"

"Mr. Newlin," Fred stepped forward smoothly and offered his hand. "I'm Frederick Conway, grandson of the deceased. I agree with you entirely, it was a wonderful service, and it's all thanks to young Mr. Harvey here. He's a credit to your company."

Once again Jason was hoping for that Guatemalan sinkhole to appear, but Mr. Newlin seemed to let the obsequiousness seep right in as Fred stepped behind him and motioned around his own mouth. Jason frowned, and Fred, clearly impatient at his idiocy, pointed to Newlin.

And smeared in a corner of Mr. Newlin's mouth was the telltale sign of chocolate from Sweets to the Sweet.

"Maybe you should go and get a coffee, Mr. Newlin," Jason said, pushing him towards the door.

"Yes, that sounds good."

"And then go home."

Newlin suddenly snapped to attention, and the unfocused glaze of his eyes seemed to clear. "My wife's going to kill me! I have to get home!"

"Have a good weekend, Mr. Newlin!" Jason yelled after him as he ran out of the room.

"See you on Monday, Harvey!" his boss yelled over his shoulder.

Jason turned back to Fred, and held up his hands in consternation. "Well, I don't know what the fuck's going on."

"It looks like your job's safe, anyway."

"I think we should go and see if that damn shop is still open," Jason said.

"I can think of much better things to do," Fred said with a glint in his eyes.

Jason pushed him away stubbornly. "I want to see Chance. God, what kind of drugs do you think he put in those damn things?"

Fred looked hurt, but Jason couldn't afford to make him feel better at the moment. If everything was all due to the chocolate, what did it say about what had happened between him and Fred? Rather than face up to that possibility, Jason would rather take on Chance.

※ ※ ※

THEY DIDN'T SAY a word as they locked up the Newlin Funeral Parlour and walked the short distance around the corner and up the road to Sweets to the Sweet.

They almost walked past the storefront, which was dark and dusty.

"Uh…" Fred said, pulling Jason back.

Jason hadn't even recognised it. The shop as they knew it was gone—as if it had never been there. The newspaper stuck on the inside of the glass window was old and yellowed by the sun—the date at the top of one of the pages was from eight months ago. In fact, now that Jason thought about it, that was how long the store had remained empty before Sweets to the Sweet had opened up in there.

"Should I start humming the theme from *The Twilight Zone*?" Fred asked.

"It's impossible!" Jason exclaimed. "We know it was here. We both saw it. We sat in there, and there was a shop!"

"Well, it's not there now."

Jason was irked by his matter-of-factness. "This doesn't worry you?"

"You think we should be worried?"

"In case you didn't notice, a whole funeral party went crazy today."

"Look on the bright side. Nobody died."

Jason slammed his hand against the window. "Can you try taking this a little more seriously?"

Fred's attention was captivated by something stuck to the front door. "Uh, Jason, there's a letter here for us."

Jason pushed past him, and sure enough, there was an envelope with their names on it. He felt Fred's chin rest upon his shoulder, and it felt warm and comforting.

"If you won't open it, I will," Fred threatened.

Jason ripped the envelope open and pulled out a small piece of notepaper. The words were written in an elegant hand:

Hey, kids, try not to stuff this up.

He shrugged Fred off his shoulder and turned to face him. "Okay, you can hum the *Twilight Zone* theme now."

"I think it's best not to question it," Fred said. "Strange things happen all the time, for no reason. Just go with it. This is one of those good, strange, things."

Jason wished he could believe it that easily. After all, what did he really know about Fred? But then, really, what did anyone know about anybody when they first got together?

But it still niggled at him.

"What are you thinking?"

"Honestly?"

"It's kind of the best basis for when you start something with someone."

"Okay, What if we…just felt what we did because of the chocolate?"

Fred sounded a lot more confident than Jason felt. "I think its effects will have worn off by now. They did with your boss. And seeing as I haven't had a call from the cops asking me to pick up Adele, I assume she's now okay as well."

"That's not what I'm asking."

"Are you asking if I still feel the same about you as I did before?" Fred reached for his hand, and Jason was reminded of how good he felt with just the simple handshake between them when they first met. Despite hardly knowing him, Fred just *felt* right with him. "Well, I do. What about you?"

"How do I feel about you?" Jason asked.

"Yeah."

"You're okay, I guess." Jason couldn't hold on to his laughter for long and it rang out into the empty street, genuine and heartfelt.

"Good," Fred seemed pleased with his response. "I don't handle rejection well."

Jason kissed him. It started as a small peck that turned into a longer, full-fledged kiss. He felt his blood burn as Fred's fingers travelled up his cheeks and guided him in closer.

Fred pulled away. "And you stress too much."

"You told me that I'm cute when I stress."

"I did, didn't I? I guess I'm going to have to keep you on your toes from now on. Just to keep you cute."

As they kissed again, Jason could still taste the after-effects of Chance's chocolate. It could have worried him, but he chose not to let it. If their kisses were to taste forever of chocolate, there was no way you could find fault with that.

As long as there was a hint of chilli.

About One Less Stiff at the Funeral

I was the first person in my whole extended family to be born outside Ireland. So although I get taunted by my siblings for not being Irish I feel that I have enough of their perspective and outlook on life flowing through my veins.

Irish funerals are emotional. Much drink is consumed; many tales are told. There is unrestrained laughter, and enough tears to drown by. I have been confused at times by how restrained funerals for other people can be, and I guess this is where inspiration for the service of Grace Conway comes from. The Conways need to be under the influence of something in order to express their emotions. Even Fred, the more expressive of the lot, needs this.

I grew up being told stories of people falling in open graves at the funeral service, of bodies being removed from coffins to be taken down to the local for 'one final drink'—you can mourn somebody's removal from your life, but you also have to celebrate the fact that they existed in the first place.

The title is a pun on an old joke: What's the difference between an Irish wedding and an Irish funeral?

There's one less drunk at the funeral.

So if you think Irish funerals can be over the top, there are some stories I can tell you about their weddings...including the time my mother punched out the brother of the groom. But maybe that could be another 'Petit Mort'?

CRITIC'S CHOICE
Josh Lanyon

WHAT THE HELL had he been thinking?

The minute he saw Rey's car, Cris knew he'd made a mistake.

That 1964 fire-engine red Mustang convertible symbolized everything that had gone wrong between them six months ago. That was not the car of a guy who planned on settling down anytime soon. That was the car of a player. A player in every sense of the word.

Hey, nothing wrong with that. Unless you were trying to build some kind of relationship—life—with the player in question. In which case, if you had any brains at all, you'd pay attention to the signs, which happened to be about as obvious as bad news in a goat's entrails.

Well, it was too late now.

Cris slammed his own car door shut and walked briskly up the flagstone walk to the house. The landscaping consisted strictly of grass, dark green hedges, and tall Tuscan-style cypress trees. But there all resemblance to sunny Tuscany ended. There were no flowers, no fountains, no color or life at all. It reminded him a bit of Forest Lawn. The estate itself was nearly large enough for a cemetery. Twenty-nine acres set in the hills above Sunset Boulevard.

Cris spared a grim smile for the hunched stone gargoyle peering around the dormer window three stories above. From the outside at least, the house looked exactly as you'd expect Angelo Faust's home to look: creepy.

But creepy in a severe and stately way.

The wind, one of those legendary Santa Anas that periodically scoured the Southland in the late summer and early fall, whispered through the maze of hedges. Unease rippled down his spine. He hated the wind. Would always hate the wind.

The mansion entrance consisted of forbidding wrought iron scroll double doors. Cris touched the doorbell and jumped at the sepulchral moaning sounds that bounced off the portico. That got a quiet laugh out of him at both his own reaction and the sense of humor behind the trick doorbell. The Whiterock Estate would have been a huge hit with the neighborhood kids. If there had been any kids—or neighborhood—in walking distance.

The doors swung open soundlessly. A very tall, very bony man in black trousers and black turtleneck studied Cris for a few unimpressed seconds.

"Hi. I'm Crispin Colley. I have an ap—"

"Oh, yes." The tone was more like *Oh, no.* "Mr. Faust and the other *gentleman* are in the screaming room."

Was this human fossil Faust's PA? Butler? A misplaced zombie from one of Faust's later films?

"Screaming room?" Cris let the inflection that suggested *gentleman* was doubtful, pass.

The fossil raised a single disapproving eyebrow. "*Screening* room."

Cris had excellent hearing, sharpened through years of listening closely to fuzzy, terrible old movie soundtracks. He began to be amused.

"I didn't catch your name."

"I didn't throw it at you. I am Neat."

"I'm sure you are."

Neat didn't crack a smile. "This way, Mr. Colley."

Cris followed Neat down the vast center hall. Three tall archways adorned by carved woodwork and decorative moldings offered a glimpse of a grand staircase and two corridors leading east and west.

Baguès crystal chandelier, wrought iron wall sconces, a marble bust of Louis XIV, a large marble-topped table, silver candlesticks, cloisonné boxes, and marble benches…it was nice to see that Faust had fared better financially than some of his contemporaries.

Neat, sounding like a bored tour guide, said, "To the west is Fhillips' Grand Ballroom, the Garden Retreat, Gentleman's Study and Salon d'Art. The east corridor leads to the Library, Drawing Room, Morning Room, Solarium and the Salon de Thé."

"Impressive."

"Possibly."

Cris bit back a smile, but his amusement faded as he realized he was going to have to face Rey in a minute or so. It was irritating to realize how nervous he was. He'd known when he accepted the offer from Dark Corner Studios that Rey was the other commentator on the voiceover of the legendary *The Alabaster Corpse*. The film's director, Paolo Luchino, was long since dead, so Rey would be offering his insights along with Faust, who had starred in the film. Cris wasn't sure why the studio thought they needed a third opinion, but he wasn't about to turn down the project. If it wasn't a problem for Rey, it sure as hell shouldn't be a problem for Cris.

"The theater is this way." Neat turned off another hallway, this one lined with framed posters of Faust's most famous releases, starting with 1956's *The Island of Night*.

There was no poster for *The Alabaster Corpse*, but then it wasn't one of Faust's major works. It *was* a cult favorite, having caught the critical attention of film historians and reviewers in recent years.

Cris knew all Faust's films. He'd seen them all many times growing up, and he'd watched them all again before he'd written *Man in the Shadows*, the one and only filmography of Faust's work. The filmography Faust had declined to authorize or even be interviewed for. In fact, given how steadfastly Faust had refused to contribute to the filmography, Cris had been more than a little surprised to be invited to take part in the project. Surprised but thrilled. Dark Corner was repackaging and releasing Faust's early films in a sumptuous five disc collection. The studio must have backed Rey's choice, which underscored just how much clout Rey had these days.

Rey, on the other hand, was an obvious choice for the project. The critics—with the exception of Cris—were hailing him as the new Wes Craven. There was even a rumor that Rey might be luring Faust back to the big screen.

Good for Rey, if it was true. Cris didn't grudge him his—well, maybe he did a little. Better not to go there.

Speaking of going places, they had apparently reached their destination.

An open door led into a home theater papered in old-fashioned red and gold stripes and complete with slanted floor. Thirteen plush theater seats were arranged in a half moon. Crimson draperies hid the screen.

"Mr. Colic," Neat announced.

"Colley," Cris corrected automatically. Though he was looking straight at the elderly man who rose and came to greet him, his focus was on the room's other occupant.

Rey.

Cris's heart sped up just as though he'd received a bad shock, just as though he hadn't known the whole time that he was going to see Rey again. He was not looking at him, not even watching him out of the corner of his eye, really, and yet he was painfully conscious of Rey's motionless figure. Cris suspected that even if he closed his eyes and turned around three times he'd be able to pinpoint Rey's exact location in any room. *Reydar*.

He forced himself to concentrate on the man before him. There had been a time when the opportunity of meeting Angelo Faust would have wiped out all other considerations. That needed to be true again if he was going to get through this afternoon.

Even at seventy-something (assuming the age on his official bio was close to being correct) Faust was unnervingly handsome, almost angelically so. The surprise was that he was so much smaller than he looked on the screen. Of course, people did shrink with age, but Faust couldn't have been much over five eight even in his youth. He was about five six now. His hair was still—well, no, that was a wig, actually—was thick and black and curly as it had been in his youth. His eyes, those wonderful expressive light eyes, were still bright, still so blue they made you blink.

"So you're Crispin Colley." Faust didn't offer his hand or a smile. He scrutinized Cris with those amazing eyes, and his expression suggested skepticism.

"It's an honor, Mr. Faust," Cris said, and he meant it. To finally meet Faust… all his intentions of playing it cool, keeping a little professional distance, went flying right out the window. He offered his own hand. "I've been a fan since I was…gosh. Forever."

Oh God. He was *gushing*. But maybe it wasn't a bad thing because Faust unbent slightly and shook hands, albeit briefly.

"Christ, you're young."

He wasn't really. He was thirty-three, but thanks to genetics and a very fast metabolism Cris looked younger. Sometimes it was an asset. Sometimes it was a pain in the ass. Not as much of a PIA as it had been in his twenties.

He opened his mouth to make some disclaimer, but Faust waved it aside. "No, no. I merely expected…someone different."

Who? Cris managed not to ask the question. He probably didn't want to hear the answer.

Faust turned away. "I think you know Mr. Starr."

"Rey," Cris said automatically.

Not for the first time, Cris wondered what it was about Rey. He was good-looking, but not in a Hollywood way, not in a stop-you-in-your-tracks way. He was a little over medium height, square-shouldered and compact. His face was strong and sensual. His eyes were a very light hazel, his hair dark. His hair was longer, but other than that he looked disconcertingly unchanged. What had Cris hoped to see? Shadows and pallor? Some sign that Rey had suffered a little over their breakup? Suffered as Cris had?

"Cris." Rey was holding out his hand. It seemed a little formal, a little weird to be shaking hands with someone you'd once—but really he didn't want to start thinking like that. Did *not* want those images in his mind any more than he wanted to slo-mo through *Texas Chainsaw Massacre*.

Cris pressed his palm to Rey's, tightened his fingers. The mechanics of a handshake. The last time he'd touched Rey it was to take a swing at him. The swing had not connected. Rey had grabbed him and then let him go, and they had never spoken directly—let alone touched each other—again.

It was strange to hold hands, to feel that warm, strong grip, even for a few fleeting seconds. Strange, the memories that seemed to be waiting in the wings to rush the stage of this moment.

It was Cris who let go. Cris who stepped back.

"How do you like the setup?"

"What?" A second later it dawned on Cris what—duh—Rey meant. "Nice. Very nice. It will be great to see this on 35mm at last."

Rey turned to Angelo, though he was still addressing Cris too. "Okay, just to run over the basics. The plan is to record this as a feature-length, screen-specific commentary in one session this afternoon. The studio is hoping for an extempore but informative audio track. They've been slammed for the commentary on some of the other releases in the Tales from the Vault series, so they're hoping to recoup a little credibility here."

"Once again looking to me to bail them out," Faust said.

Rey didn't even blink. "Angelo, you're doing anecdotal stuff and reminiscences. Cris, you're doing the film background, significance to the genre, et cetera, and I'm talking about the film from a technical aspect. Is that pretty much what everyone expected?"

Cris nodded.

Angelo said, "No drinking games?"

Rey laughed. "Maybe later in the film."

Angelo winked at Cris. Cris smiled back with as much enthusiasm as he could muster. Everyone liked Rey. He was easy to get along with. Sincerely charming. He liked people and they liked him. The fact that he was a two-timing, cheating adulterer was beside the point. It really *was*, because other than the fact that Rey couldn't keep his pants zipped, he was a great guy—and a very good director. Including Crispin in this project had been typical of him. He liked to stay friends with his ex-lovers. Hell, when it was possible he liked to stay friends with people he'd fired from sets. He was a nice guy. A nice but tough guy. That was the word in Hollywood.

They weren't in Hollywood now, though.

"We have two options. We can watch the film first, make notes, and then record our commentary on the second viewing. Or we can just view it cold and say whatever pops into our heads."

"I haven't seen this film in over thirty years."

"It's a *great* film," Cris couldn't help saying, and that time Angelo actually beamed at him. Yes, it looked like the ice was breaking. Too late for Cris's book, but it would make for a better audio commentary.

"Personally, I think it'd be great to get your first reactions on seeing this film again after all that time." Rey turned to smile at Cris. "And knowing Cris, he's already viewed the film a couple of times and made his notes on it."

Given the fact that Rey was smiling, and that making digs wasn't his style, he probably didn't mean that in a derogatory way, but Cris was nettled all the same. It just underlined the difference in their styles. Cris liked to do his homework and Rey liked to wing it. Or, in other words, Cris was staid and uptight and boring and Rey was creative and innovative and exciting. No news there.

"If it'll float your boat," Angelo said breezily.

Cris recognized that too-grave expression on Rey's face and his own mouth twitched in an automatic, quickly repressed, grin.

"Anybody have any other questions?"

Cris shook his head.

"Then let the curtain rise."

They took their seats in the front row behind three mic stands. Rey sat down next to Cris and began to explain how to use the high-powered mics. Angelo sat on the other side of Rey.

It was too cozy with all of them lined up in the front row; Cris would have preferred they spread out a little, but it would have entailed repositioning the mics and in any case, would have surely looked ridiculous. Why *weren't* they doing this in an editing bay at the studio? Not that he seriously objected to getting to visit Angelo in his lair.

Angelo pressed a button on the remote control. The overhead lights dimmed.

He pointed the remote and the crimson velvet curtains slid slowly open to reveal a 130-inch screen.

Rey settled back and stretched his long legs out. His arm brushed Cris's on the rest. He asked quietly, "You have enough room?"

Cris moved his arm away. "Yep. I'm good."

Rey smiled at him.

Don't. Just don't. Cris smiled politely back and stared straight ahead.

Angelo pressed the remote again.

Anticipation of the movie relieved some of Cris's uncomfortable awareness of his proximity to Rey. Whether he liked it or not, it did feel very natural sitting here like this. They had watched a lot of films together.

Angelo pointed the remote again.

The screen before them stayed gray and blank.

Angelo swore and pointed the remote behind him at the light in the small projection room behind them.

Still nothing.

Rey began, "Is there something I can do?"

"No." Angelo hit the intercom in the center console. "Neat!"

Silence.

"What the hell is he doing?"

A rhetorical question if there ever was one.

"Why don't I take a look?" Rey began. "I have a lot of experience with everything from projectors to—"

"No. No. Absolutely not." Angelo punched the intercom button again. "*Neat!*"

With an exclamation of impatience, he rose and left the theater.

"Run, Neat," Rey murmured as Angelo disappeared down the hall.

Cris acknowledged with a little huff of amusement.

A couple seconds passed. It was so quiet he could hear Rey's wristwatch. How weird was it to sit here side by side alone in the dark? But to get up would be obvious. Cris forced himself to relax his limbs, to at least offer the illusion that he was at ease and perfectly comfortable—and wasn't jumping every time his arm brushed Rey's.

It wasn't easy.

And it didn't help that he was trying to present this picture of ease to the person who knew him better than anyone else in the world.

"How've you been?" Rey's voice sounded abrupt.

"Fine. You?"

Rey nodded. He turned his face and Cris caught the gleam of his eyes. "You look good." The glimmer of his smile was rueful, flattering. "You look great."

"Thanks." Grudgingly, Cris added, "Congratulations on the Saturn Award nomination."

"Thanks." Rey rubbed the edge of his thumb against the tip of his nose. One of his little mannerisms when he was bored or nervous.

He clearly wasn't nervous, so…good. Polite chitchat out of the way. Cris slid lower on his spine and stared up at the in-ceiling speaker system.

"I heard you're working on a book about Hammer Film Productions."

"Just Hammer Horror. The gothic films."

"You'll be going to England for research, I guess?"

Cris nodded.

"When? I'm going over in October for the British Horror Film Festival."

"I haven't decided." Cris continued to study the shadowy ceiling with its decorative moldings and seven mounted speakers.

Hopefully Rey would get the message. It probably wasn't very sophisticated of him, but Cris didn't want to be a good sport about their breakup. He appreciated being included in this project, but he didn't want to be friends with Rey. He didn't want to let bygones be bygones. Rey had broken his heart and maybe that was a cliché, but it still hurt like hell. He still wasn't over it. He was still angry—although that probably wasn't rational. Like being mad at a cat for chasing mice.

They could work together. Cris was a professional after all. A grownup. But they weren't going to be pals. He wasn't going to be another Teddy or Evan or Mark or Phil.

He couldn't handle it. He wasn't built that way.

The speakers suddenly crackled and ominous organ music poured from the sound system overhead. Both Cris and Rey jumped—and then laughed sheepishly.

A hooded figure flickered on the screen, time code numbers burned in at the bottom of each frame. The figure began pouring potions from jeweled flasks. The camera panned slowly to skulls littered on the floor of a tomb. The hooded figure hurried past and spared a kick for one of the skulls.

Cris had always loved that shot. It was so outrageous. Especially for 1963.

Rey reached the remote control as the credits flashed up. He pressed and the screen froze on the image of the hollow-eyed flying skull.

Angelo returned. He was a little out of breath but impressively spry for a man of his age. He took his seat. "What did I miss?"

"We're fine. We can re-sync the audio. I just want everyone to remember that the mics are hot. So if you don't want it potentially on the audio track, keep it to yourself."

"Got it," Cris said.

Angelo waved a lazy hand.

Rey pressed the remote. The credits began to roll, the jagged graphics looking like the black and white embodiment of a migraine.

TWO

"Hey, I'm Rey Starr and I direct horror films, some of which you may have seen or at least heard of. It's my great honor to introduce one of my all time favorite scary movies, *The Alabaster Corpse*. I'll be doing the audio commentary on this classic shocker, and I'll be joined by the film's star, Hollywood and horror legend Angelo Faust."

Rey paused. Angelo said nothing.

Rey continued, "This is a rare privilege. Angelo and I are sitting here with Crispin Colley, noted film historian and critic for *Phangloria* magazine. Cris is also the author of *Man in the Shadows*."

Rey nodded to Cris.

Cris leaned forward. "Nice to be here, Rey."

"Friends, Romans, Countrymen," announced Angelo. He giggled.

Cris threw a quick look at Rey.

Rey cleared his throat. "It's unusual to see the kind of prologue we're watching now in a horror movie—in any kind of movie of the period, actually. The director, Paolo Luchino, was trying to make sure the audience understood that we're watching a story about the decay of society rather than just a standard horror flick."

"*Si*," Angelo said, and rattled off a string of Italian.

Cris studied the tip of his Kenneth Cole boots, and tried not to laugh. Angelo was definitely a wild card. Watching the film first and roughing out a general script probably would work better, but Rey liked to fly by the seat of his pants. And he generally got good results, so….

"The film was made in 1963. It was based on a novel by James Gasper called *Death Merchant of Venice*, which came out in 1960. Although Gasper's novel was critically panned, it was a huge bestseller, and just watching these opening scenes, which follow the book closely, you can see how visual and dramatic a story it is."

"The film was shelved for two years," Angelo said. "I was very disappointed about that. It was supposed to be my big breakthrough. A lot of people in Hollywood saw it. Everyone had their own private projection rooms in their homes, and everyone kept saying it was going to be a smash hit, and the real beginning of my career, but the head of Europix didn't like the film, didn't understand it, and it was locked away.

"Finally, Carlo Grossi, the picture's producer, decided *fuck all that, fuck the American release.*"

Cris felt Rey's wince at the objectionable F-word, though he didn't attempt to curb Angelo's enthusiasm.

"The film opened in a little theater in London of all places, and got terrific reviews, became a tremendous success as a nihilistic classic. Then, of course, the American studio wanted their piece of the pie and the film was finally released over here. Two years late. I have to say American audiences never really did *get* it the way European audiences did. But the American filmgoer is generally simple-minded, don't you think?"

Rey said, "Er...."

Cris grinned inwardly. Poor Rey.

The plot of *The Alabaster Corpse* was pretty generic. The usual fiendish madman was busily preying upon lovely young girls in 1960s Venice. Dragging them off to his tomblike lair in the crypt of a monastery submerged beneath the canals—one of the best all time horror movie settings in Cris's opinion—the fiend murdered the damp and unlucky mini-skirted damsels, embalmed them, and finally posed them like classical statuary in the garden of his palazzo. Unfortunately for the cloaked fiend, he set his screwy sights on the fiancé tour guide of a nosy reporter—played by Angelo.

Cris tuned back in to hear Rey say, "Angelo, you were saying earlier you haven't seen this film in thirty-plus years?"

"That's right. Not since the director yelled *cut!* After filming was over, I came back to the States, back to Hollywood, and Jack Mart of Universal called me right away and asked me to do *Haunted Red Sea.*"

"*Red Haunted Sea,*" Cris murmured automatically. He didn't mean to correct Angelo—it was the last thing he intended—but he was obsessive about accuracy and it just…popped out.

There was a pause. Angelo said, "No, I don't think so."

Rey's knee bumped Cris's. Not that Cris was crazy enough to argue with Angelo, let alone on tape.

Angelo, sounding a little annoyed, continued, "Anyway, *that* became my big breakthrough. I made that picture with Anita Boyd. What a mouth on her! I forgot all about *The Alabaster Corpse*. I never liked to see my own work." He leaned over and said pointedly to Cris, "I never read my reviews."

"No, I don't read mine either."

"Make that three," Rey said.

They all laughed, though Cris's was a little strained. He'd met Rey when Rey had contacted him over his review of the remake of *The Mummy of Soho*. Rey had loved that review. Nearly as much as Cris had loved the movie.

"Cris, did you want to add s—"

But Angelo was now off and running on the beauties of Venice. "Have you been there? If you do ever go, my recommendation to you is you lose yourself in the city for a few hours. Wherever everyone else is headed, you go the opposite way. That's how you discover Venice. The real Venice. Not that gondola ride and glass-blowing crap. I don't think it can have changed that much."

Rey forged steadily on. "Now, in this shot we have—"

"Why don't we stop the movie here," Angelo interrupted.

"Uh…" Rey leaned forward and hit the record button. "Okay. What's up?"

The film continued to play on the screen in front of them.

"It's lunch time."

Cris nearly laughed at the expression on Rey's face. Priceless. For all Rey's fooling around when he was off the clock, when he was working, he was all business.

Rey checked his watch. "It's eleven."

"That's right." Angelo rose. "I'm an old man. I like my meals on time."

Rey looked at Cris with an expression that on anyone else would have to be described as "helpless."

Cris, still struggling to keep a straight face, shrugged and stood up.

They dined in the loggia off the main dining room. It featured high ceilings, tile floors, and an enormous arched leaded-glass window that looked over the mansion's windy south terrace. Cris could almost smell the creamy blossoms of the olive trees painted in the full-size wall mural of a sunny Tuscan garden.

Angelo sat at the head of the table, which was appointed with simple but elegant white linens and white china. Rey sat directly across from Cris, and each time Cris looked up, Rey's eyes met his. It made him uncomfortable, but it also set his blood pounding. He knew that look of Rey's.

"One thing the Italians do very well is lunch," Angelo said as Neat moved around the table, ladling creamy soup into each bowl. "In Venice they like a lot of fish and vegetables. Neat, let's have the Torrontes with our meal."

Neat muttered something that sounded uncomplimentary, and departed. He was back a short while later with a bottle of white wine and crusty, warm bread. The wine was crisp, the bread delicious dipped in olive oil.

Angelo directed his comments solely to Rey, though he kept all of their glasses topped up. Cris sipped his wine and kept his mouth shut. It seemed clear that Rey and Angelo knew each other pretty well.

The soup was really excellent. Cris spooned it slowly and watched the clouds scudding over the palm trees. The wind seemed to be picking up. No wonder he felt tense and off-kilter. He forced himself to concentrate on Rey and Angelo's talk of films and art. When had Rey met Angelo? It must have been fairly recently, but it was typical of Rey to win over even a difficult personality like Angelo.

The soup and bread was followed by chicken Florentine. In some peculiar way the chicken and spinach reminded Cris of the Florentine-style pizza he and Rey used to order in on summer evenings and eat while they watched movies on the landscaped rooftop deck of Rey's house high atop the Hollywood Hills ridgeline. The movies were projected onto the house's exterior wall and the image quality had been pristine. Not that the viewing experience was what Cris missed most about those evenings. Nor the pizza. Nor the fabulous smog-enhanced sunsets.

Who had Rey invited over for pizza and movies last summer?

"I did read your book, you know." Angelo said suddenly.

Cris shook off his unproductive speculation to find both Angelo and Rey gazing at him. "Oh. Yes?"

Angelo topped off their wine glasses yet again. "It would have been a better book if I had cooperated."

"I know," Cris said ruefully.

"It wasn't bad, though." Angelo held his glass up as though judging the clarity of the pale gold liquid. "I'm amazed you got that old buzzard Macy Carl to contribute. Although you shouldn't have believed half of what he told you."

"I tried to verify when and where possible." Cris was careful to keep his tone neutral. It *was* sort of aggravating, given how many times he'd tried to approach Angelo, but that was genius for you. You couldn't expect the Angelo Fausts of the world to operate on the same wavelength as everyone else.

"You even had *Vulcan's Shadow* listed in there. I didn't think anyone remembered that picture."

"Nothing escapes Cris's attention." Rey's hazel eyes met Cris's.

Was that supposed to be funny? Was Cris supposed to have reached the stage where he could chuckle over the memory of finding another guy's zebra print thong beneath the passenger seat of Rey's car? The car currently parked out front of this mansion?

"I've got a good memory too."

"Yes, you must." Angelo handed around a box of chocolates. The gold box label read *Sweets to the Sweet*.

Cris slipped the lid off. "Is this that new place on Wilshire?"

"I wouldn't know," Angelo made another of those airy gestures. "People send me things. Little presents. I'm not forgotten. Even now my fans remember me. Not that there are so many left. We're none of us getting any younger."

"This film collection will change that." Rey put a hand over his glass to prevent Angelo from refilling it yet again.

Cris selected a piece of chocolate and took a cautious bite. He closed his eyes in instant bliss. Real chocolate. The real thing. Cocoa, butter, sugar, cream…and nuts. It was the kind of stuff he secretly loved. None of that trendy stuff everyone served now flavored with green tea and wasabi. These chocolates reminded him of his early childhood when everything had still been safe and happy. This was the real thing. Rich, sweet, peculiarly satisfying—especially with the merlot they were now drinking.

"What's your personal favorite of all your films?" Cris asked, emboldened by the wine and Angelo's relative approachability.

"*Haunted Red Sea*. What's your favorite of my films?"

But enough of me. What do you *think of me?* It was such a classic example, Cris's gaze automatically went to Rey. Rey's mouth pursed in that way he had when he was trying to keep a straight face.

"*Murder Tavern*."

"One of my later efforts."

"I think my favorite's *Fatal Hour*. Frances Sullivan did a masterful job making that script human." Rey reached for a piece of chocolate.

Angelo's forehead wrinkled. "But that was a spoof."

Rey assented. "That's what was brilliant about it." He took a bite of chocolate. "Wow. What's in this stuff?"

He and Angelo bickered amiably for another minute or two and then Rey charmingly but firmly shepherded them back to the screening room. Angelo insisted on bringing the wine bottle and the box of chocolates, which he placed on the table near the bank of mics.

They were no sooner seated than he was on the intercom ordering Neat to bring more glasses.

Rey's expression was wry, but after all an element of spontaneity contributed to the success of some of the greatest commentaries out there. Who could forget Monty Python's *Soundtrack for the Lonely: A Soundtrack for People Watching at Home Alone*.

Cris had to admire the tact and patience with which Rey dealt with Angelo, but there was no question Rey was good at his job, and a lot of that job was about effectively dealing with people.

The film had continued to play while they were in at lunch. It had reached the climactic scene between the reporter played by Angelo and the cloaked fiend played by Gin Todesco.

Rey checked his notes. "Take it back to T.C. 012213."

Angelo was speaking into the intercom, requesting Neat.

Silence.

There was more punching of buttons, muttering, and then finally Angelo departed cursing quietly.

Rey picked up the chocolates and offered the box to Cris, who selected a truffle.

"Are you seeing anyone?"

Having his mouth full of chocolate gave Cris a few seconds to consider his reply. "Yeah."

Rey's eyes narrowed. "That didn't take long."

Cris stared at him in disbelief. A number of responses went through his brain. He kept his jaw clamped on them all.

Rey stretched out his legs, leaned back in the comfortably padded seat. "But then you always were all about the white picket fences."

"Fuck off." Cris said under his breath, aware that Angelo was going to walk through that door any minute. Rey seemed to have no such concern.

"Why? Have you changed your mind about what you want?"

"No. Have you?"

Rey had an odd expression. "You didn't stay around long enough to find out what I wanted."

"It felt more than long enough from where I stood."

Overhead, the organ blasted out its ominous intro. In front of them, the now familiar images flitted across the screen as the movie began to roll again. Cris stared stolidly at the screen as Angelo returned to the room.

He flung himself down into his chair. As an afterthought he reached for the remote and dimmed the room lights once more.

Rey pressed record. "Cris, I know this film is one of your favorites. Can you give us an idea of where it ranks with other classics of the period?"

Cris sat forward. "The sixties were a particularly rich period for horror movies. We start the decade with *Village of the Damned*, Mario Bava's *La Maschera del Demonio* and *Little Shop of Horrors* and end with *Night of the Living Dead* and *Rosemary's Baby*."

"*The Birds* in '63."

"*Mill of the Stone Women*."

Rey was laughing. "From the sublime to the ridiculous. I've never understood what you see in that flick."

"It's a great flick!" Cris was laughing too, his earlier anger forgotten as they gained the safety of common ground.

"You just dig the windmills."

"I do, yeah. The windmills are original, visually haunting. The whole film is atmospheric and stylish. The use of Technicolor is surprisingly effective. You don't expect it. Those eerie blues and fiery reds. Arrigo Equini's art direction and Pier Ludovico Pavoni's photography are nearly impressionistic. It's one reason why I regret Paolo Luchino opted for black and white in The *Alabaster Corpse*."

"You two used to live together, is that right?" Angelo interjected.

Cris snapped back to unpleasant reality. "Turn it off," he told Rey, and Rey jumped to hit the recorder.

When he was sure he was no longer being recorded Cris said, "We need to set some ground rules."

"What did I say?" Angelo seemed surprised.

Cris's attention was all on Rey. "I know you like that whole cinéma vérité approach but I'm not going to be part of some—"

"I know that."

"Our personal life—*my* personal life—is not up for home entertainment viewing."

"You don't have to say anything else." Rey said. "You already know this isn't scripted. Conversations…naturally evolve."

"I don't want any conversation evolving in this direction."

Rey's face tightened. "Okay. Relax. We've all got the message."

Angelo said huffily, "If I've overstepped—"

"You haven't," Rey said.

Cris refrained from comment. It wasn't Angelo's fault. It wasn't anyone's fault, really, but that didn't change the fact that no way was he discussing his personal life on this film's commentary track.

"I find it interesting." Angelo directed his comment to Cris. "In my day you couldn't be a known homosexual in Hollywood and still have a career.

You're luckier than you know."

"Great. Let's go with that." Rey kept a wary eye on Cris. "I mean, of course, keeping it general and focused on Angelo. There's no secret that we're gay, right? Regardless of what happened between us, we're not in the closet."

Cris nodded. Both Rey and Angelo relaxed, which left him feeling unhappy and uncomfortable, as though he'd flipped out over nothing. Doubly embarrassing, because it probably looked like he wasn't over Rey if he couldn't casually laugh off the fact that they'd once lived together.

"So you're coming out officially?" Rey was talking to Angelo. "You're going on the record?"

Angelo snorted. "Is it supposed to be news? Does anyone give a damn what my sleeping arrangements are these days?"

Rey hit the record button again.

"Fuck off," Cris's recorded voice said quietly, fiercely.

Rey lunged for the recorder again. "What the hell?" He looked bewilderedly at the buttons. "I-I don't get it. I must have hit rewind when I thought I'd hit play. Or record when I thought I'd hit…" he trailed off, still frowning at the buttons.

"How much did we lose?" Angelo asked.

"I'm not sure. I can't understand what happened."

"Take two." Angelo waved a vague hand. "Let's just go from here."

Rey looked at Cris. Cris shrugged. It was almost worth the wasted time to see Rey this flustered.

Rey let out an exasperated breath and carefully pressed record. "Let's talk about the homoerotic overtones in this film and a lot of your other films, Angelo. The friendship between your character, Dino Raniera, and the police inspector…."

"Christian Tavella," supplied Cris.

Rey threw him a quick smile. "Right. Played by the talented Gabriel Caswell, who died so tragically young."

"He was a hop head," Angelo said casually.

Cris, who had reached for another piece of chocolate, choked, then coughed to try to cover.

Rey drove determinedly on. "The relationship between cop and reporter is probably the most important in the film. I know the first time I watched it, I was struck by that friendship, which seems much more intrinsic to the plot then the relationship with the Bella Philbrook character."

"Don't you think we should rewind the film?" Angelo inquired. "That was a very good bit of acting you just missed commenting on."

Cris couldn't help laughing out loud at Rey's expression. Rey threw him a quick, uncertain look.

It was going to be a long afternoon.

Three

THE WIND WAS still gusting in warm, tired sighs when Cris left the Whiterock mansion after eight o'clock that evening.

Against the odds, the film commentary had ended up going pretty well, but he still felt hungry, tired, headachy from too much wine, and a little depressed. Angelo had invited him to stay for a late supper, and if Rey had taken off, Cris would have grabbed that opportunity. But Rey had also been invited to supper and seemed inclined to accept, so instead Cris had said goodnight.

By the time he was walking down the flagstone steps to his car, he was sure he had made a mistake. When was he going to get this kind of opportunity to talk with Angelo Faust again? He was letting Rey scare him off—and it was especially foolish because Rey had been friendly, even deferent at times.

And yet…he couldn't bring himself to turn around and go back inside.

Cris had nearly reached the bottom courtyard when he heard a whisper behind him. He glanced over his shoulder. There was nothing there. It was the wind making that unsettling sound, like a cloak dragging along the stones.

He felt a flicker of impatience with himself. He was not easily spooked. A lifetime of watching scary movies had pretty much hardened him to anything resembling *atmosphere*, but he was edgy tonight. Edgy for a lot of reasons. And letting it get to him.

As he continued down the stairs, he pulled his keys out, and tossed them from hand to hand as he crossed to his car.

The wind fluttered and scraped as though something invisible was scuttling behind him. Cris resisted the temptation to turn around and take another look. Funny how underused wind was as a device within the genre. Granted, he had particular reason to hate it, but the only movie he could think of off the top of his head was *The Red House* with Edgar G. Robinson and Judith Anderson. In that film, the wind made a creepy and effective ploy: the rising murmur of old ghosts crying for justice.

Well, there was *Horror in the Wind*, but that was entirely different. He smiled, remembering—until he reflected that the last time he'd watched that one had been with Rey.

He unlocked his car, got in, and sat there for a few seconds, feeling the gusts shake the vehicle. After a few seconds he recalled himself, and turned the key in the ignition. As he started down the drive, the headlights picked out the smooth indifferent face of the classical statuary behind the hedges. The blank, blind faces reminded him of the macabre garden in *The Alabaster Corpse*.

The road uncoiled in loose, black loops, snaking down through the arching tunnel of trees. It seemed a long way to the gate. Longer than it had seemed when he'd driven up that morning.

Cris's eyes were on the road, but his attention was back at the mansion, as he relived each frame of the afternoon in his memory. Mostly what he remembered was the painful delight of seeing Rey again after all this time. Maybe more painful than delightful, but…there was no denying it had shaken him.

Well, he had loved Rey. Loved him so much it had frightened him sometimes. And no wonder given the way things had turned out.

His headlights died.

One moment the road was illuminated in the ghostly haze of his high beams, the next moment he was flying along in complete and utter darkness. The trees beside the road stood like darker shadows against the night.

Then, the car engine cut out.

The only sound was the tires gliding along the road and the wind.

"What the…?"

Cris checked the blacked-out dashboard, pumped the gas to no effect, and quickly steered to the side of the road. The car rolled to a silent stop.

The engine ticked, strangely loud in the windblown silence.

The battery usually gave some warning before it went. Cris knew this because he'd had plenty of experience. Which meant—shit!—the alternator. Much more expensive. Terminally expensive, in fact.

Cris tried the key again, knowing it was the wrong thing to do.

Nothing. Not a damn thing.

The dashboard remained dark and dead.

He got his cell phone out.

His initial relief that it still worked—and why wouldn't it?—faded at the sight of the single lonely little bar. No signal.

"Oh come *on*."

It wasn't freaking Black Hills Forest, even if it did look like it here in this Delphian tunnel of trees.

For another disbelieving couple of seconds Cris sat motionless.

Okay, well…he couldn't be that far from the front gates. The only problem was, it was about four miles to help if he figured in the walk back to Loma Vista Drive, then east on Doheny Road, then the march back to Sunset Blvd. The chances of anyone picking him up this time of night—anyone he'd be willing to climb into a car with—were growing slimmer by the minute.

No. Better to walk back to the house. It couldn't be much more than a mile away.

He climbed out of the car, ignoring the instant and instinctive unease at finding himself at the mercy of the elements.

One element. Wind.

The trees around him groaned as though they were being tugged by their roots. The leaves rustled noisily overhead, millions of whispering tongues. Cris closed his ears to them, locked the car, and started back toward the house.

Once he was outside the tunnel of trees, he tried his phone again.

Still nothing.

Ohhhkay. Maybe a little trope-ish, but people did break down on lonely, deserted roads and their cell phones failed to work. That was why movie tropes became…tropes. The recognizable reality within the fiction.

Cris started walking again, firmly ignoring how dark and isolated it was, considering all those colored, twinkling lights in the valley down below.

He walked with an uneasy eye on the creaking, swaying trees lining the road. He was slightly amused at his own reaction to the dark, but he'd never pretended to be the outdoors type. Not that you could really call a Beverly Hills estate, no matter how isolated, The Outdoors.

His heart jumped at the sight of distant lights shining through the trees.

Then he realized he couldn't possibly be that close to the main house. Besides, the lights were too far to the north. It couldn't be the carriage house. Maybe a caretaker's cottage? Faust seemed like a guy who'd have a caretaker on the payroll.

Cris was distracted by the appearance of bright headlights coming swiftly down the road toward him. He heard the familiar growl of a sports car. Not any sports car. A vintage Mustang.

Rey.

He hadn't stayed for dinner after all. Cris moved to the middle of the road, waving as the headlights swept the road, spotlighting him.

The Mustang braked in slow swoops, swerving neatly to the shoulder and gliding to a stop.

The top was down. Rey rose from behind the windshield. "Hey. What happened?" he called.

Cris approached from along the side of the road. "My car broke down." He hooked a thumb over his shoulder indicating where he'd left his vehicle. "Can you give me a lift down the hill?"

"Of course. Hop in."

Cris, came around, opened the Mustang door, and slid in.

Rey faced him. "You sure this isn't just a ploy to get me alone?"

"Very funny."

Rey's grin was white in the moonlight. "I can dream, can't I?"

Cris spluttered but refrained from comment. Too dangerous.

After a pause Rey said, "You're very hard on my ego, Cris."

"The fan club's plenty big enough without me."

Rey started to answer. Cris said, "Are we going to sit here trading witty dialog all night or can we get moving?"

In reply, Rey shifted the stick into drive. They bumped off the shoulder of the road and the Mustang molded itself to the road as they sped away.

"You left in a hurry this evening," Rey observed as they rounded the first bend.

"Places to go, things to do."

Rey decelerated into the next curve, accelerated out, headlights swinging across the black road. "So what's the matter with Chitty Chitty Bang Bang now?"

Cris acknowledged the crack with a reluctant quirk of his mouth. "Who knows? Maybe the alternator. Maybe a belt slipped. You're the mechanic of the family."

Cris heard the echo of *the family* and shut up.

"You should trade that heap in."

"Not all of us need something new and different every five minutes."

"Why do I get the feeling we're not talking about your car?"

Cris gazed out the side, watching the pale tree trunks flash by. He was reminded of Rey's white picket fences dig and annoyed with himself for that sour—and revealing—comment.

Not getting a response, Rey asked, "Who's this guy you're seeing now? Anybody I know?"

"No."

"How can you be sure? I know a lot of people."

Cris laughed. "No kidding. In every sense of the word."

"Ouch." Rey started to add something but stopped as Cris's car appeared in the Mustang's headlights a few yards down the hillside.

Rey tapped the brakes, slowing. "Do you want me to take a look at it?"

"No. If you can just drop me off somewhere on Sunset."

"I can do better than that—"

"I don't need you to do better than that. Just drop me off at the first pay phone."

"Why don't you just use your cell phone?"

"*Oh my God. You know, I never even thought of that!* Because I can't get a signal."

After a distinct pause, Rey said, "I don't ever remember you being such a surly bastard."

Cris made a face that Rey probably couldn't read in the dark.

They continued on down the hill, and Cris's misery escalated with each yard. Why *did* it have to be like this between them? Why couldn't Rey have been everything he'd seemed at the start?

More importantly, why couldn't Cris stop feeling this way? It was over. His mind was made up. Why did he still have to feel—

"Jesus fucking *Christ*."

Cris wrenched his gaze forward in time to see one of the giant oaks by the side of the road come crashing down ahead of them. Leaves and dirt drifted in the wind, white on black, the image as stark as a film negative.

Rey hit the brakes, but it was too late. Cris felt the impact as one of the front tires hit something—a rock? A branch?—and exploded.

Belatedly, he remembered he hadn't put his seat belt on, realized that he was probably—ironically—going to die with Rey, and then the Mustang was careening across the narrow highway. Numbly, he watched a wall of tree trunks loom up on his right. He tried to brace for impact.

Rey twisted the wheel, hand slapping over hand, tires and brakes screeching. The Mustang spun out, made almost a full circle, and skated to a lurching stop.

Slowly, in shaking disbelief, Cris let go of the dashboard and sank back in the bucket seat. His blood beat a dizzy tempo in his temples, his heart hammered in his throat. All that adrenaline and no place to go. He felt almost sick in the wake of that violent surge.

He had been so sure. The wind…the car out of control…exactly like before…like his mother….

Rey was speaking to him, voice urgent. "Cris? Are you okay?"

Cris turned his head and stared at him.

"Are you okay?"

Cris nodded. He turned back to stare at the fallen tree. Leaves and twigs still floated lazily on the breeze.

Rey jumped out and walked to within a few feet of the tree. Cris shoved open his door and followed.

Side by side, they stared at the fallen giant, the huge snarled roots dropping great clods of earth. The fender of the Mustang just reached the leaves and outstretched twigs.

A few seconds earlier and they would've been under that monster. It seemed unreal, impossible that they weren't—nearly as unreal and impossible that the tree should have come down at all—yet here was the evidence a mere inches from their windshield.

"Talk about a freak accident," Rey said, his voice sounding bizarrely calm. "That oak must be a couple of hundred years old and it picked now to come down?"

"It's the wind. The fucking wind."

Rey reached out and gave his shoulders a quick, hard squeeze. Cris squeezed him back. Whatever was wrong between them, he was very glad Rey was okay.

That they were both okay.

Rey let him, go, pulled his cell out and was checking for signal—with predictable results.

"*Shit.*" His gaze was black in the glare of the Mustang's headlights. "I don't believe this. What now?"

Cris shook his head. "I guess we walk back to the house. I sure as hell don't feel like hiking down to Sunset Boulevard in this."

"No." Rey put his phone away, considered bleakly, and then went back to the Mustang. He retrieved his keys from the ignition. "So much for me coming to your rescue."

"It's the thought that counts."

Rey laughed.

They started up the winding road, the occasional pebble skittering from underfoot.

It was cold, but not unpleasantly so. The main nuisance was not being able to see more than a few feet ahead—and the wind, which made conversation difficult. Not that there was a lot to talk about.

Was there?

"Cris—" Rey began after what felt like half an hour or so.

"How long do you think we've been walking?" Cris asked at the same instant.

"Ten minutes?"

"It feels longer."

"You're out of shape."

That was probably true. Without Rey there to nag his ass he didn't swim or jog or play squash anymore. He still went for walks on the beach, that was about it. They were shorter walks these days.

He refused to let the memories hurt. "The thing is, right before I spotted your car, I saw lights through the trees. Now I don't see them anywhere."

"You mean over there?"

Cris's gaze followed the direction Rey was pointing and sure enough, there was the friendly winking glitter of light through moving leaves. He stopped walking.

That was weird. How had he missed those lights?

"Yeah. That's it."

"What do you think it is?"

"Guest house? Gamekeeper's cottage?"

Rey made a sound of disbelief. "Well, whoever it is, they seem to be home."

"Maybe their phone's working."

In accord they climbed the low bank and cut across the grass. Through this stretch the trees provided a natural windbreak, and it was quiet enough to hear themselves speak—assuming they had anything to say.

Once again Rey opened his mouth.

Once again, Cris interrupted, "You know, if this was a movie, we actually would've died in that accident and we wouldn't know it."

Rey broke off whatever he had started to say. "Like *Carnival of Souls*." He sounded amused.

"Yeah."

"But it wasn't an accident. I stopped in time."

"We *think* you stopped in time. But in fact…."

Rey laughed. "If this was a movie, there would be someone waiting for us—moonlight gleaming on his knife blade—in that little clump of trees ahead."

Cris shuddered and laughed quickly. Rey gave him another of those casual sideways hugs—letting him go quickly this time, feeling Cris's instinctive resistance.

"How are the dreams?" he asked

"Under control."

Rey was the only other person in the world who knew about the dreams. The only person Cris had ever trusted enough to tell, to share that weakness. To hear him speak of them now seemed unsettling, almost a betrayal. But that was silly. Why would Rey instantly forget just because they weren't together?

"The wind doesn't bother you anymore?"

Cris said aloofly, "Sometimes."

His bad dreams had never been about vengeful ghosts or psychos with knives. Those things didn't frighten him. No, the dreams—nightmares—had been about loss and loneliness. Sad, ordinary, shabby little dreams. Dreams about waiting and waiting for someone who never came. Waiting on a night like this, a night when the wind howled like a hungry animal, and when the doorbell finally rang it was police officers. In his dreams he relived the death of his mother, relived waiting for his father to show up and save him from foster care, relived moving from family to family, afraid to let himself love.

Now Rey was part of the bad dreams.

But for all that had happened between them, he'd never tell Rey that. Never hurt him with that. Regardless of how it had all turned out, Cris couldn't forget how it had been for those months, how it had felt to belong to someone, to have someone of his own. That had been his own personal concept of heaven… waking up from the old bad dreams to find himself in Rey's strong arms, hearing Rey comfort him with the sweet, foolish things you could only say in the dead of night. It had meant everything knowing that at last there was finally someone to rely on, to trust.

Into the silence that had fallen between them, broken only by the thud of their feet on the grass, Rey began tentatively, "Cris…."

Cris shook his head. "Don't."

"Can't we at least be friends?"

He knew Rey well enough to know that it was meant sincerely, that there was no intent to hurt. So he checked the bitter words and said only, "No."

"You can't—it's not right—to cut me off without a word. To not let me at least explain—"

There was genuine pain in Rey's voice. Real and deep hurt. It was hard to hear. It undermined Cris's anger to know that Rey was suffering too. He preferred to think of Rey as hard and callous and unrepentant. But that was unrealistic. Just as unrealistic as Rey thinking a few sincere words of explanation could make it all better. For all that Rey was tough and savvy, there had always been that streak of naiveté. Maybe because Rey had grown up secure and loved; it was bound to make a difference. Rey truly believed that there was no problem so big or so complex that talking it all out couldn't set it right.

Cris knew better. There was no fixing some things. There was no fixing this. He said again, "No."

This time Rey didn't protest, didn't try to argue. He walked beside Cris without speaking, although Cris could feel all the unspoken arguments buzzing in Rey's silence.

It was probably due to his preoccupation that Rey stepped wrong and went sprawling. He landed face down, full-length on the grass. It was so astonishing, and he looked so uncharacteristically uncool, flailing as he went down, that Cris nearly laughed.

He caught it back in time, alarmed when Rey didn't move for a couple of seconds.

"Rey? Are you okay?" He knelt.

"Shit," Rey muttered. He began to push up and then yelped.

"What's wrong?"

Rey sat up, shifted awkwardly, painfully onto his butt. He swore. "Talk about scenes from bad movies."

"What? What is it?" It was impossible to see in the darkness.

"I can't believe my goddamned luck. I think I sprained my ankle."

Cris drew back, resting on his heels. "You're kidding."

Rey shook his head. His big hands circled his ankle. What Cris could see of his downturned face was screwed up with pain.

He put his hand on Rey's shoulder, squeezing in comfort. "How bad? You want me to go ahead and bring help?" The lights of the caretaker's cottage, or whatever it was, weren't far now.

Rey rocked forward and back. He shook his head.

"You can't walk on a sprained ankle."

"It's not that bad. If you'll give me a hand I can make it as far as that house."

"Are you sure?"

Rey nodded, reaching out an arm. Cris put his shoulder under Rey's arm and helped him to his feet. Rey stood swaying, his arm hooked steadfastly over Cris's shoulders. Cris slipped his own arm around Rey's waist.

"I've finally got you where I want you," Rey got out from between clenched teeth. It was a line straight out of *The Alabaster Corpse*.

Cris made an amused sound, although he didn't find this particularly funny. "I think this is a mistake. You can't hop on one leg for a mile."

"Mile? It's only a few yards." Rey gave an experimental hop and Cris had no choice but to move with him.

It was distracting, no doubt about it, to have Rey plastered against him, shoulder to shoulder, flank to flank, hip to hip. Rey's muscular arm clutched Cris's shoulders. The light scent of his perspiration mingled with that of his aftershave. The aftershave was new. Something expensive and musky.

It troubled Cris, though he didn't know why.

"Is it pretty serious, you and this other guy?" Rey sounded breathless, probably from all the hopping.

"It could be."

Hobble. Hop. "You don't have any doubts?"

"About what?"

Hobble. Hop. "Ouch. About us?"

Cris stopped walking. "No. I don't have any doubts."

He tried to put a little distance between them—did they really have to be melded together to move forward?—but Rey clung like a limpet. "And yet you were sure we could stay together forever. Forsaking all others. That was the rule, as I recollect."

"You proved me wrong."

"Maybe *I* was wrong."

Cris shook his head. "No. You were right. For you. I still believe it's possible to be in a committed monogamous relationship. Straight guys do it all the time. I refuse to believe being gay means being sexually promiscuous."

"I never said that."

"Yeah, you did. You said monogamy was an unrealistic expectation for an adult, sexually active male."

The wind rifled through the treetops, throwing silver shadows over Rey's face. He bit his lip as though he was in pain.

"Why don't you wait here and let me get help? It's not that far to this cottage or whatever the hell it is."

"No." Rey's arm tightened. "This night is too fucking weird. We need to stick together."

Cris laughed. "What do you think could happen here in what's technically Angelo Faust's front yard?"

"It's just wrong," Rey said stubbornly. "Your car going dead. That tree coming down. Lights out here in the middle of nowhere. It's all wrong. At the least, you have to admit it's very weird."

"Maybe you should stop watching all those scary movies."

"Funny." Rey took another hobbling step. "Come on."

Cris shifted his arm to better support Rey's weight and they shuffled on.

As they drew closer Cris could make out the yellow light shining from behind diamond-paned windows. A gold and red sign hung above a rustic-looking door. *Sweets to the Sweet.*

"It's a shop," Cris said in disbelief, stopping short. "It's the candy store."

"It looks like they're open."

"But…how can there be a shop here?"

"We must have wandered off Angelo's property."

That wasn't possible. Cris opened his mouth to object, but Rey had let go of him and was hobbling to the front door.

Surely it would be closed. But even as Cris's thought took form, Rey was pulling the door open.

He held it for Cris.

Had he hit his head? Was he unconscious and dreaming? Because this was…nuts.

Hesitantly, Cris walked forward, stepped past Rey into the shop and registered the lush and complicated aura of chocolate. His eyes widened even before he saw the cases and shelves. That smell was more than fragrance, it was atmosphere, it was ambiance, it was…alive.

He stared at the glass cases, at the trays of gorgeous, handcrafted candies. He remembered that he hadn't had dinner and that he'd drunk more lunch than he'd eaten. Maybe that explained—

"Whoa." Rey's comment sounded heartfelt.

"What is this place?"

"Sweets to the Sweet." Rey was studying one of the black and gold boxes.

"But it's like something from…I don't know…Hansel and Gretel?"

Rey grinned. He called out, "Anyone here? Hello?"

"Don't say that!"

"What?"

"It's the equivalent of *Who's There?* and that's fatal."

Rey laughed. "Don't worry. I'll stay out of the basement."

"Shh. Wait." Cris's hand closed on Rey's arm. "I'm not kidding. There's something—"

The lights went out.

The last image Cris had was Rey frowning as he turned. Cris's breath caught raggedly.

He felt the breeze as the door behind them, still standing open to the night, suddenly flew forward and slammed shut with a force that shook the small building.

For a strange wracked instant, Cris wondered if he was going to suffer some kind of psychotic break, just completely short out in a surge of pure, unadulterated panic. He must have made some naked sound. Rey's arms locked around him, held him tight. His voice was warm and definite against Cris's ear.

"Don't. Don't, Cris. I won't let anything hurt you. I swear it."

It was like missing a step, only to have a hand reach out of the darkness and save you from a headfirst tumble. The solid relief of it was far greater than the shame of giving into animal fear. He hung on to Rey.

The door behind them swung open again and leaves swirled inside on a blast of wind.

"What *are* you doing?" inquired a light, male voice.

Vaguely, Cris was aware that Rey had stepped in front of him, partially blocking him from the newcomer.

The overhead light flashed on. A young man with long dark hair stood in the doorway, keys in hands. "You're going to have to find some other place for *that* sort of thing. We're closed. I was just locking up."

His voice was a very pleasant voice, but the bright light reflecting off the windows and glass cases made it difficult to get a clear view of his face. Cris could see that he wore jeans and a leather jacket, that his hair was long and dark, but beyond that he had only an impression of shining eyes and a pale face.

"We didn't realize anyone was still here. Could we use your phone?" Rey asked. "Our car broke down."

That was certainly easier—and a lot more believable—than explaining what had actually happened.

The young man said, "Sorry. This windstorm must have knocked a couple of phone lines down. My phone's been out all evening. Can I drop you somewhere?"

"You can't get out through the gate," Cris told him. "One of the old oaks came down. It's blocking the road."

"I go out through the back."

Cris and Rey exchanged uncertain looks. "Could you drop us off at the main house?" Rey asked.

"Sure. Why not? My car's just around the back." He gestured for them to follow. They stepped outside, waiting while he turned out the lights once more and locked the front door. "My name's Chance, by the way."

"Rey," Rey said. "This is Cris."

"Hi, Rey. Hi, Cris." Chance gestured for them to follow. "This way."

"You're really out in the middle of nowhere," Cris commented as they rounded the small stone building and spotted Chance's black VW. "Do you get a lot of business?"

"I always get a lot of business." Chance opened the VW door. "Just squeeze in the back there, Cris. Rey, you can ride shotgun."

Four

"How's Angelo?" Chance inquired as the VW whipped through the obstacle course of trees and shrubs. "I need to pay him a visit, but things keep cropping up."

Cris's head grazed the ceiling of the car as they bounced over a rut. He unstuck his eyelashes, saw gleaming red eyes captured in the crazily sliding headlights, and squinched his own shut again. He was vaguely aware that he was clutching Rey's shoulder with his right hand, but he didn't care. He didn't even care when Rey gave his hand a reassuring pat.

"Is there a road through here?" Rey was asking doubtfully.

"Of course." Chance spun the steering wheel and they hurtled around a giant oak. "There's always a road. You just have to look for it. Oops. Sorry about that."

Cris fell against the side of the car interior, righted himself, and cautiously opened his eyes again. There was a scrap of paper attached to the visor over Chance's head. Despite the darkness of the car's interior, he thought he could almost make out the words.

Chance said, "If you limit your choices to only what seems possible or reasonable, you disconnect yourself from what you truly want, and all that is left is compromise."

"What?" asked Rey, tearing his gaze from the wall of trees rising before them.

"Cris was trying to read my quote of the day." Both Rey and Cris gasped as Chance's hand left the wheel so that he could point up at the paper pinned to his visor.

The VW bounced as it left the grass and hit the paved drive. Cris's head bonked the ceiling again. Rey threw him a quick look.

They sped on up the road unfurling like black smoke before them.

"Quite a storm," Rey said, apparently feeling some conversation was required.

"I've seen worse. How about you, Cris?"

"Yes."

"Here we go." Chance said cheerfully as the VW tore into the lower courtyard. He circled twice as though seeking the exact right parking place and jerked to a halt. "Safe and sound."

Rey got out of the car, and pulled the seat forward for Cris, who unfolded painfully. "Are you coming in?"

"Not tonight," Chance said. "But give Angelo my best."

Cris looked back over the slanted seat, but all he could see was Chance's Cheshire grin.

"Thanks for the ride." He could hardly believe they were standing there in one piece. His legs felt weak with the relief of being on solid ground once more.

"Not at all. Sweet dreams!"

The VW was in motion even before Cris pushed the door shut.

"And I thought the night was weird before," Rey said as the VW's buzz died away into the night. "If I didn't know better—"

"I'd say Angelo spiked our soup with hallucinogens."

Rey laughed. "Something like that."

"You're not limping," Cris observed as they headed for the stairs.

Rey misstepped. "Yeah. Well, my ankle's a lot better now. I must have just strained it."

Cris stopped walking. "Wait a minute."

Rey stopped too.

"Were you *faking*?"

"I…yeah. I was."

Cris's jaw sagged. "Are you fucking *kidding* me?"

"Er…no."

"*Rey.*"

"I know." Rey's face was apologetic. "Sorry."

"Sorry? That's so…so *childish*."

"It was. I know. Too many bad movies."

Cris scraped the windblown hair from his eyes. "Why? Why would you pretend to sprain your ankle? My God, it took us twice as long to walk up that hill."

Rey said shortly, "You know why."

"Oh come *on*."

Rey's face was set in stubborn lines. "I miss you. I miss you all the time. Is that so hard to believe?"

Cris missed Rey too, but he didn't want a part time lover. And he didn't want to be with someone he couldn't trust.

"It isn't hard to believe," he said quietly. "But it's beside the point."

Even in the moonlight he could see how that hit Rey, and he had to look away.

In silence they went up the flagstone steps and rang the doorbell. The ghostly moans echoed through the house.

No one came to the door.

"Do you think Angelo's in bed?"

Rey rang the bell again. "The entire staff can't be in bed. Besides, the lights are still on."

Cris winced at the macabre cries reverberating off the stones of the portico. At last, lights came on from old-fashioned sconces. The iron scrollwork doors opened.

Neat stood before them, weaving slightly. His hair stood up in tufts and he was wearing a dressing gown and slippers

As though on cue, one of the small decorative gargoyles slithered from the roof over the walkway, knocking its way down the tiles to fall in front of them with a dusty thud.

Neat peered nearsightedly down at the broken gargoyle and then looked at them.

"What are you doing back here?"

"Sorry to wake you. Our car broke down," Rey said.

Cris couldn't stop looking at the broken statuary. If that thing had landed on one of their heads, the unlucky guy would have been brained….

"Why hello there!" Angelo appeared behind Neat. He was also in dressing gown—embroidered black silk in his case—and leather slippers. "The party's not over after all!"

He sounded three sheets to the wind, in Cris's opinion. Not that there was anything wrong with that in the privacy of his own home, but he was a little startled when Angelo slung his arm around Neat's shoulders and smirked at them.

Rey launched into an explanation of their adventures, but Angelo waved this away, beckoning widely them to follow.

Rey looked at Cris. Cris shrugged.

They followed Neat and Angelo as they wove their way downstairs to a beautifully appointed wine cellar. A large wooden table sat in the middle of the room. On it were several open bottles of wine. The table was set for two with bread and cheese and olives and meat.

"We were just having a little snack," Angelo informed them. It came out more like *werejushhavinglilshnack*.

Neat eyed him, then wearily pointed to a sideboard. "Get yourself plates and glasses."

They moved to obey. Cris could see this whole scenario was tickling Rey's sense of humor. It *was* funny now that they were back to the relative safety of Angelo's house of horrors. He wouldn't have wanted to be on his own, though. Suddenly Cris remembered that terrifying moment in the candy store when reality had seemed to snap. Rey's arms had fastened around him and for an instant Rey had seemed to be the only thing tethering him to sanity.

He glanced at Rey and Rey, feeling his gaze, looked back and smiled. Warmth washed through Cris. Yeah, it was embarrassing to have come so noticeably unglued over a little windstorm, but it had meant a lot that Rey had been there for him—and that he didn't think any the worse of Cris for his meltdown.

He remembered too when the door had flown open and Rey had stepped in front of him. Rey hadn't known what was on the other side of that door—and he hadn't cared.

Cris carried his plate to the table and sat down. All at once he was starving.

In the end, the evening was one of the best that Cris could remember in a very long time. Angelo reminisced and told a number of funny stories—

especially funny given how much wine they were drinking—and boozily confided to Cris that he'd enjoyed his book and was sorry he hadn't cooperated. Even Neat, who turned out—among other things—to have been Angelo's private secretary for most of his career, had a number of dryly entertaining tales about their travels.

Every time Cris looked across the table, Rey seemed to be looking his way, smiling, sharing a private joke with him.

Finally Angelo invited them to spend the night and call for a tow truck in the morning when the phone lines were back up. Neat briefly disappeared and then returned to escort them to their rooms.

"No one can hear you scream," Neat informed Cris after Rey had closed the door of his room.

"What?" Cris stared.

Neat looked at him like he was losing it. "Your. Room. Is. In. This. Wing." He clearly enunciated each and every word.

"Oh."

Neat led him a short way down the hall and pushed open the door to a room furnished in dark wood and shades of blue and gray. "Good. Night," he said with that same exaggerated care.

"Deep screams," Cris bade him.

Neat smiled primly and closed the door.

Alone, Cris stood for a moment listening to the wind outside. He went to the window and looked down. Carefully placed spotlights illumined cypress trees and a Grecian-styled swimming pool. He watched the silvery water ripple in the wind for a few moments, before turning away.

He turned out the light, undressed, and climbed into the large and surprisingly comfortable bed. The sheets smelled freshly laundered

Despite his fatigue, his brain kept turning over the events of the evening. He couldn't tune out the knowledge that Rey was just a couple of doors down the hall. It was hard to believe that Rey, who couldn't help jumping everything in pants and claimed he still had feelings for Cris, wouldn't make some move.

Cris considered this idea irritably and realized that at least part of his irritation was that Rey had given no indication that he had any such idea.

He remembered again that strange moment—was there a moment that hadn't been strange?—in the candy shop when Rey had instinctively moved to protect him.

Of course there hadn't been any danger, and Rey had probably realized that before Cris—

He stopped himself. Why was it so important to try and convince himself that the gesture had meant nothing? That Rey's feelings for him meant nothing? Rey had his faults, but he wasn't shallow and he wasn't cowardly.

Cris stared moodily up at the shadowy outline of the molding. He could feel a draft from the window across the room, the wind still whispering to him, telling him he would always be alone.

He closed his eyes. He didn't want to think about any of this, didn't want to start remembering. Where had he read that the nervous reflex of worrisome thoughts before sleep had been conditioned into man's Stone Age brain to keep him from falling too deeply and dangerously asleep?

That's all this was. His unconscious effort to keep a T. rex from having him for a midnight snack.

And yet here he was, once again remembering the night his mother died. He'd been nine. The woman from upstairs had been staying with him. Funny he couldn't recall her name, because she was the one who usually babysat for him when his mom worked late. His father had taken off when he was three. Cris had only the vaguest memories of him. He wasn't even sure whether they were true memories, or stuff he'd made up to comfort himself. It had been just him and his mom for as long as he could remember.

That night he had been waiting up to show her a clay dish he'd made at school. What had ever happened to that little dish? Lost in the aftermath, probably. He had waited and waited, but she never came. It was a cold, windy November night, and to the day he died, he would never forget the melancholy jangle of the chimes blowing on their little porch.

Finally the police had come and told them, Cris and the lady whose name he could never remember, that there had been an accident and his mother was dead.

That was all. Worse things happened to people. He had gone into foster care. It wasn't that bad. No one had hurt him. But no one had loved him. He had not come first for anyone. No one had fought to keep him when he was moved to other homes and other families. For a long time he had reassured himself that none of it mattered because his father would come for him. Once his father knew what had happened, he would come for him....

But his father had never come. He'd never heard from his father at all. Maybe his father had never known. Maybe he had known but hadn't cared. It was hard to say which scenario hurt more, but in the end it didn't matter. In the end it was all the same.

It had gotten a lot better once he was an adult and on his own. Being alone wasn't nearly as lonely as being with people who didn't love you. And for a time he had thought maybe he would find someone of his own to love, but somehow it just never quite worked out.

Until Rey.

And it turned out Rey couldn't be happy with just Cris.

But Rey did still care for him, was willing to step in front of a T. rex for him....

Cris jerked back to alertness. He realized he had been on the verge of falling asleep. He'd heard something. What? The draft from the window stirred the draperies, moved the door in its frame. He raised his head, listening.

Not the wind. Someone was tapping at his bedroom door. He threw back the covers and went to the door.

Rey stood in the hallway. He was still dressed. "Hey."

Cris, standing in his underwear, blinked at him. "Uh, hey."

"Can I come in?"

Well, this was certainly predictable. "Rey...."

"I didn't come here for sex."

"I should hope not. Sex is a death sentence in horror movies." The truly irrational thing was Cris actually felt a twinge of disappointment. About the sex, not the death sentence.

"You know, we're not actually in a horror movie."

"After the night we've had, I'm not so sure. Why *are* you here?"

Rey flicked him a funny, self-conscious look. "Because. Because you have trouble sleeping in strange beds, and because it's a windy night and you hate the wind."

True. All of it true. It touched him. It was probably meant to—he knew firsthand how very good at seduction Rey was—but…it was effective, nonetheless.

He said more sturdily than he felt, "Thanks. I'm okay though."

A glimmer of Rey's charming grin. "Okay, then you can protect me."

Cris rolled his eyes, started to shut the door, but Rey stepped forward, slipping his arms around him, halting Cris's automatic retreat.

It felt good to be in his arms again. Too good. Cris said dryly, "That's more like it."

He felt Rey's quick shake of denial. "No. Not fair. I meant what I said. It's not like I don't know the difference between love and sex."

Cris opened his mouth, but then he let it go.

"Come on. It's freezing," Rey coaxed. Cris sighed and led the way.

Bedside, Rey paused. "Okay if I take my jeans off to sleep?"

"Whatever." Right on cue.

Rey dropped his jeans and they climbed into the bed, sheets still warm. Rey stretched out. He put his arm out and Cris moved next to him, resting his head on Rey's shoulder.

Rey said, "This feels right."

Cris sighed again, but not as loudly as before.

"I've missed you."

You already said that. But Cris stopped himself. Why shouldn't Rey say it again? It was what Cris was thinking too.

Rey touched his hair lightly. It felt good. It felt familiar. "You can relax. I'm not going to do anything you don't want."

Cris grunted, but he was quietly processing. Rey had a partial erection that he was politely doing his best to avoid imposing on Cris's crotch, and he was confining his caresses to Cris's hair. That was certainly different.

After a couple of peaceful minutes, Rey's fingers stilled. He leaned over and kissed Cris's temple.

"Good night."

Cris said at last, "'night."

He could feel Rey's body relaxing, growing heavy against him. Lying here like this brought back a lot of memories, good memories of nights when they'd lain awake talking till dawn. The sex had been good too, the best, but it had been the companionship Cris longed for most.

For the first time he considered his own part in their breakup. Had he been too emotionally needy? He wasn't sure. Rey had never come right out and said it, but now Cris wondered. He'd recognized the depth of his feelings for Rey right away and he'd started pushing for commitment.

Maybe it was growing up in foster care. Maybe he *had* pushed too hard and too fast for security, stability.

That still didn't excuse what Rey had done. He could have just talked to Cris. Told him he was pushing too hard.

Right?

"Okay?" Rey sounded half-asleep.

Cris nodded. He blinked uncertainly into the darkness.

Apparently they *were* simply going to go to sleep.

Five

The room seemed gilded. Lovely, flickering autumn gold. It danced over the polished furniture and turned even the dust motes to something magical.

Sunrise. Ah, the traditional end of a horror film signifying the return to the natural order of things.

Cris smiled faintly. He turned his head. In sleep, Rey's face was relaxed and young as it never was when he was awake. His erection was prodding Cris's hip, but it didn't bother Cris. He'd had a night of surprisingly pleasurable dreams—most of them featuring Rey.

In fact, he gave a gentle push of his hips.

Rey's eyelashes flickered.

Cris gave him another nudge. His own body had been up and awake for some time. He leaned in, turned Rey's bristly cheek his way and kissed him deeply, thoroughly. Rey's arms came around his shoulders, his hands rubbing the muscles of Cris's back, kneading his spine as their tongues met. Cris murmured, surprised at the pleasure it gave to taste Rey again. He arched back into the willing and ready arms.

They kissed again, deeply, wetly. Cris's fingers twined in Rey's hair, Rey's hands brushed lightly down to cup Cris's buttocks and pull him closer.

Cris nodded encouragingly, just in case there was any doubt that he was fully vested in this. He liked the feel of Rey's smooth, flat chest against his own. Running his hands over Rey's muscled back, he slipped his tongue between warm parted lips. Rey responded with tightened arms, his mouth working hungrily against Cris's.

Rey stroked one hand down Cris's flank, then slipped his hand between them, curving his palm around Cris's cock. Cris murmured huskily and pushed forward into the warm grip. "Yeah, I want it…that feels…." His own hands grew more restless, more urgent. He found Rey and did his best to reciprocate. It was awkward with hands bumping against hands, and hard to concentrate when Rey was touching him just the way he liked, giving him just the right amount of pressure at just the right speed.

He thrust hard into the slick tunnel of hands Rey made for him. Beneath his own frantic, quick breaths he could hear Rey's choked moan, and he tightened his hold, trying to give at least a fraction of the pleasure he was getting. His hands pumped Rey's stiff cock faster, their voices blurring together.

And there it was. That hot, sweet release like no other, spurting between Rey's fingers, and Rey coming a few heartbeats after….

※ ※ ※

CRIS LEFT THE steamy bathroom. He picked his Levi's up, shook them briskly, and pulled them on. Finding his cell phone, he checked for the signal. Beauty.

He glanced over at Rey, still lying on his side, sheet modestly draped over his hip. Rey was frowning.

"The bathroom's all yours."

"Jesus. Can't you take a minute to…."

Cris stopped. "To what?"

"To talk."

"About?"

Rey's frown deepened. "There isn't anyone else, is there?"

Cris stared at him.

"You wouldn't have made love—"

Cris's brows arched. "Made *love*?"

Rey stared.

"It was just sex. And I quote."

Rey whitened. "You don't mean that."

"Why wouldn't I mean it? That's your philosophy, isn't it?"

Rey sat up. "Why are you doing this?" The pain on his face was too real, too raw to ignore. It drained Cris's resolve.

He sat down on the edge of the bed. "I'm not…I'm trying to be a realist."

"I don't want you to be a realist. I want you to be you."

Cris laughed. "Great. Thanks." He shook his head—mostly at himself.

Rey covered his hand with his own. "What do you want?"

Cris felt the warm strength of the fingers laced with his own. He tried to imagine freeing himself, telling Rey that this morning had truly been the last time, that they would never hold each other again, never kiss again. "I want the last six months never to have happened. I want the thing with Terry never to have happened."

"The thing with Terry meant nothing."

"It meant something to me."

"I know." Rey grimaced. "I screwed up. I can't turn back the clock, but I promise you I'll never screw up again. At least…I'll never screw up that way again. I may screw up other ways."

"Rey, you know me well enough to know I *can't*—"

"Listen to me. I want to be with you. I want that more than anything. Everything happened so fast between us we never really discussed our expectations until we were already moving in together. When I realized you believed that we'd be exclusive—"

Cris tried to free his hand. "What did you think moving in together meant?"

"I don't know. I just wanted to be with you all the time. I *should* have realized before, I know, but I wasn't thinking that far ahead. It wasn't even that I *wanted* to be with someone else. I wouldn't have moved in with you if that was the case. But knowing that I couldn't, that that part of my life was over… it's like deciding to give up smoking. All you do is think about cigarettes."

"Yeah, I get it. I got it six months ago. You weren't ready to give up that part of your life."

"But I was. That's the thing, Cris. I *was* ready. My head had to catch up with my heart, that's all."

"Which head was that? Because—"

"I'm serious."

Cris sighed. "Why didn't you tell me? Why didn't you talk to me? Why did you have to do that? And then let me find…." His voice gave out. Six months later it still hurt enough to knock the wind out of him.

"I don't know," Rey said. "It was stupid and gutless. I knew if I even suggested an open relationship, you'd be packing your bags."

Cris didn't deny it. "You still should have told me."

Rey's mouth twisted. "The truth? If I'd told you what I was feeling maybe you would've decided you had a right to screw around too. I couldn't take that."

Cris's laugh was short. "Well that's honest. Twisted. But honest." He didn't want to know the answer but he had to ask. "How many times was it? How many times did you cheat on me?"

Shamefaced, Rey said, "Just the once. I swear to God. I didn't go looking for it. Terry was coming on to me all the time."

"But you struggled madly? Yeah, I've seen that movie."

"Listen. Even if it doesn't change anything for you, let me say it. I owe you this much."

Cris pulled his hand free and that time Rey let him. "Interesting way of looking at it. You owe me the chance of forcing me to listen to you spill your guts so you can clear your conscience."

"That's not what I mean. It's not an excuse. It's an explanation. Terry was offering and I figured maybe I'd get it out of my system."

Cris nodded. "How'd that work out for you?"

"You know how it worked out. Terry decided we were starting an affair and before I could get rid of him, you found out about the afternoon at the beach house."

"That's the way I remember it too. Glad we cleared that up."

"I fucked up."

"Literally."

"But I've learned from that. I'm not saying it was a good thing, but maybe it was a necessary thing. It helped me understand that it's you I love and that what we had was real and it was meant to last."

"It didn't."

"It should have. It still could. I want you back, Cris. And I think, as angry and as hurt as you are, you still love me too."

The lie would have taken more energy than Cris possessed. He stared, silent, ahead.

Rey put his arm around Cris's shoulders. "You know what? You're telling me everything you're afraid of. What do you *want*?"

Cris was silent. Everything he was afraid of was the same thing. That Rey would fuck up again and break his heart. He wasn't sure he could survive being hurt that much twice. As for what he wanted? He wanted safety, security, commitment. And he wanted Rey. And he wasn't sure those things were mutually compatible. Rey without safety, security, commitment was a frightening proposition. But safety, security, and commitment without Rey would be like being buried alive. He might as well be one of the statues in The Alabaster Corpse.

"I love you," Rey said. "I'm not perfect, but I'll always be here for you."

Studying Rey's face, the sincerity there, Cris remembered his thoughts before sleep the night before. Remembered that Rey had braved monsters for him and held him safe against bad dreams. Rey loved him. No, he wasn't perfect, and perhaps they would hurt each other again, but he believed Rey when he said he would be there for him.

It was as much as anyone could hope for. Life was not a movie after all.

He took a deep breath. "I want…us to try again."

Rey's arms locked around him. His kiss was sweet.

❃ ❃ ❃

Angelo was at breakfast when they went downstairs to say goodbye. He was reading the paper and holding his coffee cup up to Neat to refill.

Both men stared as Cris and Rey walked in.

"The tow truck is on its way," Rey said. "We thought we'd—"

"What the hell?" Angelo stared and then turned to Neat. "I thought they left last night?"

Neat shrugged. He finished filling Angelo's coffee cup.

"Well," Angelo said. "Nice to see you again, of course. You said something about a tow truck?"

"The Auto Club is on the way. Cris's car broke down last night and my…" Rey stopped. "I'll call you later," he finished.

"Of course. I'll look forward to it." Angelo waved them off vaguely.

"I'm telling you," Cris said as they headed for the vast center hall with its three tall archways, "this was the weirdest—"

"Tell me over breakfast," Rey said. "We've got plans to make." His gaze slid to meet Cris's. Cris smiled back, but his smile faded.

He stopped.

"What's wrong?" Rey asked, stopping too.

"Oh no."

"What? What is it?"

"You don't think this is one of those *it was all a dream* endings, do you?"

About Critic's Choice

One thing I have little patience with are romances where the conflict is all based on some big misunderstanding or an artificial issue two intelligent people could resolve in about five minutes of honest dialog. My characters usually screw up big time and then the challenge is to see how they might realistically resolve those problems. I believe sincerely in the power of love—and that being able to forgive is one of the best gifts you can give yourself.

In Critic's Choice, Cris still loves Rey, but he's been badly hurt and the idea of taking another chance on love is more frightening than having to watch an all-day Godzilla marathon.

WISHINK WELL
Jordan Castillo Price

Chance's fingers drifted to his throat. His red bandanna was gone. Strange…he hadn't realized he'd grown so enamored of it.

His shop was gone, too. No subtlety whatsoever. There one minute, gone the next. The Fates must have been in quite a hurry. The thought of them scrambling, breathless and frantic, to fling everything into place for his next task—that notion pleased him. He smiled to himself.

The hall in which he now stood was plain. A hint of disinfectant that was supposed to smell like something pleasant, but didn't, lingered. A bank of vending machines spanned the wall. On the corner of the plexi that covered the front of the nearest machine, a gold sticker read:

Sweets to the Sweet Vending Co.
Comments? Complaints?
Call 1-888-CHOKLAT

Cute.

Chance supposed it explained the hand truck stacked with boxes in front of him, and the butch work clothes—black, of course, with his name embroidered in red over the place his heart would have been. English, like the sticker. American, to be precise, judging by the toll-free number. He ran a hand through his hair. It was long enough in front to tuck behind his ear, short in back. Then he peered down at his shoes: steel-toed work boots. Terribly butch, indeed.

While the hall was empty, for the moment at least, the sounds of humanity were close. Voices, a television, a phone ringing. Chance opened his senses. The place felt good. It felt right.

Which was more than he could say for most places.

He tore open the top box, and the smell of cheap, commercial chocolate momentarily blocked the scent of chlorine and phenols. As he stared into the box, a couple rounded the corner—no one he needed to concern himself with. They stepped around him like he was invisible, and fed some quarters into a nearby vending machine. The machine whirred and clunked, a cup dropped into place, then syrup mixed with hot water and sprayed into the cup. Chance saw the workings of it as it went through its motions. It made him miss his espresso machine, all steam and bombast.

Ridiculous. He unlocked the machine directly in front of him and began stocking the plastic-wrapped cupcakes with sure, economical movements, and he told himself that sentimental nonsense about the espresso machine was unacceptable. He was perfectly at ease here in this—what was it, a clinic? A hospital? He didn't *miss* the shop.

"It's nice here," the woman said to the man as he waited for the spout to stop dripping. Accent? Midwest. Ohio, maybe. Michigan. The flat, nasal A and hard R danced at the edge of Chance's tongue, should he need to speak. "Homey," the woman went on. "And the staff is so nice." The man nodded. If he answered her, Chance saw, he would cry. Once his cup was ready, they stepped around Chance again, blowing on their coffees, and disappeared around a corner.

The gluttony, the dirty, secret pleasure, the want, the need. Missing those things from the shop was understandable. Wherever he was now, though…it reminded him of other things he missed, too. The weight of human mortality settling around his shoulders was comforting, like the embrace of an old lover whose leaving would always be a mystery. He'd enjoyed his old vocation. He'd been good at it. And yet….

He squeezed a pair of plastic-wrapped cupcakes packaged side by side on a cardboard strip. They sprang back into shape the moment he released the pressure.

One didn't want to become stale.

It had been a long time. He'd come a long way. Farther than he would have ever thought possible. So many people, so many pleading faces, all of them yearning for one simple thing. Love.

The tempered glass had gone opaque. Frost rimed the interior of the vending machine, sparkling on the crimped edges of the plastic packaging. Chance wondered how long he'd been lost in his thoughts. If anyone had come or gone while he'd been wandering down memory lane, he hadn't noticed them, nor they him.

They weren't The One.

Since the cases were refrigerated, it took quite a while for the glass on the first machine to clear. Traffic in the hallway was not exactly bustling. Chance began to work more slowly. With his shop, it was at least more obvious what he was supposed to do—tend the counter. If The One didn't show up, eventually Chance would lock the door and make candy. The next day, he'd do it again. Sometimes The One showed up within a day, or a week—then again, it might take months. But surely it would only take so long to re-stock the vending machines. And then what?

⁂ ⁂ ⁂

Blip. Blip. Blip. Blip. Blip. Beeeeee….

Eddie glanced at his heart monitor. Funny, he didn't feel dead. He'd always imagined halos and wings and a chorus of harps. Or maybe a long tunnel with a light at the end.

A couple of months ago, once the laundry lists of diagnoses had begun, he'd tried to shape his vision of the great hereafter into something a bit more exciting. Men with washboard abs, tanned skin glistening under the sun as they mopped their brows with the T-shirts they'd just peeled off. Doing some sort of non-specific construction work, he supposed, although why they would need hot, gay builders when St. Peter could just wave his hand and make it so, Eddie hadn't quite worked out.

…eeeeeeeee…

If there even was a heaven. Eddie wasn't exactly sure, because his boon pal Leah always said he was made of "source," and that he and everyone else were all "source" having experiences, and when his experience was over, he would be re-absorbed into the energy that was everyone, and everything. Conceptually, it intrigued him, but the thought that Eddie Flynn's thirty-eight years of life on the planet would add up to the same shapeless, formless energy as everyone else's—including the bacteria who died their quiet deaths every time the cleaning crew hit them with Lysol—made him feel melancholy, and preemptively disappointed.

...eeeeeeee...

A face poked around Eddie's doorjamb. Travaughn, his day nurse. Travaughn looked more like a gang-banger than a nurse. Whenever his sleeves rode up, Eddie couldn't help but ogle the do-it-yourself ink, indigo against brown skin, and wonder what all the blotches and symbols were supposed to mean. Probably nothing good, given that Travaughn had ended up with the spooked look of someone who'd seen more death than even a hospice nurse was supposed to.

...eeeeeeee...

"Sorry, man. We had a power surge. Knocks everything all crazy." Travaughn leaned across Eddie's bed railing and turned off the monitor.

...eep.

Eddie took the clip off his forefinger and set it on the tray beside his untouched tapioca pudding. He felt too hot to do dairy. Especially tapioca. He'd never been clear on what that stuff actually was.

"You been up for your walk today?"

Eddie would have sighed, except that it hurt to sigh.

Travaughn looked him over. "You makin' that face that say no."

Eddie almost did sigh. And then he almost coughed—and coughing was the worst, because even though the doctors said the shunt in his right lung was nowhere near any nerves he should be able to feel, he swore that when he coughed, he could feel it stabbing him, tearing his lungs up from the inside. "Can't I just lie here and listen to the chorus of a half-dozen heart monitors malfunctioning?"

"You could…but you'd feel better if you get yo' ass outta that bed and walk."

Eddie loved Travaughn. He wouldn't say as much—undoubtedly it would just be awkward. Travaughn: straight, black, alive…Eddie: gay, white, and barely.

Travaughn said, "I'll come get you once I let everyone know what's happening."

Eddie pushed down his bed rail and swung his feet over the side of the mattress. His slippers felt cool, for a moment. And then, like everything else his fevered body touched, they warmed. "No, s'okay. I'm good to walk."

Pop would hit the spot. Either he could drink the thing—no need to worry about the dangers of high fructose corn syrup anymore—or he could roll the can around on his body, at least until it grew as warm as everything else he touched.

Travaughn pulled the I.V. stand around so Eddie could use it to steady himself, and when it seemed that all systems were go, left to help the other patients discover that they were not yet dead, either.

Walking. Such a pain in the ass. Yes, he knew he would feel better afterward—even though it was looking like the COPD or one of its many complications would finish him before bedsores set in. But walking meant breathing, and breathing meant that little fucking shunt tearing him up from the inside out.

Minor commotion in one of the rooms. Evidently they'd taken the heart monitor's word over the evidence of their own two eyes. Maybe. Or maybe someone had actually died. The first time it had happened, Eddie freaked out—quietly, to himself, without a lot of heavy breathing. But after the second or third, he'd come to terms with the fact that dying was what people came here to do, so being a drama queen about it would get old, fast.

Eddie walked to the end of the hall, turned, and made his way through the double doors that led to the public areas. The sound of the few heart monitors still bleating silenced as the doors swung shut behind him. Lights clacked on overhead, one by one, activated by an energy-saving motion detector, and a gentle fluorescent tube buzz filled the newborn silence. Eddie turned another corner.

Hel-lo.

Too bad his heart monitor wasn't on, because the guy filling the vending machine looked suspiciously like the last gasps of a dying brain, and the reality check would have been welcome. Because if it was all a wish-fulfillment fantasy, Eddie would have liked to take a big, deep breath. Shout, sigh, wolf-whistle. All of the above.

Pain, however, had made Eddie more cautious, as pain tends to do. He took a careful breath. It hurt.

Too bad. Eddie had been hoping it might be a fantasy. Because then some music would have piped in, the hot vending machine guy would have turned toward him, grinding his hips, and the strip show would begin. Instead, the guy glanced at the ingredients on a candy bar wrapper, shook his head in disgust, and stuffed the candy into the corkscrew-shaped dispenser.

It wasn't that Eddie thought he could cruise someone in hospice—especially given his 15% lung capacity. More that old habits died hard. And that maybe it was beneficial to check someone out—like walking. He didn't technically need to do it. But it did feel good.

Suddenly the I.V. was an embarrassment, like maybe he should have hung a few jackets and a hat on it and pretended he just happened to be leaning against a coat tree. But the vending machine guy hadn't noticed the clack of the wheels against the tile, nor had he acknowledged Eddie's approach.

Probably for the best. After all, with his arm tubed to the I.V. with a six-inch midline catheter, it wasn't as if any sort of fantasy, however brief, could come to fruition. He couldn't act as if he was there visiting a dying friend because he was such a great guy. He couldn't pretend he was skinny because he liked the way it made his ironic T-shirts hang. And seeing the look on the vending machine guy's face once he got a load of the I.V. would not likely be something Eddie wanted to dwell on.

Eddie fed his quarters into the pop machine and pressed a button. A series of elaborate clunks sounded. A wisp of frosty air escaped the flap on the bottom. But no can.

Great. Now he'd have to talk to the cute vending guy, I.V. or no I.V. "Excuse me."

The guy—"Chance," according to the embroidery on his shirt—turned and locked eyes with Eddie. He didn't look startled. He didn't look dismayed. He didn't look…much of anything. A blank slate. A very pretty blank slate. A blank slate Eddie would have cruised in a heartbeat, if his gaydar bleeping like a heart monitor on the fritz was anything to go by—if not for the damned I.V.

Oh well. He'd settle for a can of pop. "The machine ate my quarters."

Chance considered Eddie's statement with profound gravity, and then he swiveled his gaze onto the offending soda machine as if he expected an explanation from it. His brow furrowed—great eyebrows, wickedly peaked—and then he pulled a slip of paper and pen from his pocket as if he'd only just realized they were there. "Here you are. Fill this out, and the company will send you a refund in four to six weeks."

Eddie couldn't help it. He laughed—and dear God, how it hurt. He held his breath, pressed his eyes shut against the pain, and sagged against the side of the machine. "Are you kidding me? I don't even have four to six *days*."

Chance cocked his head and looked at Eddie again, a soul-deep look that made the hairs on Eddie's forearms stand at attention. "Funny, how that works."

"Funny weird. Not funny ha-ha."

"No. Not really."

"All I want is a Pepsi."

Chance narrowed his eyes. "Why?"

"Don't tell anyone I told you, but if you pull that ring on top, you can get to the fizzy sweet stuff inside and drink it."

Undaunted, Chance eased forward. Eddie stared. If it weren't for the I.V. propping him up, he would have sworn he was getting cruised in return. "What I meant," Chance said, "before you bowled me over with your oh-so-rakish wit, was that I wonder why a Pepsi is *all* you want?"

"Color me a realist. I find it more useful to want things I have some chance of getting." Eddie's gaze dropped to the open vee at the neck of Chance's work shirt. Tendons played under the ivory skin of his throat. He looked profoundly smooth. Eddie wanted to lick him, right there where his top button was open, and feel the sublime smoothness beneath his tongue. He wanted it much more than he wanted a soda. But he was indeed a realist. "Can't you just open up the machine and nudge the can the rest of the way down?"

Chance pushed the pen and paper, both cool to the touch, into Eddie's hand. He turned toward the soda machine and gave it a long, critical once-over, then whacked it on the side. It shuddered and groaned. A Pepsi dropped from the chute. Vapor rose from the aluminum as Chance held it out to Eddie, and white frost spread from the bottom of the can halfway to the rim.

The frost inside the machine must have stopped up the works. But Chance didn't seem keen to investigate.

When Eddie reached for the can, Chance pulled it back and smiled a teasing smile. "Be careful what you wish for. Isn't that what they always say?" Eddie looked deep into Chance's eyes, though he couldn't say for sure exactly what color they might be. "And yet…I'm not so sure I agree. Why is it such a crime to get what you want?"

The can was so cold it hurt Eddie's fingers to touch it when Chance finally held it still enough for him to take it. He wanted the pop, yes. But more than that, he wanted to lean in farther and close that distance to Chance's lips; he wanted to do so even more sharply than he wanted to take a long, deep, pain-free breath. And he'd been wanting to breathe for months. As Eddie hovered on the cusp of initiating the kiss, he agonized about how, and what if, and why even bother when it wasn't as if it could lead to anything…and the pause stretched just a moment too long.

Inside that pause, Chance backed away. He smiled his goodbye, kicked his hand truck back on its wheels, and carted his stack of half-empty cardboard boxes down the hall.

Eddie watched the spot where Chance turned a corner and walked out of sight. He shook his head. The sexy vending machine guy would have kissed him, he realized. A pit of hurt blossomed in his chest that felt something like the shunt in his right lung, but filled more deeply with regret.

TWO

THE PLASTIC BAG sloshed as Eddie tried to figure out where he could position it that it wouldn't hurt. Not only did he feel hot, but he felt hot in the most uncomfortable places. Around his incision and his I.V. shunt; at his feet, forehead, crotch and armpits; and worst of all, deep down inside where no half-melted bag of ice could ever cool him.

"Are you sure I can't bring you another book?" Leah's round face was creased with concern. Eddie hoped that once he was too far gone on morphine, pain, and the whole dying thing, he never came right out and told her that she looked like one of those dried apple-head dolls. Or if he did, that she'd understand.

"I hate reading. I've always hated reading. Why would I suddenly start liking books now?"

"There has to be something from your apartment I can get you—something that would make you smile."

"I dunno." He gazed out the window and wished, for once, he had a view of Hospice House's parking lot. Instead, he saw a lawn dotted with dandelions. "Maybe a different shirt."

Leah brightened. She might be spiritual, but sometimes the best way to bolster the spirit was to care for the body. "Okay, I'll bring you a shirt. A certain one?"

"Yeah, it's ah…I got it in New Orleans. Kinda trendy, some blues, some greens, dark…." Something he looked really good in, that he wore only on special occasions, like when he really wanted to wow a first date.

"You got it, kiddo. A shirt."

"And some shoes. I'm tired of wearing slippers."

Leah grabbed a pen from the nightstand and handed it to Eddie, along with a paper napkin. "Write it down for me. The trendy blue and green shirt you got in New Orleans, and which shoes?"

Eddie considered the pen. Most pens had white plastic barrels and the logo of some business or another on them. This one was plain, shiny and black. It was the vending machine guy's pen. Chance. Eddie tapped it against his lips as if he needed to think about how to write up his favorite shirt, and gave it a surreptitious sniff. Not too deep, though, since he could only inhale so far.

It smelled like any other pen—plastic and ink. But you couldn't blame a guy for trying.

"I think I feel like wearing my Doc Martens."

"How will I recognize those?"

"There's a tag at the heel that says *Doc Martens*."

Leah stood and crossed the room to his dresser. "If only everything in life were that simple."

Eddie pulled off the pen cap. A fountain pen? He wasn't even sure he knew how to write with one. He tried a few strokes on the napkin. At first, the ink didn't flow. Eddie rested the napkin on the sidebar of his bed and scribbled. He dug a circular trench into the napkin, bordered by a few whiskery traces of ink. One of the many books Leah had been trying to woo him into the land of reading with rested on his nightstand, something about living in the "Now" that he simply couldn't fathom. He grabbed it and used it to support the napkin while he scribbled the ink into action. Blue-black ink wicked into the torn paper and formed a dark splot. There. He'd gotten some use out of the book.

Under the ink-blob, he wrote *Doc Martens.*

Beneath that, *blue shirt I got in New Orleans.* The napkin absorbed a lot of ink, which made the writing thick and childlike, but it was legible enough.

Eddie considered adding *a life* to his list, but figured it would have been a selfish way to get his kicks at Leah's expense. Leah was one of the only ones who hadn't stopped visiting. Not that he blamed his old friends and lovers and all the combinations thereof. If their situations were reversed, he doubted he would have had the heart for more than one or two visits, either.

Leah opened the dresser drawer and said, "Wait a minute. Are you talking about the shirt you wore to Annie's bachelorette party?" She pulled something from the drawer and held it up. "This one?"

Eddie squinted—though she was only three feet away from him, and he didn't exactly need to bring the leaf-pattered fabric into focus. "Yeah, but…I don't remember bringing it here." He remembered bringing T-shirts, sweatpants and underwear, all that only grudgingly. He'd agreed to enroll in hospice care for one reason, and one reason only: the morphine. At the time, his rationale had been that he was going to spend whatever time he had left rotting in bed, so what else could he possibly need?

And yet, there it was. The trendy shirt that always seemed to end up with a bunch of phone numbers in its pocket.

"It's got creases in it from being folded in that drawer," Leah said. "I'll hang it in your bathroom and let the shower run a few minutes. The steam will straighten it out."

Leah opened the closet door, where several empty plastic hangers clicked together on the pole. She crouched, gathered something from the floor, and turned to face the bed. Her expression was bewildered, but then she forced some brightness into her voice. "These must be the Doc Martens. They have those tags on the heels."

Eddie's stomach knotted as he realized Leah probably thought his mind was going. "Whaddaya know?" His cheer sounded forced, too. "There they are."

"Maybe Jeremy came to visit," she suggested, "and he brought some clothes for you."

"Doubtful. My brother only stops by on Tuesday afternoons." On Tuesday afternoons, Jeremy worked at his company's west side branch, which meant the hospice center was on his way home. On one hand, Eddie resented that convenience even played a role in their final few visits. On the other, at least he didn't have to feel any more guilty about their relationship than he already did.

"Maybe he brought them last Tuesday."

"And I didn't happen to notice them for six whole days?" Eddie regretted the question as soon as it was out of his mouth. Leah would think his mind was starting to go for sure. "Maybe someone was cleaning the room," he said, "and they moved some stuff around. While I was sleeping." He didn't actually believe that—no one had any reason to move his clothes around—but it sounded plausible enough that it would allow them to drop the subject.

Leah worked the knot from the laces of Eddie's left Doc Marten and slipped it on his foot. It looked ridiculous without a sock, and it was a lot looser than it had been the last time he'd worn it. Not just because of the missing sock, either. Even so, the sight of the knobby-toed boot in his bed made him smile. "I wish there was something I could get you," she said.

"There is…one thing."

Leah looked at him with an expectant and anticipatory half-smile on her face.

"Ask when they expect the guy to come and fill the vending machines. I'm dying to find out."

THree

So, Eddie thought. This is what it feels like to be nervous.

It had been a while.

Maybe he was reading into things, but he thought Travaughn seemed pleased to unhook the morphine drip and help him into the trendy shirt. Eddie took the pulse monitor from his forefinger to button the buttons himself. "I think I want to stay unplugged for now," Eddie said. "It gets in the way when I walk."

Travaughn nodded. "You going for a walk? Where at? I'll come check up on you."

"I dunno…."

"You go outside, hate to say it, but them damn mosquitoes will eat you alive."

It had never occurred to Eddie to leave the Hospice Home building. At any point. "No, no, I'll stay inside."

"You going to the lib'ary?"

"Why does everyone suddenly want me to read? No thanks." He pointed at the "Now" book. "I got that covered, should the urge strike."

"Psh. I'm talking about a *good* book. People shooting each other for treasure maps an' shit."

"Maybe later."

"I get it." Travaughn crossed his arms and looked Eddie up and down slyly. "Uh huh, I know why you being so funny."

Eddie breathed very carefully, so as to avoid the lung-jab of his internal shunt. "You do?"

"What's the worst thing that can happen. You have a little fun?"

He could only hope. "I, uh…I guess."

"You better get a move on. They only got five easels, and they fill up fast."

Eddie turned that idea around a few times, then finally admitted, "I have no idea what you're talking about."

"Expressive therapy. The painting class."

"Oh, uh…right. I'll swing by there and check it out." It was on the way to the back hall vending machines, after all.

Eddie did indeed spare a look into the class. Old ladies, mostly, with their blue hair freshly coiffed from the visiting hairdressers. Funny, how some of them looked perfectly fine, like they could be at the park, or the dentist, or the grocery store, while others really did look like they were at death's door. The appearance of imminent death, skin either too taut or sagging, yellowed eyes, brittle nails, those things didn't bother Eddie. The paintings, though. Flowers. Lots and lots of flowers.

Flowers belonged in the ground, not on top of a casket in big, tacky arrangements. He wondered if he'd remembered put a "no flowers" statement in his obituary. He'd have to ask Leah.

All afternoon, Eddie had been so keen on donning his trendy shirt (albeit with black sweatpants instead of jeans, since none of his jeans fit anymore) and presenting himself by the vending machines, that it hadn't occurred to him the hallway would be empty.

Overhead, the fluorescent lights buzzed softly.

Three upholstered chairs—institutional, but attempting to look as if they weren't—hugged the wall beside the pop machine. That was one good thing about Hospice House. Always a chair when you needed one.

Eddie's head spun from a combination of morphine and exertion, and the sickening heat of the infection that refused any and all attempts to clear it out with various courses of antibiotics spread through his chest like a malignant sun. It would probably be the infection that killed him, Eddie thought, even though it had been the advanced COPD—the wreck of his lungs—that had gained him a bed in Hospice House to begin with.

Foregoing the morphine had probably been a bad idea. It hurt now, a dull kind of ache. But that was nothing compared to the pain he'd feel when the current dose wore off completely. Eddie sat, feeling the morphine slowly ebb, stared at the ceiling and wondered how he'd managed to convince himself beyond the shadow of a doubt that fantasy-boy Chance would be there, right there, posing for his ogling convenience the moment he rounded the hallway corner. Maybe it was true: his mind really was starting to go.

The walk back to his room seemed twice as long, and several times he needed to locate the nearest institutional-looking chair and avail himself of its support. All the while, he berated himself for slogging all the way to the back hall without bringing any change for the machine. Because now he was burning up.

The figure, framed in the window by midday brightness, was probably a fever-dream. Or maybe it was actually the end, after all. Eddie stood blinking in the doorway to his bedroom, gathering the reserves to stand up straight, and he squinted against the backlighting. His voice, when he spoke, had only enough breath for a whisper. "Chance?"

The figure turned. "Where were you?" Not Chance. Eddie's brother, Jeremy. The mingling of disappointment and relief—yes, relief, because Eddie couldn't fathom what he would actually do if it *had* been Chance in his room—flooded him, and left him rubbery-limbed and lightheaded. He found another of those institutional chairs in his room, two of them facing each other across a small round table, and sank into it.

"Pop machine." Even being so economical with his words, Eddie struggled to find breath enough to say them. Jeremy leaned against the wall by the window and crossed his arms while Eddie sorted out his confusion and said, finally, "It's Monday."

"Yeah."

"You come on Tuesday."

Jeremy seemed annoyed that Eddie had spotted his pattern. "Yeah, I wanted to…do you need anything? A magazine or something?"

Why on earth was everyone so fixated on getting Eddie something to read? He shook his head. It wasn't worth wasting his breath.

"What are you all dressed up for?" Jeremy asked. Eddie thought his brother seemed irritated by the thought of him strutting around in something other than an old T-shirt.

Eddie shrugged.

"Christ, you're sweating." Now, with a clear vision of something he could physically do to help, Jeremy marched into the bathroom, soaked a washcloth in cool water, wrung it out and handed it to Eddie.

Eddie mopped his forehead. He hoped if the time came where he couldn't wipe his own brow, it happened between one Tuesday and the next; his relationship with Jeremy had never been tender. It didn't seem right for his dying to change that.

Jeremy perched awkwardly on the opposite chair. "Anyway. I came to tell you. Anne is pregnant."

Eddie sucked in a breath before he could catch himself, and it sliced him from the inside like a thousand razor blades. His enlarged heart pounded hard, straining to carry oxygen to the rest of his body, but the oxygen wasn't there. Fresh sweat broke out on his forehead, and he coughed a few small, gaspy, unsatisfying coughs, and sopped up the sweat. "That's great," he managed. "That's so damn…great."

"Don't tell anyone. I dunno who you'd tell, but…Anne's funny about telling anyone. She wants to wait until…."

Eddie nodded and held up a hand for Jeremy to stop. He didn't blame Anne, after the first time—what was it, five years ago? Her sending out that email that she wasn't having a baby, after all.

"We were hoping to have an ultrasound to show you. But the nurse said if anything was visible at this point, all it would be is something called a gestational sac. And our insurance wouldn't pay for it yet—"

Eddie shook his head. "S'okay. I'm happy."

"Good. Thanks." Jeremy stood and wiped his palms on his slacks. "So, uh, listen. I will actually be driving right by here tomorrow on my way home from work. I can bring you some pop." He glanced down at the refrigerator they hadn't bothered to stock with anything, not for the few days Eddie had left. "Here, how 'bout this? You make me a list, I'll stop at the minimart on the way here." He pulled a business card from his pocket, *Jeremy Flynn, IRA Planning,* flipped the blank side toward Eddie, and handed him a pen from the nightstand.

Chance's pen.

"I gotta go sign something at the nurses' station, then I'll be right back."

Eddie felt pretty good about the idea of giving Jeremy something to do. No doubt his brother would be happier with an assignment. The fountain pen made much cleaner strokes on the business card than it had on the napkin. It almost looked like Eddie's handwriting. He wrote *Pepsi*, and beneath that, *cake*. Which seemed like a weird thing to request from a convenience store, he realized. Especially since he'd always been one for cocktails more than dessert. Ding Dongs, Twinkies, even a donut—something like that would have made more sense. And yet, when Eddie poised the pen to cross out the word, he imagined a triangular slab of spongy, moist cake covered in sugary frosting, and he decided to leave it as it was. The convenience store probably sold something that fit the bill. Even if it wasn't triangular and it came in a box.

Pain crackled through his lungs as he took his next breath, and he wrote *morphine* on the list. Which, he realized, was pretty macabre. He slipped Jeremy's card beneath the moss-covered Styrofoam base of the fake plant behind his chair. When Jeremy asked him for the list, he could simply say, *Never mind. I don't need anything.* In the grand scheme of things, while a Pepsi really would have been nice, he wouldn't miss it all that much longer.

"Knock knock," Travaughn called from the hallway, and although it wasn't yet time for dinner, he was wheeling his meal cart. "Mary Lou Montagna's ninety-five years young today, and she spreadin' the love."

The top of the cart was covered in slices of cake, trailing frosting and moist chocolate crumbs on little white paper plates.

Eddie stared. His fingers and toes went tingly. He wondered if he was about to black out.

"Now, I don't wanna hear you're not hungry. Take a piece and at least try to eat it. Mary Lou won't have it any other way."

Eddie nodded. He didn't have the breath to explain that he was more baffled and stunned than anything else.

"And what kinda Coke you want—orange? Root beer? Or Pepsi?"

It felt like the world tilted. Eddie took a very slow, careful breath, and said, "What, no diet?"

"Diet, my ass," Travaughn laughed. He reached into a plastic tub on the second tier of his cart, sloshed his hand around in it, and pulled out a dripping wet can of Pepsi with a few shards of ice sliding down the aluminum. He tossed a napkin onto the table and set the can on top. Water stained the napkin dark, and caused it to wrinkle and bunch.

"You feeling okay? You been off your drip for too long. Here, lemme plug you back in."

Travaughn wheeled the I.V. stand over. Eddie leaned forward and allowed him to roll up the sleeve of his trendy shirt and attach his morphine drip. "You wanna get up and walk around again," Travaughn told him, " just ring the bell. I'll take care of you, a'ight?" He wheeled the cart out of the room and down the hall.

Eddie listened to the sound of the squeaky wheel receding, and the warm narcotic tingle began. He hadn't realized how much pain he'd been in until it dulled. The Pepsi was deliciously wet and cold—and that was just holding it in his hand, not even drinking it. He rolled it over his forehead, and squinted against its searing iciness until he couldn't stand it anymore, and then he rested the can on his thigh, where it left a dark stain of wetness that didn't much matter, as it was hard to see against the black sweatpants.

He slouched in his chair, fit the chair back into the curve of his neck, and stared up at the acoustic drop-ceiling as the morphine sank deeper. It wasn't bliss, exactly. In fact, it felt a bit sickening. But he preferred it to the pain.

What the hell had just happened?

"Okay, so..." Jeremy stood in the doorway, lingering there like he was worried the room might suck him in if he crossed the threshold. "You got that list?"

"Gimme another business card."

Jeremy looked puzzled as he pulled it from his pocket and handed it over.

"The other one got wet," Eddie explained.

"Oh."

A bead of ink spread over the back of the business card as Eddie pressed into it and considered what he should write—but what exactly had it been that made a slice of cake, a Pepsi and a morphine buzz appear on command? The ritual of planting of the card? Eddie's firm statement to the universe of what he wanted? Or was it something as simple as the pen itself?

Maybe the blue shirt hadn't been in that drawer all along. Maybe the pen had made it appear there.

"I, ah…never mind. I don't need anything." Eddie tried to smile reassuringly. "Tell Anne congratulations for me."

He stared at the ceiling and made the seams between the tiles go in and out of focus as his brother's footsteps receded down the hall. The shirt, the Doc Martens, the Pepsi, the cake…hell, even the morphine. Every single thing he'd written with that pen had landed right in his lap.

Magic, or coincidence? It wasn't as if the chocolate cake had simply appeared from thin air. A bakery created it. One of Mary Lou's family members—probably her daughter-in-law, who seemed to be the one in charge—paid for it, brought it to Hospice House, cut it into slices and told Travaughn to spread it around. So if it really was a magic pen, it wasn't the sort of "abracadabra—poof—there it is" magic that could make something out of nothing.

But if the trendy shirt had been in the bedroom closet at Eddie's apartment, which was where he'd last seen it, by what mechanism had it traveled to his drawer at Hospice House? Had Leah, in some sort of magical trance, stuffed it in her bag the last time she was picking up Eddie's mail, and then folded it into the drawer while neither of them was paying attention? If so, that would mean the pen could function outside of time. Or had the molecules traveled from one end of Columbus to the other and reassembled themselves in Eddie's hospice room? That explanation would make distance irrelevant.

Eddie popped the tab of the Pepsi can and took a long swallow. It was cool, but just barely. His body heat had tainted it already.

He placed his index finger on his brother's business card and drew it across the surface of the table so he could reach it. Curious to see how the magic pen would deal with an abstraction, he wrote, *Relief from this heat.*

Then he settled back into his chair, and he waited.

Four

THE NOISE WOKE Eddie. Another power surge, he thought at first, as the whine of a flatlining heart monitor cut through the nap he'd never intended to take. Footsteps on linoleum, not as urgent, he imagined, as they might be in a hospital. In hospitals, there would be crash carts, grimly efficient nurses, and urgent pages to the physicians. Things were different at Hospice House. Quieter.

I am so glad I skipped the hospital.

He sat up, rolled a kink out of his neck, and saw it was almost time for dinner…but he'd forgotten about his cake. He took a bite. The edges of the cake had dried while he slept, but the frosting, beneath the thin, waxy outer skin, was still creamy and sweet. It coated his teeth like butter. No, he wasn't really one for sweets, but it seemed important to notice the grain of the cake, the glide of the frosting, and the way it clung together in his mouth. The second bite was better. Moister, since the center of the slice hadn't yet begun to dry out. Eddie worked his way through the layers, prodding, sampling, comparing and contrasting, until nothing remained on his plate but a shell of dried chocolate cake, part of a candy flower and some smears of frosting.

He hadn't even realized he was hungry.

The first slug of Pepsi was a bit flat, but then Eddie found the fizz again. Strange, how the pop tasted nearly dry, like champagne, after the sweetness of the cake. He drank it in long, greedy swallows, enjoying the crackle of carbonation against the roof of his mouth, until he realized he needed to breathe. He slammed the near-empty can down suddenly, and drew air in small, rapid, careful gasps.

Travaughn stood in the doorway with a desktop fan in the crook of his elbow, watching Eddie recover from his Pepsi. "You okay?"

Eddie nodded. His eyes watered.

"Dorine in room twenty passed away."

Eddie kept nodding. He hadn't known Dorine long. She'd moved in after he did. What a thought.

"Her daughter thought you could use this." He moved a withered flower arrangement and set the fan down instead, plugged it in and turned it on. "How you like that?"

"Good." It was a minimal reply, and not only because Eddie was short on breath. The last thing he'd written—*Relief from this heat*—it couldn't possibly be a coincidence. Granted, Dorine had inoperable throat cancer. But how could Eddie know if today was really supposed to be Dorine's last day on earth…or if he'd killed her with the magic pen?

Travaughn's going to think I'm crazy, Eddie realized. If he had all the breath in the world to explain himself, maybe he could have described what was going on in a way that didn't make him sound like a lack of oxygen had killed off some important part of his brain. Undoubtedly, a demonstration would be effective—but not at the risk of killing someone over something as common as a twelve-dollar plastic fan.

"You don't look so good." Travaughn crossed his arms and considered Eddie. "You want a sponge bath? Alcohol rub? Cool you down some?"

Eddie took a few slow, careful breaths, then said, "A shower." It was harder to speak than it had been while Jeremy was there only a few hours before.

"If you feel up for it, let's get to it." Travaughn ushered Eddie into the small bathroom, I.V. stand and all, and while the water warmed, he slipped the trendy shirt off of Eddie with only the smallest interruption in the morphine drip. He taped plastic over the incision on Eddie's side with as little tape as possible—just enough to waterproof it without taking off half his hide when he peeled it back off. Shoes, socks, sweatpants and underwear came off, and then Eddie was seated on the plastic bench. He didn't suppose he'd ever get used to showering sitting down. He didn't suppose he'd have much more time to acclimate.

He soaped himself up with one hand—he could at least do that much for himself—while his I.V. arm rested on Travaughn's shoulder, away from the handheld sprayer. "Colder," Eddie whispered in Travaughn's ear.

"It's already too cold."

"Please."

Travaughn nudged the water temperature down. Eddie closed his eyes. It was indeed cold. The spray actually ached wherever it touched him. As it moved over his body, down one leg, over his feet, up the other leg, over his crotch, his stomach, around to his back, it left behind a stinging trail that felt deliriously good, once the sting wore off. But only for a moment. And then Eddie was hot again.

"Do you believe in magic?" Eddie asked.

Travaughn wet Eddie's hair. The spray felt wonderful against his scalp. Travaughn picked up the shampoo and flipped open the top with his thumb. Eddie took the bottle from him. He surrendered it easily. "It depends on which day of the week you ask me. Sometimes, I feel like every moment on God's green earth is a miracle. Sometimes," he shrugged. "Dorine and me, we didn't talk too much. Even still, I hate to see her go. Sometimes, it feels like it's too hard."

Although that wasn't the sort of magic Eddie had meant, he supposed he could have done worse than to come off as rhetorical. He lathered his hair one-handed, waited for Travaughn to rinse away the suds, and said, "Does everything have a cost?"

Travaughn took the shampoo from Eddie, squeezed more directly onto his head, and looked at him sideways. "You goin' all philosophical on me, ain't you?" He sighed. "Could be. Maybe not right away, but somewhere down the road. Yeah. I think so."

What Eddie had meant, he supposed, was that if magic did indeed exist, was it possible to create something from nothing? Or was this thing called magic bound by some set of rules or laws, perhaps a mystical form of physics, where every action caused an equal and opposite reaction. He scowled, even as Travaughn's fingers worked *their* magic on his scalp.

"Why you ask?" Travaughn rinsed Eddie's hair again. It felt squeaky. "You feeling guilty 'bout something?"

Eddie caught himself before he could gasp. Travaughn *knew* about the pen?

Travaughn nodded slowly as he considered his next words. "I get what it's like to feel guilty."

Oh. He was still coming from the philosophic conversation. Not the batshit-crazy-dying-brain discussion Eddie'd been participating in.

Travaughn said, "When I was young and stupid, mostly stupid, I did some things." He sighed a heavy sigh. "Every day, I pay. I keep on paying. Sometimes it don't seem like I'll ever be done paying." He turned off the tap. "I try, though. That's why I'm here."

Eddie stood, allowing Travaughn to steady him, and considered what kind of self-imposed penance Travaughn might be doing that he needed to work in a place like Hospice House. It felt like a steel I-beam had fallen on Eddie, and was crushing his chest.

"If you got to tell anyone you're sorry," Travaughn said, "you call 'em and let 'em know. While you can."

Eddie glanced toward the phone, but couldn't think of who he would call.

"You smoke?" Travaughn asked. "A lot of my patients with lung cancer, emphysema, they feel so guilty about smoking, I think it's the guilt eating them faster than the sickness."

Eddie shook his head. He'd quit. Ten years ago, even. Though of course it hadn't made up for whatever he'd inhaled from the ages of fourteen to twenty-eight.

The conversation was veering into territory that seemed to wound the both of them more than it healed. Eddie struggled to find a few simple words to express, "Never mind, Travaughn. You've got it all wrong. I was just trying to figure out how the magical pen works, and if I feel guilty for anything, it's that my desire to stop stewing in my fever juices made Dorine in room twenty check out before she was ready." But no words came to him, and instead he turned his hands palm up, helpless.

Travaughn swiped unscented hospital lotion over Eddie's elbows and knees. "You want your clothes back on, or pajamas?"

Eddie had never worn pajamas at home. The set he'd been wearing all week was Jeremy's. Still, the trendy shirt was probably pretty ripe after he'd sweated on it all afternoon. "Just boxers," he said. He wasn't expecting Jeremy or Leah, and if the doctor swung by, no doubt she'd seen worse.

Travaughn went through the motions of disapproval, rolling his eyes and shaking his head, but he caved in pretty easily. "You the boss."

He made a big show of arranging the fringey cotton throw, as if he needed to remind Eddie of its existence. The frustration of not being able to express himself, of not even being able to *try*, prompted Eddie to say, "Okay. Thanks." Since he was unaccustomed to dismissing people, especially people as decent as Travaughn, he did his best to nod and try to look grateful—although he suspected he just appeared to be wincing.

"I'm here 'til eight. Lemme know if you need anything else."

Eddie nodded. Travaughn seemed to understand that he didn't have the breath to speak. Maybe he also knew Eddie wouldn't have known what to say if he had.

※ ※ ※

THE NIGHT NURSE was not Travaughn. She was very tall, coolly professional, and always struck Eddie as being exceedingly competent. The fact that he didn't even know her name, however, was a pretty good indication of the level of their bonding.

"Are you still awake?" She peeked around the privacy curtain that Eddie had drawn, not so much for privacy, which he found he suddenly cared very little about, but for the sake of sparing others the need to see him in his boxer shorts.

Eddie shrugged. Speaking would have taken too much out of him.

The nurse looked from Eddie, to the fan, and back to Eddie again. She frowned, and came closer. Her hand, when she pressed it to his forehead, felt cool. "Would you like something for the fever? I can call…."

Eddie shook his head, feeling guilty that he didn't have it in him to thank her for her concern, and maybe to apologize for never finding out what her name was—because maybe, deep down inside, she was just as special as Travaughn. Likely, they all were.

He closed his eyes. If he'd known how much guilt was involved in the whole dying thing, he would have considered jumping off a bridge a month ago.

"Feeling too weak to talk? Can you write?"

Eddie's eyes flew open.

The nameless night nurse pressed a notepad into his hand. "Here." She dug in the pocket of her navy scrubs and came up with a regular pen. "Now you can let me know if you need anything without playing charades." She smiled. "The I.V. always gets in the way."

A surge of panic caused his heart monitor to bleep faster, and Eddie cast around in the dim light for Chance's pen. Not on the round table. Not on the nightstand. Wait a second—there, on the tray table, hugging the ridge around the edge like a shadow. A wisp of a sigh escaped him. He hadn't realized he'd grown so attached to it.

Once he was assured the magic pen was still within reach, he took up the thoroughly (he hoped) non-magical pen the nurse had given him, and wrote: *I don't need anything, thank you. What's your name? I'm Eddie.*

The nurse took the pad, smiled again—more deeply this time, he noticed, and said, "I'm Krista."

She gazed at him for a moment. Eerie how many of the people who worked around there could do that, just look at a dying person without looking quickly away. Her dark hair—black or brown, he couldn't tell in the low light—was pulled back in a plain ponytail. She looked to be about his age, somewhere approaching forty. She was mostly angles and planes, and looked like she would have been at a loss to fill out a cocktail dress. But when she smiled, really smiled, she was beautiful. "I'll leave the pad with you," she said. "Buzz me if you change your mind."

With the bedside lamp on its lowest setting, Eddie had to strain a bit to see, but the notepad Krista had given him was bigger than the backs of his brother's business cards, and easier to write on than a napkin. He pulled up his knees, even though the position seemed to squash his already-compromised lungs, planted the pad on his thighs, and concentrated.

Whatever he wrote, he was certain it would have consequences. A small thing like a shirt barely rippled the surface of reality. The cake and Pepsi were a happy coincidence. And yet the fan…had he been too greedy? Or maybe too vague?

His chest hurt. Badly. Even with the morphine. He could scribble down a wish to be released from his pain, but look what had happened when he'd asked to be cooler. Not a safe request. Not without knowing the rules. It occurred to him to ask that he know the rules…but who said that would be safe, either? What if someone else died to get him that knowledge?

Of course, there was always the option of ignoring the pen and letting nature take its course. It seemed like the responsible thing to do.

Or was it?

What if the pen fell into the wrong hands once Eddie was gone? Someone who didn't give a damn about the consequences could cause a lot of damage. And what about someone who wanted to actually *cause* damage, someone who wanted to get back at an ex-lover, or a rival at work, or…anyone, really. The owner of the pen could become the world's most ruthless, deadly assassin without ever getting a drop of blood on their hands, and no one would ever be able to prove a thing.

Eddie knew what he needed to do. No one would go rooting through a dying guy's wastebasket for a broken pen. He reached for it, fully expecting it to roll away from him or burst into flames, but nothing like that happened. It was just a pen.

Until he grabbed it two-handed and attempted to snap it. No luck.

He presumed he was just weak. However, when he duplicated the efforts with Krista's pen, it bent immediately. He stopped short of breaking it, and tried again to snap the magic pen. Nothing. In fact, the point dug into his palm and drew blood. He turned his hand open to assess the damage, but found he hadn't actually been wounded. The wetness crawling along the lines of his palm was black. Ink, not blood. And the pen? It hadn't even cracked. Maybe it was just a nicer pen than Krista's. Made out of a higher grade of plastic…oh, who was he kidding?

That damn pen was unbreakable.

If Eddie'd been at home, he could have bought some cement and interred the pen in the base of a new birdbath. But at Hospice House? Throwing the pen out the window, hiding it in the toilet tank, attempting to flush it…nothing Eddie could do from his room seemed permanent enough to keep innocent people safe from the pen.

Although, if he couldn't bury the thing himself....

He picked up Krista's pen, checking it multiple times to make sure it really *was* Krista's pen and not the other one, and he began to write.

Dear Leah,

In case I don't get to see you, there's one more thing I want you to handle for me. It's got a lot of sentimental value—a black fountain pen. Sounds silly, I know, but I was hoping you could make sure you put it in my hand during the viewing so it's with me when I'm buried. I'm slipping it under my pillow right now for safekeeping.

Oh, and in my obit, can you make sure people don't send flowers? It's so fake. Instead, people could put money into a fund for....

Eddie debated whether it would count as blabbing about Anne's pregnancy if he told Leah about his future niece or nephew. Probably.

Damn it, he thought. *Why does everything always have to be so hard?* He dropped his head back on the pillow in frustration—and then flinched when he realized a figure was standing at the edge of his privacy curtain, watching him.

Chance.

Eddie's heart monitor raced as he tried to get hold of himself. How stupid of him. How could Chance possibly be there in the middle of the night? It would just be Krista, in her navy scrubs, checking up on him. He knuckled his eyes and looked again.

No. It really was Chance.

Five

EDDIE FLYNN WAS practically naked. Chance hadn't been prepared for that. His proportions were beautiful—thinner now than they had once been, no doubt, but all the better to showcase the delicate sweep of his collarbone, and the waist's serpentine curve that led to the rise of his hip and the long, lean stretch of thigh.

Chance was so involved with the shadow cast by the luscious dip of Eddie's navel that it took him a moment to notice…he'd been seen.

Eddie said nothing—he couldn't—but his eyes went wider. The machine beside his bed began to beep more rapidly.

No sense lurking in the shadows, then. Chance stepped forward and allowed himself another long look. It made no sense that Eddie was still there—and yet….

A fleeting thought: was it possible, Chance wondered, it was his fault?

Absurd.

Death never waited for love. Besides, Chance had roamed the halls, the grounds, even the neighborhood in search of someone to nudge toward the trajectory of Eddie's room. There simply wasn't a lover for Eddie Flynn anywhere.

Eddie's mouth worked as he struggled for air to speak, and his chest heaved with the strain of not being able to cough. Whatever was happening here, it was unacceptable. Chance had done every single thing he could possibly do—and if there was nobody appropriate to strike that final spark against Eddie's dwindling flame, what sense was it to allow the poor man to suffer so?

How would *they* like it if Chance stopped doing *his* work? He spun out a small fantasy in which he ignored all the cues and clues, crossed his arms and simply did nothing. But, no. The only ones to suffer would be the lovelorn and the lost. And in the end, it wouldn't really prove anything at all.

Eddie's back arched with the strain of not-coughing, and his ribs showed in delicate relief while his muscles tensed and twisted. It was some sort of test, then. Some ploy to prove Chance was incapable of letting go of old duties to embrace the new.

They'd certainly chosen delectable bait.

Eddie thrashed against the bed until Chance could stand it no longer. He placed his finger to his lips, and whispered, "Shh."

The wracking ghost of a coughing fit abated. Eddie settled against the hospital bed, blinking away tears the strain had brought to his eyes. His wet lashes formed shiny spikes that framed riveting pale eyes.

Chance was not in the habit of apologizing, but in this particular case, he truly was sorry. Not that he thought he'd done anything wrong—but he regretted that some capricious twist of the Fates had resulted in Eddie dangling between life and death in anticipation of a lover who would never come.

Apologies would do no good, though, not like action. Eddie might be Chance's first failure, but if the only lasting damage would be sustained by Chance's pride, then so be it. If his replacement wouldn't finish Eddie, then he would. He stretched forth a hand in an old, familiar gesture, and as it often happened, Eddie reached for him in return.

Chance blinked in surprise. Eddie *wasn't* reaching toward him after all; he was holding up the black pen.

※ ※ ※

"Take it," Eddie said—or attempted to say. He formed the word with his lips, but he didn't have enough breath in him to give voice to it.

Chance stared at it for a moment, then plucked it from Eddie's grasp. "I presume you noticed it was…?" He shrugged.

Eddie nodded. And he hoped he looked good and serious, too.

"And you're done with it?"

Eddie nodded again. Firmly.

"Fascinating. Obviously, you haven't checked out of hospice and booked yourself a Caribbean cruise…so what *did* you ask for?"

Eddie yearned to explain that whatever he'd gotten from the pen, it had been an accident. A fluke. He'd never really thought it was magical. And he'd never meant to kill anyone over a desktop fan. But all he could force out was a single, whispery word—and a lie, at that. "Nothing."

Which Chance ignored, because he was busy pressing the pen to his ear so he could listen to it. "Cake? Seriously? What a pity. If I knew where my shop disappeared to, I could ply you with the world's most decadent ganache." Was he teasing? He didn't look like he was teasing.

Chance's gaze shifted, and his gloriously peaked eyebrows drew down and furrowed. He looked into his other hand as if he hadn't realized there was something in it. A tiny paper cup rested in his palm.

A pill—something to put Eddie out of his misery? Maybe a cyanide tablet wouldn't be such a bad thing. Not if Chance followed it, ever so carefully, with that kiss Eddie had missed out on before.

Chance leaned over the bedrail until his face was only a few feet from Eddie's, and said, "Well. Aren't you in for a treat." He stared at Eddie for an uncomfortable, overlong moment, and then turned his attention to the paper cup. The heart monitor's blip grew perky with anticipation as Chance frowned down into the cup's interior. "It's not much," he said finally. "But perhaps you will…enjoy it."

He fed the small, smooth oval to Eddie as a priest might give Communion, and the scant brush of his fingertip on Eddie's lips was cool. Eddie tried to swallow, but whatever coating was supposed to seal the tablet had already melted, and it stuck to his furred tongue, and then the roof of his mouth.

It melted fast as he struggled to force it down, suddenly frightened that maybe he would manage to get dying as wrong as he'd gotten living, and that by allowing the suicide pill to melt in his mouth, he'd slide into a coma for a few days instead, and deplete whatever meager estate he was leaving his family that much sooner.

"Food of the gods," Chance murmured.

Eddie forced his watering eyes open. He wasn't dead. Nor was he in a coma. And the bitter, earthen-sweet taste of chocolate had surged up to fill his awareness.

"Theobroma cacao." Chance pronounced the Latin words as naturally as he'd said the phrase in English. "*Food of the gods* is the literal translation.

Funny, how glimpses of truth do manage to shimmer through men's minds… on occasion. Funny strange. Not funny ha-ha."

Saliva flooded Eddie's parched mouth as his body reacted to the exquisite blast of chocolate like it was a panacea, and finally he did swallow, once, twice, three times. He opened his mouth to gasp for air, and found he could actually breathe, if only a bit. "Did you…?"

"Cure you? No." Chance smiled sadly. "I have…many talents. But that's not one of them." He dropped the paper cup. It bounced off the bedrail, slewed along the edge of the mattress, then fell to the floor and rolled under the bed. "I am curious, though." He waggled the pen. "Why didn't you cure yourself?"

"You can't get something out of nothing." Eddie's voice was small, but thanks to the soothing balm of the chocolate, he could speak. "If my time was up, and I asked for more…." He imagined his brother's wife, Anne, sending out another one of those emails to however many people she'd sworn to secrecy. Maybe she wouldn't even need to compose a new one. She could cut and paste the sad news from the last time.

"I wish I had more to leave to her," Eddie said, as if Chance had been able to pluck the knowledge of his niece—yes, he'd decided it was a girl—straight from his mind. "I wish I'd never picked up smoking."

"It wasn't the smoking," Chance said, as if he really had been privy to Eddie's very thoughts. "It was the summer you spent in East Cleveland."

How could he know about that? Eddie tried to work himself up over the absurdity, and found he wasn't terribly surprised.

That summer. All this time, Eddie had thought he'd paid many times over for the folly of skipping out on his family when he was seventeen, leaving town with a guy who claimed to be thirty (but had probably seen several birthdays since then) only to end up flipping burgers in the world's greasiest greasy spoon to scrounge up enough bus money to get home.

The things you do for love.

"How?"

"The cooking gas was tainted."

And to add insult to injury, the "thirty"-year-old had run off with one of the busboys.

"So you see how much use it's been to anguish over your cigarettes."

Strangely enough, it really did feel good to know that small part of the burden was no longer Eddie's to carry. When he forced himself to seek Chance's eyes, he found Chance gazing down at his chest. Looking right through him to the infection, he supposed. Although a healthier man might have thought Chance was staring at his nipple. The fringey blanket was wadded at the foot of the bed. Eddie considered covering himself—but if getting ogled was the last action he'd ever see, he decided he might as well enjoy it.

He felt a smile creep over his expression, heavy-lidded, and even a touch naughty. He would have thought his mortal coil would have given up the mechanics of cruising this late in the game, but it was comforting to know it hadn't. And maybe the release of the guilt had made room for an emotion Eddie didn't mind savoring for whatever time was left.

"Would you do something for me?" he asked. Chance's shrewd gaze flicked up to meet his. Eddie gathered his courage—it was easier now that he had so little to lose—and said, "Would you unbutton your shirt?"

Chance's eyes narrowed. He was incredibly still for so long, Eddie began to wonder if maybe he was a hallucination, after all. But then his hand moved over his chest, startling-pale against the black of his shirt, placed the pen in his shirt pocket…and lingered at his top button.

Eddie's heart monitor galloped. He unclipped the sensor from his forefinger, reached over and turned the machine off.

"I shouldn't." Chance's voice was hardly a whisper now, too. The chorus of heart monitor bleeps from down the hall almost drowned out their conversation.

"Shouldn't? Or don't want to?"

"Oh, I want to."

If Eddie's heart monitor had still been connected, its blips and bleeps would have staggered into an odd syncopation. He mirrored the slit-eyed gaze back at Chance, and said, "Then what's the holdup?"

Chance closed his eyes. Incredibly long, black lashes cast a fringed shadow over the harsh angles of his cheekbones. The pause stretched, as heart monitors chirruped gently, far away, like a flock of contented pigeons.

And then, with an easy flick of Chance's white fingers, the button fell open. Eddie wheezed a gentle sigh.

"I really shouldn't," Chance said, unbuttoning a second button, and a third.

"I won't tell if you don't."

A smile quirked the corner of Chance's mouth. "If only things were that simple."

The final button was undone, and the silky black shirt slid open. His chest was statuary-smooth. Eddie let his gaze roam down the subtle curve of his chest, skim the arch formed by his ribs, then linger at the abs, gently defined. And although Chance had humored him more than he'd ever dreamed possible, he still wanted more. "Your...jeans?"

Chance rolled his eyes...though not in a way that suggested he couldn't be persuaded.

"Just...the button. And maybe, y'know. Touch yourself. While I watch."

"And that will satisfy you?"

"Uh huh."

"I doubt it." Chance slipped a hand down the front of his black jeans and rearranged his package. Eddie's eyes went to the new and prominent bulge alongside the fly. Hot damn, Chance was actually getting *hard* over their little cat-and-mouse game? Unbelievable. The urge to touch himself in response was brutal, but the feel of the I.V. tugging at his arm was enough to keep him from mimicking Chance's hand.

"You're right," Eddie whispered. "Not satisfying at all. C'mere and show me what those hands of yours feel like."

Chance pulled his hand from his pants. "I knew talking to you again would be a slippery slope."

"And yet, here you are."

"Here I am." Chance grasped the bedrail and jerked it down with a practiced click.

He stepped closer. Close enough for Eddie to touch him. Eddie reached out, and the I.V. line snapped taut. He glared at the tubing, and tried to remember exactly how Travaughn had unhooked the line without spraying blood and morphine everywhere. It seemed like it should have been easy, like unplugging a lamp, but he couldn't tell how it was all connected. He gave the line a tug anyway, but since the whole point of the midline catheter was for the thing to stay in his arm, it held.

Until cool, pale fingers covered his, and an easy twist caused the morphine line to fall free. "You won't be needing that anymore."

Eddie's heart felt ready to hammer out of his chest. "Really?"

"Don't play coy. You knew it was coming."

While Eddie supposed that was true, he'd never imagined dying would be *quite* like this. Chance began to straighten up again, but Eddie caught his hand—so incredibly cool—and pulled him forward. After a token resistance, Chance gave in and let himself be drawn down toward the mattress.

Eddie pressed the back of Chance's hand to his lips. The longer he held it, the colder it felt. The knuckles were smooth and chill enough to pass for marble.

He'd only meant to graze those knuckles flirtatiously, but they felt so good against his hot lips that he held Chance's hand there, breathing the buttercream scent of the skin…and before he knew it, he allowed himself the smallest of tastes, merely to see if Chance really did taste like he smelled—glaciers and sugar and dew on the windowpane. Because his hand sure as hell didn't smell like a human being's hand.

Didn't taste like it either.

Chance's breath hissed in. Was that good or bad? Eddie tried to read him—ridiculous, obviously, because he might as well try to read the fine print on a cell phone contract on a moving bus. But he hoped the reaction was good. He slid his tongue over one knuckle, then another, and then eased it into the silky vee between Chance's fingers.

Chance groaned, shifted his hips, and reached down with his opposite hand to resettle the bulge in his jeans again. "Yes." Eddie said it so quietly, it was more the shape of a word on his lips than an actual utterance. He'd had that effect on men all the time when he was well. But now? He hadn't even realized how much he'd missed the dance of seduction until he'd revisited the old steps he thought he'd forgotten.

The bed frame creaked as Chance slung a leg over Eddie and planted his knee into the mattress, then shifted his weight onto the bed. Would the bed hold? It hadn't been built for fucking—though surely plenty of patients weighed more than Eddie and Chance put together. Still…Eddie smiled against the backs of Chance's fingers. It might be amusing to demolish one last bed.

Once Chance climbed into place, he hovered there with his knees on either side of Eddie's thighs, a hand planted beside the pillow, and his open shirt and the front of his hair hanging down to cast him in shadow. Eddie reached down with his free hand to get to work on the jeans.

He felt around more than was strictly necessary to get the lay of the land. Very nice package. Definitely hard. Chance's breathing shifted when Eddie grazed his shaft through the black denim. Sensitive, too. Good.

"If you have a no-kissing policy," Eddie said, "I hope you'll make an exception."

He thought he saw a smile flit across Chance's shadowed features. "Lucky you…you're already the exception."

Chance lowered himself so his body touched Eddie's in a dozen places—but gently, with sublime tenderness. He fit his lips to Eddie's, and they were as cold as his fingers. He paused like that, lips barely brushing, in the way he seemed to pause and consider everything, like celestial voices were telling him what, or what not, to do. And then he slid his cool, wet tongue into Eddie's mouth.

Better than morphine. Better than any illicit thing Eddie had ever toyed with, in fact. A pleasant chill spread over his tongue—sweet, yet dry, like Pepsi after birthday cake—and he shivered in anticipation. Before he realized what was happening, Chance had shifted the grasp on his hand to weave their fingers together, his cold, smooth palm against Eddie's fevered skin, and pressed Eddie's hand back into the pillow beside his head. Eddie gasped now, and breathing in the air that Chance exhaled was like stepping out of an overheated apartment on a sub-zero day in February and filling his lungs with the scent of an oncoming blizzard.

His hips bucked up before he could temper his reaction, and he squeezed Chance's fingers, pleading for a bit of understanding—that usually he would let events unfold more slowly, to savor them. But not now. He didn't have that luxury now.

Chance squeezed his fingers in return, and kissed him with such tender thoroughness his mouth went tingly-numb.

He wrestled Chance's jeans open one-handed and pushed at the denim, hungry now to feel a stiff cock in the flesh. Chance had one free hand too, and together they managed to shove his jeans out of the way, and then, the flimsy barrier of Eddie's boxers. Jeans and boots and underwear teetered over the side of the bed, and hit the floor with a couple of clomps and a hiss of sliding fabric. And everywhere Chance's skin touched Eddie's, it was cold. Even the hard length that now rested against the crook of Eddie's thigh.

"You feel amazing," Eddie said, when Chance ended the lingering kiss that threatened to leave him with brain freeze.

"You, too."

"Oh." It hadn't occurred to Eddie that fucking him was anything more than a lark, that he had anything to offer Chance in return. He barely stopped himself from adding, *really?*

Chance shifted down to lay a chill kiss at the base of Eddie's throat, a kiss that sent delectable shivers down Eddie's spine when he thought he'd never feel another shiver again. With exquisite slowness, Chance trailed kisses down Eddie's collarbone and shoulder, following each kiss with a wintry caress. Sweet, cool relief blossomed wherever Chance kissed him, and touched him, and kissed him again.

Eddie's skin sparkled so with the effervescent aftermath of Chance's caresses, by the time Chance reached the incision, Eddie hardly felt its itchy stiffness. Even so, the caress of Chance's lips, even a hint of tongue, bathed the two-inch wound in a wave of blessed numbness. Chance lingered there for a moment, and then kissed an exquisitely cold trail back up to Eddie's sternum.

When Chance finally released Eddie's fingers, they were cold enough to stay that way. Now, with both hands free, Chance lavished his cold caresses over Eddie's aching ribs, trailing cool fingers lower, and lower still, to skirt the pubis, the thigh, and finally, finally....

Eddie tensed every muscle, from his jaw to his toes. When Chance's fingers slipped around the base of his cock, that most intimate touch was indeed frigid. But it wasn't, as he'd feared, excruciating.

It was glorious.

As Eddie soared towards the brink and his back arched up off the bed, Chance put his cool lips to Eddie's ear and whispered, "Don't worry…I'll make it last."

He could do that?

Still straddling him, Chance stroked his cock lightly with one hand, and burrowed down deeper between his legs with the other, exploring his balls, the crease of his thighs, even his taint. Eddie felt his sphincter clench as if he would shoot his load any second, and when he tensed, those facile, cold fingers stroked his clenched ass with an unhurried gentleness that would normally have made the dam burst.

Only it didn't.

Eddie gasped—a small gasp, but the biggest one he could muster. "Tight," Chance murmured appreciatively. A single fingertip breached the pucker, and Eddie's hips flailed as if he was coming, and coming hard. Only, he wasn't. Not yet.

"You're much tastier wracked with pleasure than with pain."

More than likely, Eddie thought, he looked about the same either way. His face was currently screwed up against the intensity of the sensations, bolts of cold racing up and down his spine, plunging down to his nuts and setting his whole groin a-tingle, then flitting across his chest and abs and down his limbs, to finish as pins and needles in the tips of his fingers and toes.

Chance left off fingering Eddie's ass, and began lavishing deliciously cold tweaks and caresses on his nipples. Eddie made a strangled sound as parts of his body that he hadn't even realized he'd been ignoring blazed into awareness. He felt like the Visible Man pullout in the old encyclopedia he and Jeremy had shared as kids—the stack of acetate illustrations of the human body you could peel from one another like the layers of an onion. Skin, muscle, organ, bone. If Eddie were the Visible Man, he'd be the giant, pulsing network of nerves.

All the while his hands made magic over Eddie's body, Chance never stopped kissing him. He rounded the curve of Eddie's ear, left trails of coolness over his scalp, and finally settled their foreheads together to pause the kisses and gaze into Eddie's eyes, too close to properly see. His hand slowed on Eddie's cock, but didn't stop. Eddie's body ached bone-deep with the need to come.

"I can't wait anymore," Chance whispered. "I wanted to draw it out longer…but I want you. Now."

What a relief. Any more waiting, Eddie thought, and he'd turn himself inside out.

Chance raised himself on his knees, and Eddie stared up at the pristine, white smoothness of his chest, framed on either side by the open black shirt. His face, too—his breathtaking face, serene, but with undertones of a fathomless sorrow—framed by the stark black of his hair. Though his hands were no longer working their magic on Eddie, the tingling pleasure they'd left behind still crackled over Eddie's skin. Chance turned and rifled through the drift of junk that had accumulated on the bedside table; Eddie's heart stuttered when he saw Chance pull the institutional tube of unscented lotion from the pile.

"Wait." Eddie closed his hand over Chance's as he thumbed open the tube. In so many ways, it was the same thing he'd done before too many times to count. And yet, it was nothing like those times. Not only because of the hospital bed and the distant sound-texture of heart monitors bleeping down the hall.

Chance's cock, rigid, jutted over Eddie's stomach, foreskin pushed back to expose the delicately flushed head. Eddie took the lotion from Chance, squirted some into his palm and drew his now-slippery hand over the shaft and around the tip. Chance caught his lower lip between his teeth.

It felt like a regular cock—Eddie had touched more than few—and yet, it didn't. Maybe it was the coolness of the skin, or maybe it was just the thought that this was the last cock Eddie would ever handle. He allowed the notion of being able to bareback for this one final ride to amuse him. Chance smiled as Eddie finished the thought.

Their thighs brushed as Chance positioned one knee, then the other, between Eddie's legs. His cold skin felt divine against the fevered heat between Eddie's thighs. Eddie stroked Chance's cock, slippery strokes, staring into his eyes to see what felt good to him. It was difficult to tell how he liked to be handled. Mostly, he was watching Eddie.

Once the traces of Chance's chilly touches began to fade from Eddie's skin, and he felt like he was able to feel that stiffness inside him without exploding from the sheer intensity of it, he angled his hips and guided Chance's cock toward his ass.

Even though Eddie'd been expecting the cold, it was a shock.

The blunt pressure definitely *felt* like a cock, but the chill, while welcome, reinforced with suddenly clarity that whatever Eddie was doing in that bed, it was far, far outside reality as he knew it.

Chance planted his knees, with the very tip of his cock prodding into Eddie's ass, and repositioned himself so he could press in with a deep, sure thrust. Mingled pain and pleasure surged through Eddie's overtaxed nervous system. What a relief Chance hadn't taken him gently. It was so much better to go out like a man.

Once Chance was buried deep, he shifted his stance once again, so their bodies were touching up and down, fire against ice, and when he moved, drawing back, pushing in, over and over, every place their skin touched buzzed with sensation.

Chance wrapped his arms around Eddie's head, weaving cool fingers through his hair, and pressed his mouth to Eddie's ear. He took a breath as if to say something, but then a particularly deft and satisfying thrust knocked the words from his mouth, and instead all he could do was moan his pleasure. Eddie gasped before he could check himself, but where he expected the stab of the shunt in his lung, now there was nothing but a frosty numbness—a release from the pain that would allow Eddie to shift the focus from his own body to Chance's.

Even with Chance's cock plunging in and out of him, Eddie worried that being so forward as to actually touch him would be the height of impudence.

He did it anyway.

He went slowly, as if by sneaking the touches in, he could convince Chance to allow it. He slipped his hands under the black shirt and around Chance's waist. Muscles rippled beneath smooth, cool skin as Chance thrust into him, and thrust again. Emboldened by the fact that Chance hadn't jerked away and demanded to know where a mere mortal such as Eddie got the audacity to actually paw him, Eddie planted his hands more firmly against Chance's back, fanning the fingers, and reveled in the feel of his body.

Eddie traced the curve of a vertebra, then ran his fingertip along the jut of Chance's shoulder blade. Other than the cold, he felt like a person, if a bit too perfect, with no stray hairs or bumps that needed to be ignored. Chance ground his face into the side of Eddie's hair, breathing hard now as his hips found an angle that sent far-reaching shocks up and down Eddie's spine with every driving thrust. Chance's breathing was low and rough, sharp against Eddie's earlobe like winter. It hurt, the cold, so relentless and intense. The pain sparkled brightly against the hum of excruciating pleasure rolling through his core in wave after wave after wave.

Long past the point at which he should have peaked, Eddie clung to Chance, dug his nails into his back and stopped fighting the sound that pushed past his clenched teeth. He would have been screaming, if he'd had the air to scream with. Even so, noises slipped past his constricted lungs, the two of them reduced to grunting and panting like a pair of animals while the hospital bed shuddered.

Someone will hear, Eddie thought, with a remote corner of his mind. He didn't care. The red-hot pleasure inside peaked harder, surely at a tipping point now, then hummed at the edge of an icy white nova.

Chance clasped Eddie's head so hard Eddie thought he might crush it, his frostbite gasps erratic. The idea that Chance, whatever he was, could find his own release in someone as mundane as Eddie Flynn was actually the thing that nudged Eddie toward that final height. He teetered there on the precipice, only vaguely aware that, yes, something did give way in the headboard that caused the bed to list toward that corner. And the I.V. stand had clattered to the floor—surely loud enough to draw a night nurse's attention. Mostly, his awareness had stuffed itself deep down in his own core, where the friction that should have crested long minutes before had evolved into a field of raw, unnameable sensation.

Something warm spilled on his stomach; belatedly, he realized it was his own seed. The contortions of his body held little interest, now that he was truly soaring. Chance's breathing went desperate, and he turned Eddie's head to force their lips together. His breath was less like February now, and more like March, with a hint of rain and maybe a timid green bud forcing its way out of a winter-dead tree limb. Chance's body stiffened under Eddie's fingers as he found his own release, not nearly as cold inside Eddie's body as he'd imagined it would be. Maybe, Eddie thought, his fever had warmed Chance enough to raise his temperature.

Chance gasped into Eddie's mouth as he emptied himself with a final, deep thrust—and then held him like that, perfectly still, to float in the nimbus of their euphoria. The semen on Eddie's belly cooled—and how strange that was, when every other fluid that had touched him in the last week had warmed, instead.

When Chance finally moved again, it was only his mouth, lips fitting against Eddie's for a delicate, unhurried kiss. Eddie meant to kiss him in return, only he couldn't find the energy to do it. His hands slid from Chance's back, though he didn't feel it when they fell back onto the skewed mattress.

Rather than worry about where his hands were, or why his mouth no longer seemed to work, it felt better to simply bask in the bliss of Chance's kisses…and to delight in the fact that he was growing so pleasantly, deliciously cool.

About Wishink Well

Eddie's character arc was always at the forefront of my mind: a guy who's basically selfish, maybe not maliciously so, but a guy who's always put his own urges and impulses first, gets a magical wish on his death bed. What does he wish for? Don't we always think, "More wishes!" And yet, like most of us in this day and age, Eddie Flynn's familiar with The Monkey's Paw and all the other morality tales wearing horror stories' clothing. He doesn't expect something for nothing. He never has.

And now Eddie's all about the consequences, in a way he never has been up to this point.

Other themes I considered: that it's not the building that makes something like hospice what it is. It's the people. So the building might be plucked right out of the perpetual cafeteria hall of my brain, with institutional furniture and buzzing light fixtures, and the activites might be cheesy, and the tapioca pudding questionable...but the people. My God. I don't know how they do it. I can guess—I know someone who quit her waitressing job to manage the cafeteria at a hospice. And she just seemed like the kind of person who would do that. A decent person with a strong moral compass.

Would it surprise you if I said the sex scene in this story was hard to write? It was hard to write. Way hard. It involved a lot of journaling, a lot of rewriting and a lot of pacing around muttering to myself.

I think it's critical to keep taking risks, and I have no idea how the story will be received, but it's important to keep reaching. Otherwise, the work will get stagnant.

About the Authors

Although SEAN KENNEDY has never been to a funeral as crazy as the one for Grace Conway, he wants to be sent off to the crematorium to the sound of a Ragtime jazz band.

JOSH LANYON has a lot of experience with writing workshops and critique groups, but he freely admits that the writers and writing groups in his stories are very much exaggeration. In fact, Josh believes one of the best things a beginning writer can do for her or himself is join a good writing group and get some objective, productive feedback. Of course, finding that group can take some time and trouble, but at least in real life it's not likely to prove dangerous.

JORDAN CASTILLO PRICE did not play with her Renegade Sam Cobra doll vigorously enough to wear out his joints. He was, however, much preferred to Ken. He also came with better accessories, though sadly, his clothes didn't come off. Perhaps that just added to his mystique.

Visit the Authors' Websites
www.seankennedybooks.com
www.joshlanyon.com
www.jordancastilloprice.com

CPSIA information can be obtained at www.ICGtesting.com
Printed in the USA
267139BV00001B/101/P